"An explanation?"

Parker nodded. "For leaving the way I did."

Ginny calmly took a sip of coffee—then set the cup down. "You don't owe me anything. It was a long time ago."

"Doesn't matter. I do owe you, and I need to get it off my chest. So, humor me?" He gave her that smile she remembered all too well.

After he'd left, how many nights had she spent weeping over that bone-melting smile that had gotten her in trouble with him in the first place? And now it was making a mockery of her defenses. Darn him.

It just wasn't fair. She wasn't a naive eighteen-year-old anymore and she didn't give a fig about making him feel better... "All right, go ahead." She dragged her gaze away to look at the wall clock. Mostly so she wouldn't be dazzled by that stupid smile. "You have five minutes."

Dear Reader,

Welcome to my very first Harlequin Heartwarming book! Some of you might have met Ginny Landry in my Harlequin Superromance, *The Navy SEAL's Rescue*. Now Ginny finally gets her own hero, Parker Nolan. Their story has been in my head for a couple of years now, and it was a joy to finally see it come to life.

Ginny was supposed to become a concert pianist and travel the world. Parker was supposed to be a civil rights attorney. Both their plans were thwarted when Meg, Parker's sister and Ginny's childhood best friend, disappeared just after high school graduation.

Parker had gotten close to Ginny after Meg vanished, then did his own vanishing act shortly after. Ginny never knew why the man she loved had left her so cruelly. But she has her own secret, one she can never reveal to anyone— especially Parker.

But when their secrets begin to unravel, it takes all his courage and her determination to make them finally see they'd always belonged together.

I hope you enjoy the book as much as I loved writing it.

All my best wishes,

Jo Leigh

HEARTWARMING

Reunion by the Sea

——

Jo Leigh

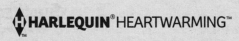

Recycling programs
for this product may
not exist in your area.

ISBN-13: 978-1-335-63378-1

Reunion by the Sea

Copyright © 2018 by Jolie Kramer

Printed in U.S.A.

Jo Leigh is from Los Angeles and always thought she'd end up living in Manhattan. So how did she end up in Utah in a tiny town with a terrible internet connection, being bossed around by a houseful of rescued cats and dogs? What the heck, she says, predictability is boring. Jo has written more than sixty novels for Harlequin. Find her on Twitter, @jo_leigh.

Books by Jo Leigh

Harlequin Blaze

NYC Bachelors

Tempted in the City
Daring in the City
Seduced in the City

It's Trading Men!

Choose Me
Have Me
Want Me
Seduce Me
Dare Me
Intrigue Me

Harlequin Superromance

The Navy SEAL's Rescue

Visit the Author Profile page at Harlequin.com for more titles by Jo Leigh.

To Debbi, for helping me every step of the way.

CHAPTER ONE

"COME ON, TILDA, get moving. You're going to be late." Ginny Landry checked the wall clock while listening to her daughter bang around in her room. "Hey, do you need any help packing?"

"No. I've got it." Another thud. "Are you trying to get rid of me?"

"Of course not." Ginny could tell by her voice Tilda was grinning. "Okay, maybe a little." Wanting a weekend for herself—well, with three of her best friends from high school—didn't make Ginny a bad mother. After all, a fifteen-year class reunion happened only once in a lifetime.

"I know you," Tilda called out, moving to the edge of the stairs. "You just don't want Kaley's mom to come in and start gushing."

"You're right. That's part of it." Ginny walked out of the kitchen and looked up at Tilda leaning over the railing. "Where's your bag?"

Tilda lost the grin. "I'm working on it,"

she said, slipping back into her room. "Dang. You're giving me a complex."

"I'll send you to therapy," Ginny called as she walked into the living room, stopping at her piano. When she brushed the keys, her glossy fingernails caught her attention. They looked so pretty.

Yesterday she'd splurged on a mani-pedi. Because she gave piano lessons, she was always careful to keep her nails trimmed and neat, but she'd gone all out, letting the woman apply a light beigy-pink color. Ginny looked down and wiggled her matching toenails peeking out from the strappy gold sandals she'd bought for the weekend festivities. She felt so glamorous. So chic. So…not like herself. But that was the point.

It wasn't at all that she was unhappy being a single mom, or to be living in the same house where she'd grown up. In fact, Ginny considered herself lucky. Temptation Bay had once been a small, quaint town tucked away on the Rhode Island coast and populated by generations of fishing families. But in the last couple of decades, the area had exploded with tourists, and summer people who'd bought up beachfront property and coveted lots along the bluffs that overlooked the water.

Ginny's family home sat on nearly an acre

on the northernmost bluff, thanks to the foresight of her great-grandfather. All the windows on the east side of the house faced the Atlantic Ocean and the bay. It was a privilege to have such a gorgeous view, and not one to be taken for granted.

She stood at the living room window, watching the sailboats glide across the sparkling blue water, wondering if her father ever missed it. If he ever regretted moving out all those years ago. Sure, his upscale Providence town house was close to his law office and he had a very nice view of the river, but really, there was no comparison.

Maybe she'd ask him now that they were on better terms. Well, they were speaking again, anyway.

"Hey, Mom, where are you?" Tilda's voice came from the top of the stairs.

"In the living room."

"Don't you think it's going to be kind of weird?"

Ginny turned away from the window. "What's going to be weird?"

"Seeing all those people you went to school with." Tilda, now wearing an oversize Roger Williams Academy T-shirt and cutoffs, stopped halfway down the stairs. "They're all going to look old, and the guys could be balding and the—"

"Oh, for… We're all in our early thirties. That's hardly ancient." She saw another grin lurking at the corners of her daughter's mouth. "Good. You're finished packing." Tilda's expression fell, and back up the stairs she went.

"You're going camping for three days, Tilda. How much stuff do you need to take?"

"I don't know. You're stressing me out."

"I'll give you five minutes," Ginny said, looking at the clock. "Then I'm taking over."

"All right already. I'm almost done."

For being extremely bright—gifted in fact— the simple act of packing had always eluded Tilda. She was just like Meg in that respect.

Ginny had been thinking of her old friend a lot lately. The reunion had brought it on, even though Meg wouldn't be coming to Temptation Bay with the rest of their classmates. And that made Ginny incredibly sad. Ten months ago was the last time her friend had contacted her. Things hadn't been going well for Meg. Not for a very long time. And after that last scary phone call, Ginny had the sick feeling Meg had finally used up all her luck.

Not a good time for her thoughts to be spiraling. She was determined to enjoy the weekend. This would be the first time the Fearless

Four—something she, Cricket, Harlow and Jade had called themselves—would be all together since graduating from Roger Williams Academy. They'd all gone their separate ways, using Facebook to keep in touch—though not nearly as often as they'd promised.

Ginny thought she heard a car. "Ready or not, here I come," she called up to Tilda as she hurried to peek out the long narrow window to the left of the front door.

"Wait! That wasn't five minutes!"

"They're here." Ginny watched Kaley get out of the Suburban, and actually crossed her fingers, hoping and praying Sharon would stay put behind the wheel.

Nope. Kaley's mom climbed out right behind her daughter.

Sighing, Ginny stepped back from the window so they couldn't see her. "Did you hear me, Tilda?"

"Coming."

"Not fast enough," Ginny muttered. Resigned, she pasted on her hostess face. She was pretty good at it considering she'd been raised without the benefit of a mother's guiding hand.

After the first doorbell chime, she counted to five, then opened the front door. "Kaley, Sharon, how nice to see you. Please," she said, stepping back and holding the door open wide, "come in."

"Hi, Ms. Landry." Kaley twirled around as she walked past Ginny, while eyeing her up and down. "Wow, you look hot. Big plans tonight?"

Ginny laughed. "Hot?"

"Oh, Kaley, mind your manners," Sharon said, doing her share of sizing up Ginny's lime-green sundress.

"It's not like I dissed her." Kaley rolled her eyes. "Mom, you're so out of touch."

Well, at least *she* hadn't called *her* mom old.

Sharon ignored her daughter and, as expected, walked straight to the living room window. "I can't get over this view. It's simply breathtaking."

"You say that every time," Kaley muttered, shaking her head and looking at Ginny. "Okay if I go up to Tilda's room?"

The words had barely left her mouth when Tilda shouted out. "Come here, Kaley! I need help deciding on a pair of jeans."

Frowning, Ginny stopped her. "You guys are only going camping, right?"

Kaley nodded, walking backward to the staircase. "She's just being lame."

Ginny had rarely experienced any trouble with Tilda. She was a model child in so many ways. And her friends were all bright, sensible kids much like Tilda. So why the niggling suspicion that something was off?

Perhaps it had nothing to do with her daughter, Ginny thought as she dutifully walked into the living room. She'd been looking forward to this weekend for months. Yes, it would be sad without Meg attending the reunion. In preparation, Ginny had given herself pep talks all week so she wouldn't shortchange the friends who would be there or cheat herself out of enjoying some adult company for a change. A little time away from the piano wouldn't hurt either. She'd been practicing like a madwoman for the past seven months, ever since the Rhode Island Philharmonic had invited her to be a guest soloist.

Sharon turned away from the window to smile at Ginny. "You're so lucky you work at home. I don't think I could drag myself away from this view," she said, sighing. "But, then, you lead such an exciting life."

At first Ginny was speechless, then she burst out laughing. "You have me confused with someone else."

"Well, isn't being a member of the orchestra exciting enough for you?" Sharon laughed. "I'd be taking out an ad in the newspaper."

"I've performed as a guest soloist twice,"

she said carefully, not wishing to let anything slip or start a rumor. "But that's all."

Sharon frowned. "I heard you're supposed to go on tour with them."

Ginny hesitated. The director had spoken with her, but nothing was actually settled. "Where did you hear that?"

"I'm not sure. Oh, wait. It was Jane Winthrop."

"Well, apparently Jane knows more than I do," Ginny said, then realized she didn't even know a Jane Winthrop.

It was tempting to ask about the woman and how she'd come about the information. Ginny decided it would be wiser to simply drop the subject. The last thing she wanted was to become fodder for gossip. She'd been there, done that after she'd dropped out of Juilliard all those years ago.

AFTER TURNING HIS rented Jeep over to the valet, Parker Nolan slipped off his aviator sunglasses. Seaside on the Bluff hadn't existed the last time he'd been to Temptation Bay. The large showy resort had replaced a small, early-1900s' hotel. But then, a lot had changed in fifteen years. Including him.

"Sir?"

Parker turned to the valet.

The young man—Rafael, according to his name tag—held up the black leather bag Parker had left on the floor of the passenger side. "Did you forget this? Or would you like for me to call a luggage attendant?"

"I don't have a reservation."

"Ah."

Parker hadn't expected to get a room at the last minute, and judging by all the cars and taxis crowding the porte cochere, he was right. "You know of any place that might have a vacancy?"

"We've got a big class reunion and a golf tournament this weekend," Rafael said, shaking his head. "Between the two I doubt you're going to find anything nearby."

"What about that old turquoise motel on Highway 1. Is it still there?"

"Yeah, but the place—" He lowered his voice. "It's kind of a dump."

Well, that hadn't changed. Parker dug into his pocket and gave the kid a five. "Thanks. I shouldn't be more than a couple hours."

Parker headed toward the glass doors, rubbing the stubble along his jaw, wondering if he shouldn't have found a room first. He could use a shower, and definitely a shave, after the long flight. Eighteen hours ago he'd been unloading the cargo he'd delivered to a backwoods town in northern Alaska when he'd received the call sending him on this fool's errand.

He wasn't going to find his sister. Not here in Temptation Bay, or anywhere else. It was obvious that Meg didn't want to be found. She hadn't surfaced in fifteen years, not even to attend their father's funeral. And then a year ago the random Facebook communications had ceased altogether. Parker's assumption that his mom had finally accepted that Meg was lost to them had shattered the moment he'd answered her phone call yesterday.

It was unclear how she'd learned of the reunion, but that wasn't important. After he followed this last shred of hope, he was going to tell her he was done. Finished. Not that she asked him very often. But this time would be the last. There was no reason to keep opening the wound. No more chasing ghosts or shadows. He and his mom had come out of hiding over thirteen years ago. She was remarried to a nice man, a dentist from Idaho who kept regular hours and put her before his job. It was time she accepted that Meg was never coming back.

At least when he'd gone to ground, he hadn't cut himself out of his mother's life completely. Meg, for whatever reason, had vanished without a word. He hoped it was because it was her choice, even if he wished she could have been kinder about it.

The important thing was that his mother was finally happy. Now, if she could just let go of Meg. Not forget her, but accept that maybe Meg was just like their old man. She'd had plenty of opportunities to reach out, give their mom some peace of mind. Instead, Meg's Facebook posts had dwindled to nothing. Keeping her secrets was clearly more important to her than her family.

The open lobby was spacious, with lots of glass, and overlooked the sparkling blue waters of the bay. People were everywhere. Spread out on the suede chairs and sofas, talking, laughing, sipping cocktails. Others stood in small groups closer to the lobby bar. A short line had formed while folks waited their turn at the reception desk.

The sheer number of people in the lobby made him want to turn around and leave. What he wouldn't give to be back in his cabin, with nothing but the stark beauty of the wilderness as his companion. Once this exercise in futility was over, he'd be better off never leaving Alaska again.

But he'd made a promise he intended to keep. With his eyes peeled, he maneuvered through the crowd, behind uniformed employees pushing carts loaded down with luggage. Off to the left of the elevators, a table was set up and manned by a smartly dressed brunette in her early thirties who flashed a blindingly bright smile and a diamond the size of Parker's De Havilland.

Yep, she looked like a product of the Roger Williams Preparatory Academy to him. He'd never understood why Meg had wanted to go there. She hadn't cared about her grades, or about hanging out with the future bastions of the upper class. In fact, she'd tended to thumb her nose at the type of kids who went to prep school. With the exception of Ginny Landry.

He returned the smile of a tall willowy blonde, and resisted the urge to glance back as they passed each other. She didn't look familiar, although he didn't expect to recognize anyone. He'd lived in Temptation Bay for only a year while attending the public high school before he'd left for Princeton.

Man, it felt like a lifetime ago.

His thoughts circled back to Ginny Landry. He wondered if she would bother showing up. Or if she was even in the country. Easy to imagine her performing somewhere in Europe, playing before the king and queen of some country that still acknowledged royalty. She'd just turned eighteen when he last saw her. He remembered since they shared the same birthday, although he was two years older.

In retrospect, at twenty, he'd still been a kid. A kid with too much responsibility to shoulder and without a clue how to handle the curveball life had thrown him. But Ginny... With all her talent and natural-born grace, it hadn't been hard for him to picture the brilliant future she'd had waiting for her.

The woman at the desk smiled as he approached. "Are you here for the reunion?" she asked, sizing him up. Her smile wavered briefly at his worn jeans. Definitely not designer. "This is the Roger Williams registration desk."

"Just what I was looking for." He gave her a smile that seemed to distract her from his attire. On the left side of the table name badges were displayed alphabetically. "Any chance I can see a list of the attendees?"

"Andrea Langston. Well, I swear..." A woman rushed up from behind him as the brunette—presumably Andrea—rose to greet her.

Parker glanced at the name badges but didn't see Meg's or Ginny's name. Although that didn't tell him anything useful.

The women exchanged silly air kisses, and he saw it was the tall blonde he'd passed a minute ago.

"Andrea, I almost didn't recognize you," the blonde said, then slid him a smile. "Hello."

Parker smiled back.

Just as she extended her hand, someone else caught his eye. Another blonde he'd once known.

"Excuse me," he said, surprised at the hitch in his breathing, and headed for Ginny Landry.

CHAPTER TWO

"How is it you haven't aged a bit?" Harlow said after she and Ginny hugged. "Seriously. You still look like a college kid."

"And you still don't know your own strength." Laughing, Ginny rubbed her arm. Harlow had once been a world-class athlete. "Can we keep the bruising down to a minimum?"

"I'll try." Harlow took her by the hand and dragged her toward a table she'd secured near the lobby bar. "This place is a zoo. I don't want to lose our spot. Have you seen anyone else yet?"

"I just got here. You?"

"Nope. Not a soul." Harlow flagged down a server. "That is, no one I care to talk to. But I haven't been here long either. I went straight to the room, hung up my dress for tomorrow night and left everything else. I wanted to make sure I scored a table."

Ginny grinned. "I'm glad you have your priorities in order."

"You got that right." Her smile was for the waitress. "A pitcher of margaritas, please."

Nodding, the young woman started writing. "Anything else?"

"Wait." Ginny frowned at her friend. "Who's that pitcher for?"

"You and me, unless Cricket or Jade shows up."

Ginny sighed. "You're insane." She turned to the server, who was setting cocktail napkins on the table. "Thank you."

The woman smiled and left.

"So, are you staying in the hotel?" Harlow asked.

"Nope. I'm only ten minutes away."

"Well, if you get too hammered, you can always bunk with me for the night."

"I'm not getting hammered."

"You sure?"

"Yes." Ginny laughed. This felt so good. In just minutes, fifteen years had disappeared. It didn't matter that they lived on opposite coasts, or that, despite their heartfelt graduation night promises, their communication had been sporadic at best. "You look wonderful, Harlow. I mean it."

Harlow shrugged. "I'm blonder."

"You know what I'm saying. I'm glad the accident didn't make you bitter."

"Oh, honey, you didn't see me after I realized I'd blown my shot at the Olympics. And my parents? I thought they were going to jump off a cliff."

She and Harlow had talked shortly after the surgery on her leg, and Ginny knew that her friend had sunk into a dark place. But she hadn't stayed there. "Come on. You're still in fantastic shape. So, good for you. Now, tell me how you like teaching."

"Only if you tell me the real reason you dropped out of Juilliard. I can't believe you're still living here and not playing a fourteen-karat-gold piano on a yacht somewhere exotic."

"What the—" Ginny burst out laughing. "You're not allowed to have any booze. None," she said and turned to see what Harlow was squinting at.

The late-afternoon sun filled the lobby with natural light, but from where she was sitting, the glare made it difficult to see.

"Isn't that Cricket?" Harlow ducked her head when someone at the next table stood and blocked her view. "In line at the reception desk?"

Ginny finally spotted her. "I'm so glad she made it. She looks great, doesn't she?"

"Like a big-shot lawyer. Oh, no...it's Troy what's-his-name behind her. He thinks we're waving at him." Harlow sank back in her chair, averting her face. "I hope he doesn't do something stupid like stop by…"

"Isn't he the guy who you—"

Harlow's glare cut her off.

"Sorry." Ginny hid a smile and turned back to tracking Cricket.

Ginny was anxious to see her, even though they'd connected twice when Cricket had come home to visit her dad, who still lived in a shack on the beach. Of the whole gang, Cricket probably knew her the best, but even though she and the rest of her friends knew about Tilda, they didn't know the entire reason Ginny had left Julliard.

The server delivered the pitcher and glasses, and Harlow asked her to bring one more.

"Have you heard from Jade? Do you know what time she's arriving?"

"Late, I think." Harlow kept her head bowed as she poured. "Where's Cricket? Getting close?"

"She has one person ahead of her."

"Is Troy still looking over here?"

"Nope. He's talking to someone."

"Good." Harlow slid the drink to her. "What about Meg? Have you heard from her?"

Ginny's stomach lurched, even though she'd

known the question would come up. "Not for a while. I seriously doubt she'll be here."

"I guess we could ask Andrea. She's checking people in and passing out name badges."

"Oh, Cricket is at the desk. I hope she doesn't go straight to her room," Ginny said, taking her first sip. The salty tartness woke up her taste buds. As for the alcohol, she'd have to watch herself. With the exception of an occasional glass of wine, she didn't drink much at all.

"She won't." After a healthy sip of her margarita, Harlow sighed, then blinked at Ginny. "I can't believe I forgot to ask… You have a daughter. She must be a teenager by now, right?"

"Oh, yes, she is."

Harlow put out her hand and wiggled her fingers. "I know you have pictures."

"You bet I do." She queued her phone, then handed it over. "Millions of them, but you only have to look at the first hundred."

Harlow's grin turned wistful as she started the slide show. "You think you might have more kids?"

"I'd like to," Ginny said slowly. She'd always wanted to have a family, a husband, at least two more kids. But the subject had the potential to raise questions she didn't want to answer. "What about you?"

"Well, I've been saying someday for so long I'm not sure where I stand. Oh, cute." Harlow held up the picture of Tilda in her first Halloween costume. "Are you in contact with her father?"

Ginny held in a sigh. "Nope," she said, hoping her tone would end the topic. Harlow returned to the slide show, and Ginny looked back to check on Cricket's progress.

Her gaze landed on a man. Tall, dark hair, muscular arms. She could only see his profile, but he looked out of place in faded jeans and a black T-shirt. He wasn't one of the golfers, although why she felt certain of that she couldn't say. And he sure hadn't been one of her classmates.

He stood near the reception desk, but he wasn't waiting in line. If he was looking for someone, he didn't seem to be overly invested in finding them. He glanced almost negligently over the crowd, then donned a pair of aviator sunglasses.

Ginny's heart rate picked up speed.

He reminded her of someone, although she couldn't place him. This guy had a swimmer's build—broad shoulders, slim waist and hips.

Probably rode a motorcycle, wrestled grizzly bears for fun and opened cans with his teeth.

"Earth to Ginny."

She jerked a look at Harlow. "What?"

"What are you doing? Did you see someone or—" Harlow gasped. "Is it Troy? Is he coming over to us?"

"No." The mystery man was most definitely not Troy. She sneaked a peek his way again, but he was gone. She looked right then left. He'd disappeared. "Oh, here comes Cricket."

She and Harlow stood at the same time and met her partway.

"I should've known I'd find you guys near the booze," Cricket said as she reached them. She raised her brows at Ginny. "Look at you in that sexy little sundress."

Sexy? Ginny rolled her eyes. "I'm so glad you made it," she said, pulling Cricket into a hug. "I couldn't believe it when I got your email yesterday."

"Ditto for me. Now, quit hogging her." Harlow threw her arms around both of them.

After a few seconds, Cricket made an odd gurgling noise. "Okay, you have to let me breathe," she said. "Seriously."

Ginny laughed and backed off first. "We better grab our seats."

After pouring Cricket a drink, Harlow said

something Ginny didn't catch. She tried to stay with the conversation, she really did. But she was hopelessly obsessed with finding the man in the jeans and black T-shirt. It was as if he'd disappeared into thin air.

Cricket was staring at her, and so was Harlow. Ginny blinked. "What?"

The server saved her from further humiliation when she stopped to see if Cricket wanted something besides the margarita.

No sooner had the woman moved on than Cricket asked, "What's going on with you? Everything okay?"

"Sure." Ginny smiled. "Other than Harlow trying to get me drunk, everything's fine."

"You holding out on us, Gin?" With a mischievous little smile, Harlow swept a gaze across the lobby. "You see something you like?"

Ginny almost spit out her sip of margarita. This was the last thing she needed. It didn't matter that Harlow was only teasing. "Oh, please," she said and looked at Cricket. "How did you manage to get a room here at the last minute? I thought they were booked."

"They had a suite left."

Harlow snorted. "You must be making big bucks."

"I'm doing okay," Cricket said, shrugging.

"Not that I'm thrilled about paying that much for a suite."

"Hey, you were always the smartest person in the class, so good for you," Harlow said, raising her glass. "You deserve your success."

Ginny raised her glass as well, and while Harlow cajoled Cricket into participating, Ginny stole a look at the bar.

There he was, standing at the end of the sleekly polished mahogany bar, drinking a beer. It seemed he might be looking back at her, but she couldn't tell for sure. Not when he was still wearing those darn sunglasses.

One thing for certain, he wasn't lacking for attention. A woman sitting on a barstool next to him was about to make her move when a blonde squeezed in between them.

He stepped aside, giving her a tight smile, along with plenty of space.

Ginny didn't know why that made her so happy.

Her elation evaporated the second she finally realized why the mystery man seemed familiar. If she had any sense at all, she'd be running in the other direction.

PARKER WATCHED HER from behind the dark lenses of his sunglasses, wondering if she'd recognized him. It wasn't so much the fifteen years that had passed. He simply wasn't the same clean-cut, idealistic college student who'd wanted to fight for justice. To work in concert with his dad—his idol—and others like him, to rid the world of evil.

Good plan, until Parker had discovered it was all a load of crap.

She looked the same, had barely aged. Her dark blond hair was a few inches shorter and now skimmed her shoulders.

And that smile of hers. No woman had a better smile than Ginny Landry. Assuming that was still her last name. He didn't see a ring on her finger, but that meant nothing these days. And with her level of talent, it was likely she was more focused on her career than a husband. Parker didn't recognize either of the two women sitting with her. They could be friends of Meg's as well, but he'd only met Ginny. Although it wasn't until after his sister had disappeared that he'd gotten to know her.

"Excuse me."

He turned to the blonde, who'd crowded him. She was the same woman he'd passed earlier, although he didn't remember the excessive perfume that was beginning to make his eyes burn.

"I practically ran you over," she said. "Let me at least buy you a drink."

"No thanks."

"Oh, come on." She tilted her head, a seductive smile lifting her too-pink lips. "Just one?"

Parker shook his head. What was it with these prep school women? Curious to take a walk on the wild side? He tipped the beer bottle to his mouth, then went back to studying Ginny. She was looking right at him. Before he could give her a nod, she turned away.

He suppressed a smile, wondering if she'd covered up the faint sprinkling of freckles across her nose. She'd never bothered to before, even though he knew she hated them. It was kind of crazy how much he'd learned about her in those few days after Meg had gone missing. He remembered thinking how odd it was that the two had become friends. Talk about opposites.

Meg was always looking for action and, yeah, a fair amount of trouble…an obvious cry for attention, he'd realized much later. His sister had idolized their dad every bit as much as Parker had, misguided as that had proved to be. It had been his first real lesson about trust and its dangers. Hadn't been his last.

Ginny had been like a beacon of light, trying to keep Meg from taking that final step into the darkness. In the end, it hadn't worked. The thing about Ginny, she might look like the carefree girl next door, but she'd never had the perfect family life either. With no mother in the picture, Ginny had been raised by a nanny. Her workaholic father had been largely absent throughout her childhood. At least Parker and Meg had had their mom to rely on. She'd been there for them through a lot of rough patches. Fielding their endless questions, for which she either had no answers or wasn't at liberty to divulge her knowledge.

Now, knowing what he did, Parker was confident his mother had been kept in the dark about her husband's whereabouts, and what he'd been doing for most of their marriage. And to be fair, the secrecy had been for their own protection.

Dammit, Meg shouldn't have punished her by running away. To some degree their mom had been a victim too. She wasn't a stupid or naive person. Parker guessed that she'd fully understood the man she'd married, but no one could've predicted his other life would end up consuming him.

Parker set his empty bottle down, then dug out some money and laid it on the bar. By the time he looked back, Ginny was gone.

CHAPTER THREE

GINNY SLIPPED INTO the ladies' room and splashed cold water on her face, trying to bring herself out of shock.

What was Parker doing here? Now—after all these years without a word, not knowing if he was dead or alive or living on the moon—he just shows up? She knew it must have to do with Meg. If the family had lost contact with her, just as Ginny had, Parker was probably hoping his sister would be at the reunion. Ginny knew his being here had nothing to do with her. And why that should hurt in the slightest was absurd. She wasn't a starry-eyed kid anymore.

After Meg had gone missing, they'd found comfort in each other's arms. That first time, Parker hadn't even known Ginny was a virgin. He'd felt terrible, had come right out and told her that giving herself should have been something special…with someone she cared about and who cared for her.

Oh, how those words, spoken with heartfelt

concern, had cut deep into her soul. Thankfully, she'd had the good sense not to admit that she'd fallen for him months before the night they'd made love. At eighteen, she'd known woefully little about the world beyond her narrow life, and even less about men.

Sadly, at thirty-two, she wasn't much more enlightened. Being a young single mom who worked at home, Ginny had barely made it around the block. Tilda had kept her—

Tilda.

Ginny gripped the counter for support.

Parker couldn't know about her. Even if he'd somehow stumbled onto Ginny's Facebook page, he wouldn't have seen anything incriminating. She'd been so careful about the meager information she'd posted over the years, including any pictures that would pinpoint Tilda's age.

Staring at her reflection in the mirror, Ginny sighed. Luckily her mascara hadn't smudged, but she looked pale. Before the girls started wondering if something was wrong, she reapplied some gloss, swept back her hair and left the restroom.

And ran straight into Parker.

Almost. He took a step back, saving them from a collision.

"Ginny…" He'd removed his sunglasses, his

tanned face bringing out the striking blue of his eyes.

"Parker?"

His slow smile sent her heart into a tailspin. "I wasn't sure you'd remember me."

Gee, why would she? "You do look different," she said, and went for the preemptive strike. "Is Meg with you? Is she here?" Ginny asked, forcing excitement into her voice and making a show of glancing around.

His expression barely changed. "I was about to ask you the same thing."

"Oh. Well, now you know the answer to that."

"My mom thought she might show up. I didn't expect her to be here."

That wasn't completely true. Ginny could see in his eyes that he'd held on to some hope. She felt a twinge of guilt for using the ploy. "Did you check at the registration desk?" she asked, tucking her hair behind her ear for the again. So annoying. She'd quit that nervous habit ages ago. "You know, for the reunion, not the hotel's."

"I figured if anyone knew whether she was coming, it would be you." He paused, studying her closely, clearly looking for something, but she didn't know what. He had no reason to think she was lying. "When was the last time you saw her?"

Ginny shook her head, the sadness resting so heavily, her shoulders drooped. "Not since she disappeared."

"Fifteen years ago."

She nodded, without hesitation, aware that the truth was more complicated than a simple yes or no. "What about you?" she asked because he would expect her to. But she already knew the answer.

"The same." His phone rang. Without so much as a glance he shut it off. "Meg must've contacted you at some point."

"She did."

"How?"

Ginny's stomach lurched. She'd be honest with him, for as long as she could, but the questions were bound to get more difficult. "Through Facebook, mostly. Sometimes she called."

"That's more than my mom got," he said with a snort of derision.

"Did Meg even know how to find any of you?"

Parker's eyes narrowed. He had the audacity to look confused.

Ginny held her breath. Why on earth had

she said that? And with that snarky tone of voice? Yes, he'd taken off without a word to her. Yes, it had hurt at the time. *Fifteen years ago*. She didn't care anymore. But that's not how it had just sounded.

She shot a look toward the bar, seeking an escape route, when she saw the exact moment he realized what she'd meant. Regret replaced confusion, which was so much worse.

"I'm here with friends and I need to get back." Refusing to look up, she tried side-stepping him.

"Ginny." He touched her arm. "Wait. Please."

"Nice seeing you, by the way." She drew her arm back and tucked a lock of hair behind her ear. A group of inattentive golfers jabbering on about their scores had hemmed her in. "Excuse me, please," she said to no avail.

"This way." Parker took her by the arm and guided her around the oblivious foursome.

"Thanks," she murmured, hoping he didn't think that had earned him any points. "I'm sure you understand this is a busy weekend for me."

"I do," he said, "but I'm not going anywhere. If you find that you have some time to spare, how about we have a drink tomorrow?"

She stared blankly at him. What did he

mean he wasn't going anywhere? "How long will you be staying?"

"I haven't decided yet. What about you?"

"Me?"

Parker smiled. "When do you leave?"

"Oh, no. I'm not— I live here." She wanted to take the words back. He looked shocked, but of course he wouldn't know anything about the unexpected twist her life had taken. If she'd stopped to think for two seconds, she would've left his misconception blessedly intact.

Questions swirled in his eyes. "You did go on to Juilliard, didn't you?"

"Yes." At least she didn't have to lie about that. She spotted Connor Foley, the pompous boor most of her classmates, including she, tried to avoid. "Connor?" She waved, catching his attention. "I'm sorry, would you excuse me for a moment," she said to Parker.

She'd taken only a few steps before Connor thwarted her escape by approaching at a fast clip.

"Ginny," Connor said, his arms open. "Ginny Landry. How wonderful to see you."

Ordering herself not to gag, she let him wrap her in a big hug. He smelled awful. Undoubtedly his cologne was expensive; everything he owned was top-of-the-line. His family was loaded. But Connor had always been short on class and good sense. She gave him a discreet hint that it was time to release her, and when he didn't, she wiggled away from him.

When Connor caught her by her upper arms, she thought she saw Parker step closer. She didn't resist, pretended everything was just fine. Maybe she was wrong and Parker wouldn't have intervened, but she couldn't risk him causing a fuss.

Connor leaned back and swept a gaze over her. "You look fantastic. I heard Alexandra and the rest of her gang are green with envy that you haven't aged." He frowned slightly. "Perhaps some Botox wouldn't hurt. Just a touch between your brows. But that's all."

Ginny blinked, then burst out laughing.

Connor's puzzled expression didn't help, but at least he'd released her.

"Thanks for the advice," she said, doing her absolute best to control herself. "I'll be sure to keep that in mind. Well, it was nice seeing you."

"Wait." Connor stepped forward, trying to regain the distance she was putting between them. "Are you here with anyone?"

She backed right into Parker.

This time it was his hands closing around her upper arms, drawing her closer. Her back met his hard chest. "Careful, sweetheart," he said, his voice pitched low and intimate. But not so low Connor wouldn't hear. "Aren't you going to introduce me to your friend?"

For a second she couldn't make her mouth work. The heat coming from Parker's body seemed to envelop her, lull her into a relaxed state. His work-roughened palms slid down her bare arms. It was entirely possible the late-afternoon sun flooding the lobby was making her feel flushed, but she didn't think so.

Just as Ginny was about to make the introductions, she realized Connor had walked away. Good grief, how long had she spaced out for?

She didn't exactly push Parker away but she definitely made a point as she jerked back and turned to him. "Why did you say that?"

"Say what?"

"That I'm here with you."

His eyebrows shot up. "I didn't."

"You implied it."

"Sorry." He shrugged. "I didn't realize you liked him pawing you."

She could still feel his warmth slipping down her spine, as if she hadn't broken contact. Her skin tingled from the roughness of his palms. Hugging herself, she rubbed her arms, trying to erase the feel of him.

"We haven't seen each other for a long time, and we were awfully young, so I can understand why you might make such a ridiculous comment," she said, irritated by the smile lurking at the corners of his mouth. "However, let me assure you, I can take care of myself just fine."

"Don't doubt it for a second," he said, folding his arms across his chest.

Why did he have to have so many muscles? More important, why was she reacting to them…to him? A man's intellect was of far greater interest to her. Not that she didn't appreciate a good-looking man.

She realized she was staring. "I really do have to go."

"Let me give you my number."

"Your— Why?"

"In case you have time for a drink. Unless you prefer to give me yours."

Ginny shook her head, perhaps a bit too quickly. No, let him think she was brushing him off. Maybe then he wouldn't stick around. But to be safe, she would make a point of getting Cricket alone to ask her about potential parental rights. She rifled through her hand-bag. The pen wasn't in its usual place.

"I can put it in your phone, if you like."

Looking up, she met his eyes. Something glinting from them sent a little shiver through her body. Her fingers brushed the pen. She pulled it out along with a credit card receipt that was blank on the back. "I'm ready," she said, the pen poised to write.

He recited the number.

She repeated it to him and then stuck the receipt in an inside pocket. Feeling a bit more in control, she shook her hair back just as something troubling occurred to her. "Are you staying here at the resort?"

"Nope. They're booked."

"Right." She tried to hide her relief. "Well, again, it was nice seeing you, Parker. Good luck finding Meg."

His penetrating gaze made her feel completely transparent. Naked. Too vulnerable. "You have no intention of calling me, do you?"

"Would you blame me if I didn't?" She tried to bite back the words but it was too late.

Regret flickered in his eyes. Not that Ginny cared. He knew exactly what she meant. A week after Meg's disappearance, he and his mom had pulled their own vanishing act.

Overnight their home had been stripped of everything personal. The whole community had been stunned. Rumors had spread like wildfire. That they were in witness protection had been the most popular.

All Ginny knew for certain was that her heart had shattered into too many pieces to count.

CHAPTER FOUR

STILL IN HER ratty old robe, Ginny left her makeup spread out across her bathroom counter and went to the kitchen to pour herself a third cup of coffee. She hoped the extra caffeine wouldn't make her jittery, but without another dose she'd be nodding off by lunchtime.

Ha. She should be so lucky.

It had been a mistake talking to Cricket. Ginny felt awful for wasting her friend's time. Not only had she jumped the gun, but she'd been unwilling to give Cricket all the facts. Ginny's only excuse was that she had panicked the moment she'd seen Parker. And now, after a poor night's sleep, she wasn't any more ready to face the day. Just knowing he could show up at the resort at any minute wreaked havoc with her nervous system.

This was supposed to have been a fun weekend, a time to catch up and relax with her friends. Social media was great in so many ways, but nothing beat seeing everyone in per-

son. And being able to show them more pictures of Tilda.

She'd been looking forward to the reunion
for weeks.

She'd actually made peace with the fact
that Meg wouldn't be making an appearance.
Once Meg had hooked up with Danny all those
years ago, her fate had been sealed. So Ginny
had been prepared for her absence. Parker,
though…nothing could've prepared Ginny
for him.

Her heart had actually raced with excitement, just like it had when she was eighteen.
Then, as the ramifications of him finding out
about Tilda had begun to sink in, panic and
nerves had taken over. Now, even without ad-
equate sleep, she realized she'd overreacted.
Even if he were to meet Tilda, which she didn't
see happening, it didn't mean he'd make the
leap that he and Tilda were related.

After filling her cup and adding sugar, she
leaned against the counter, staring out the window. Jade had arrived late last night. When it
came to causing trouble she'd always led the
pack. Ginny smiled. Her mind wouldn't have
time to wander with Jade around.

The doorbell rang.

Sighing, Ginny took another sip before
going to answer it. She knew it was Rod-

ney from next door. Practically every Saturday he conveniently hit a ball over her fence and needed to enter the property. She had no idea what was so interesting about her side of the—

It wasn't Rodney. Through the long, narrow window she saw Parker standing at the door. And he most definitely saw her. No pretending she wasn't home. But having the reunion as an excuse, she figured she could get rid of him quickly.

Gripping the knob, she took a deep breath and then opened the door. "Parker. This is a surprise."

"I know," he said, shrugging. "I would've called first if I'd had your number."

And he couldn't have taken the hint?

Instead of pointing that out, she held on to a polite smile. He wore jeans again, but they were dark blue and went well with the green polo shirt tucked in at his slim waist.

"Mind if I come in?" he asked. "I won't stay long, and I come bearing gifts." He held up a white paper bag, probably from Gustav's. Great. The bakery was off-limits to her.

"Okay," she drawled. "Honestly, I only have a few minutes. I was just on my way out."

As she stepped back, holding the door wide, his gaze slid down the front of her body.

Wondering about the flicker of amusement in his eyes as he walked past her, she looked down at herself...

Her faded, oversize granny robe had to be a hundred years old. On the left side was a hole you could drive a truck through, and it was so long the hem dragged on the floor behind her.

She bit back a whimper.

Then, as if that wasn't enough, she remembered that she'd made it through only half of her makeup ritual. She had to look like a stupid clown. Good. Maybe he'd leave sooner.

Ginny clutched the front of her robe, making sure there were no gaps, and gestured for him to go into the living room. Tilda always teased her about the robe, pointing out she was too old to have a security blanket. Her daughter wasn't too far off the mark. The robe was Ginny's go-to when she was sick or upset or just feeling a bit blue.

"I smell coffee," Parker said. "Any chance I can get a cup?"

"Sure, although if you use cream you're out of luck. All we have is milk."

His brows drew together in the oddest frown. "We?"

Ginny swallowed. Hard. "My daughter," she said, and saw him glance toward the hall. "She's camping with friends this weekend." Ginny cleared her throat. "I'll go get your coffee."

Too frazzled to think straight, she swept a swift gaze around the room as she headed for the kitchen. Sitting on the bookshelf closest to the piano were two framed pictures of Tilda, one from when she was five and the other from her twelfth birthday. They were in plain sight. Nothing short of a miracle would stop him from looking at them, which would lead to questions Ginny didn't want to answer.

Her hand shook as she poured him a cup, and she cursed under her breath when some of the hot brew burned her fingers.

"Here, let me get that..." His voice came from close behind.

She jerked, spilling half the coffee onto her hand and the floor. She clamped her lips together.

"I didn't mean to startle you," he said quietly and took the cup from her. After setting it on the counter, he picked up her hand and inspected the red skin.

"It's nothing."

"Do you have any ointment handy?"

He'd shaved, she realized, doing some close inspecting of her own. The dimple on his chin was more visible, and the sudden urge to rub her thumb over it had her pulling her hand back.

"It's fine," she said and returned the carafe to the coffee station, then went to the fridge. The second she opened it she remembered the milk was already on the counter.

"Okay to use this?"

She turned to find him holding up the kitchen rag she left draped on the dishwasher handle. She nodded and watched him crouch to wipe the coffee off the hardwood floor. "Do you clean windows too?"

Glancing up, he grinned. "With the right motivation, you bet."

Oh, no, she wasn't taking the bait. She gave him a slight smile and slid the small ceramic pot of sugar toward him as he rose. "Thanks," she said, gesturing vaguely at the floor.

He eyed the nearly empty coffee carafe.

"I'd offer to make more, but I know you don't have much time. Go ahead and finish it up. It's still fresh."

"I brought something from Gustav's…"

"I guessed," Ginny said, sighing.

Parker paused, the amusement in his eyes hard to miss. "The bag's in the living room. Are we going back out there, or should I go get it?"

"Yes, please."

His brows went up.

"Let's stay here." Maybe, just maybe, he

hadn't noticed the photos. Knowing she had a daughter was one thing. Knowing her daughter's age, well, that was something else altogether.

She went ahead and scooped up the remainder of the beans she'd ground earlier, enough for at least half a pot. Anything from Gustav's required coffee as an accompaniment. And not just any brew but the really good stuff, of which she was always sure to have a vast supply.

Parker returned quickly and made himself at home finding the small plates and setting them on the table along with forks and napkins.

She was dying to know what he'd brought, but she wouldn't ask. As soon as the coffee started to brew she turned to him. He swiftly brought his gaze up to eye level. The robe...

When he pulled a chair out from the table for her, she bit her lip as she sat down. Why was this suddenly feeling like the Last Supper?

"Go ahead and open the bag," he said, as he took a seat across from her.

"I'm not sure I should be starting the day with sugar," she murmured, even as she reached for the sack. "I drank more alcohol last night than I typically drink in a whole year."

"You don't look hungover."

Ginny peeked inside the bag and groaned. "I love anything Gustav makes, but the cardamom rolls are my absolute favorite."

"I know."

She frowned at his pleased smile. "How?"

"I asked." Parker shrugged. "I figured someone behind the counter would know you."

"I haven't been in there for months." Sniffing, she tore the bag open. She had no willpower when it came to all the ridiculous pastries they offered.

"Why not? Have you been touring?"

She put the roll on her plate and pushed the bag at him, her appetite diminishing suddenly. Something in his piercing blue eyes told her he already knew the answer to that question. She wouldn't be at all surprised if he'd been asking around about her. Despite the hordes of tourists and all the summer people, the locals managed to stay tight and connected.

"Touring?" She stared right back at him. "I teach piano. Here at the house. Five days a week."

"That's what I heard. I just didn't believe it."

"Why not? I make a respectable living, and I have a number of kids who are very serious students."

"That's not— I'm sure that's true." Shaking

his head, he sighed. "You had dreams, Ginny, big dreams, about Juilliard and about life after Juilliard. And rightfully so. We talked about them, remember? You're too talented to be… giving piano lessons…"

Heat crawled up her throat and exploded in her face. The anger and hurt building inside her nearly frightened her into silence. "What about you?" she asked, holding on to her temper by a thread. "Since we're discussing *our* dreams. Did you ever go on to law school? Are you the big shot, crime-fighting attorney you intended to be?"

"Come on, Ginny. I'm not criticizing you, and I'm sure not looking for an argument." He reached across the table for her hand but she snatched it away and clasped her hands together on her lap.

"I'll take that as a no."

"Okay. You're right. I didn't go to law school. I didn't even finish Princeton."

Ginny had willfully done the poking. She should've been satisfied with his weary expression of defeat as he leaned back in his chair. Why on earth hadn't he finished Princeton? He'd been doing well and was so excited. Had he dropped out because of Meg?

Regret lasted only until she remembered

they'd been talking about *her* broken dreams. She hadn't prompted the discussion, he had. And whether or not he'd meant to sound critical, how she chose to live her life was none of his business. He'd lost that right the day he'd made love to her, then disappeared just hours later without a word. At least she hadn't brought *that* up.

"Well, I gotta say, that's not how I imagined embarking on my explanation," he said with a faint smile.

The coffee had finished brewing.

She stood up, scanning the counter until she located her cup. She grabbed it and the carafe, relieved to see her hands weren't shaking too badly. If she let him say his piece now, maybe he'd leave. Go back to wherever it was he'd come from. At the very least, she wouldn't have to be looking over her shoulder all weekend. Nevertheless, she wasn't about to let this conversation go on too long.

After they each had a steaming cup in front of them, she sat down. "An explanation?"

Parker nodded. "For leaving the way I did."

Ginny calmly took a sip—then set the cup down. "You don't owe me anything. It was a long time ago."

"Doesn't matter. I do owe you, and I need to

get it off my chest. So, humor me?" He gave her that sexy smile she remembered all too well.

After he'd left, how many nights had she spent weeping over that bone-melting smile that had gotten her in trouble with him in the first place. And now it was making a mockery of her defenses. Darn him.

It just wasn't fair. She wasn't a naive eighteen-year-old anymore and she didn't give a fig about making him feel better... "All right, go ahead." She dragged her gaze away to look at the wall clock. Mostly, so she wouldn't be dazzled by that stupid smile. "You have five minutes."

"Thank you," he said, his voice lowered. "I mean it."

"Four minutes and fifty-six seconds."

His deep, raspy chuckle was almost as bad as the smile. "First, I want you to know it wasn't my decision to leave. I didn't have a choice."

That tactic wouldn't work on her. Ginny believed everyone had choices. Sometimes they weren't popular or easy, and the consequences could be life changing. She doubted anyone understood that concept better than she did.

"My dad used to work for the DEA," Parker

said, then paused to take a quick sip of his coffee.

"Wait. Not when you all lived here. He was an insurance investigator, right? Or was it a claims adjuster?"

"Neither. He'd been working undercover for a while by the time we moved to Temptation Bay. Meg probably told you the same story we were fed."

"I wondered why he was gone so much," Ginny said, mostly to herself. "Meg hated it."

"We both did. Mom too. According to what she told me later, it wasn't a problem at first. The assignments were low-level drug busts that kept him away for a week or two at the most. Then, as he became more involved tracking down an East Coast heroine distribution ring out of Florida, his boss kept sending him deeper into the organization. Usually for months at a time. At one point he was gone almost a year."

Ginny's eyes widened. "How was that possible? Didn't you question where he was?"

"Of course, but my mom covered for him. Once she said he was away for job training. Another time he was supposed to have gone to Texas to investigate a case of fraud." Parker shrugged. "We were young when it started and got used to the absences."

"Not Meg," Ginny said half to herself, her gaze straying toward the window. "It bothered her a lot." Ginny thought back to the week before her friend had disappeared, when she'd begun her downward spiral. "Was that why your parents were getting a divorce?"

Parker looked taken aback. "There hadn't been any talk of divorce. My mom would've mentioned it. Personally, I wouldn't have blamed her if she had left him," he said. "Why do you ask?"

This time it was Ginny who was caught off guard. Mr. Nolan hadn't just been Meg's idol, he'd been Parker's, as well. "About a week before Meg went missing she overheard your parents arguing. She told me your dad was having an affair and leaving for good."

Parker's brow furrowed. "I remember you telling me she'd heard them talking. It was the day before he left for Colombia. But I don't think you mentioned anything about an affair."

Holding her breath, Ginny shrugged. Unfortunately, she couldn't remember what she'd told him and what she'd hidden at the time. "I can't recall specifics."

"No reason you should." He let out a weary sigh. "Too bad he didn't leave for good. It would've been better all the way around."

Ginny hid behind her cup of coffee as pieces of the puzzle started falling into place. Studying the lines of tension bracketing Parker's mouth, the hardness in his expression, she was still curious about his animosity toward his dad. Everything had happened so long ago but Parker looked as if he'd just awoken from the nightmare. "The night you and your mom disappeared…?"

Parker's features eased. "The agency was afraid Dad's cover had been blown, and that Meg's disappearance had something to do with it."

"You mean, they thought she'd been kidnapped?"

"Or worse. It was a while before we found out she'd just run away."

Ginny knew there was a lot more to that story, but clearly Meg had elected not to share it with her family so neither would she. However, she still had questions. But did she dare ask? Getting him on his way was her top priority. Leaving the past in the past was her safest move. She didn't need to slip up and say something that would raise questions she wasn't prepared to answer. Ever.

"Ginny…" He leaned across the table and brushed his fingers over the back of her hand. "I didn't want to leave like that. Without saying goodbye, or at least explaining what was going on. It happened so quickly, and my mom…she was a mess, and at that point I was all she had."

Nodding, Ginny managed a smile. "You could've called me later…when things weren't so crazy." She shrugged a shoulder. "Just to tell me you were okay."

"You're absolutely right."

"It doesn't matter now. I don't know why I said that." Good grief. Couldn't she listen to her own counsel? She moved her hand back and brushed the hair away from her face.

"Ginny, please…"

She stood rather abruptly. "I guess you'll be taking off soon." She didn't offer him any more coffee and put her cup in the sink. "Oh, I should've asked…how's your mom?"

"Happily remarried. Living in Idaho." Parker got to his feet and must've noticed Ginny's startled reaction. "The old man's been dead for fourteen years."

"Oh, I'm sorry." Ginny's breath caught at the detached look on Parker's face. A wave of sadness washed over her. The Nolans had once been a close family, despite Mr. Nolan's frequent absences, and the senseless tragedy of the situation broke her heart.

"Hey, you okay?" In seconds Parker was at her side.

"Yes, I'm fine. It's just—I can't begin to imagine all the pain you and your mom went through. And for nothing. So much could've been avoided if only Meg had said something." He was standing close, his rugged good looks and musky scent emphasizing how different he was from the earnest, clean-cut young man she'd fallen for all those years ago.

"Sure, Meg lit the match by taking off like she did, but there was more to it." Bitterness tinged Parker's voice. "Turns out Dad, the big hero, wasn't the man we all thought he was."

Ginny didn't know what that meant but she wasn't about to ask him now. Her stomach churned when she realized she'd played a part in all the devastation. In her misguided loyalty to Meg, she hadn't been entirely forthcoming with Parker and the police about what she'd known at the time. It wasn't much, and probably wouldn't have mattered in the long run, but still... "Did Meg's disappearance have anything to do with you dropping out of Princeton?"

Something about the set of Parker's shoulders, the flicker of disappointment and defeat in his eyes before the mask slipped back into place, made her want to hold him close, offer him comfort. The impulse was beyond insane. That hadn't turned out so well the last time. Knowing she could've made things worse by her silence had her stomach clenching.

"Nothing went the way I planned after all that happened. But it's worked out fine. Now I have different expectations and a lot fewer disappointments."

The trace of rancor in his tone made her feel even worse. If only she'd said something. Anything. Light-headed suddenly, Ginny swayed a little and used the counter for support.

Parker put his arms around her. "What's wrong?"

"Nothing. I think the coffee might not be agreeing with me." She didn't resist. It felt good being held by him again. Too good, she thought as she laid her cheek against the warmth of his chest. Only because she couldn't look into his eyes. At least that's what she told herself.

"I didn't mean to hurt you," he whispered, his arms tightening ever so gently. "I was young, angry and stupid. And too self-absorbed. I should've called."

Ginny didn't dare move. Or speak. Tears stung the backs of her eyes. She refused to let them fall though. Thinking she heard the front door open, she stiffened.

"Don't get out the shotgun. It's just me."

Tilda.

CHAPTER FIVE

PANIC SHADOWED GINNY'S EYES as she shrugged off his arms and stepped back, bumping into the counter. Parker had heard the door and immediately gave her some space.

"Tilda?" Ginny's voice broke. "What are you doing here?"

"Um…" The girl entered the kitchen and slowed to a stop when she saw Parker. "I live here?"

"You're supposed to be camping. Why aren't you with Kaley and her family?"

The teen was tall and slim, her long dark hair pulled back into a ponytail that fell past her shoulders. Her big brown eyes went wide with surprise as her gaze bounced from Ginny to Parker. "Kaley's brother had an allergic reaction to something and had to go to urgent care."

"So the trip is canceled?"

"No. That happened yesterday. We're on our way to Sunset Pond now." She blinked at Parker, then gave him a little smile. "Hi."

Ginny cleared her throat. "Oh, Parker, this is my daughter. Tilda, this is Parker Nolan."

"Any relationship to Meg?"

He offered her his hand, which she shook with a firm grip. "I'm her brother."

Tilda's grin widened. "I haven't gotten to meet her yet, but Mom talks about her a lot. And she has tons of pictures of them from high school..." She trailed off, frowning, and turned to Ginny. "Did Meg make it for the reunion?"

Ginny shook her head.

"I was hoping she might be here, so I figured I'd show up and surprise her," Parker said with a shrug, wondering how much Ginny had told her daughter. "Guess the joke's on me."

Tilda gave him a closer look. "Did you go to Roger Williams too?"

He almost smiled at her lack of subtlety. And here he'd even shaved. "Nope."

The girl was quite a bit older than she was in the picture he'd seen in the living room. Fifteen maybe? No, she had to be younger since Ginny—

His chest tightened. He studied Tilda more intently. She didn't resemble Ginny, which didn't necessarily mean anything. She didn't look like him either, though her crooked smile reminded him of Meg. But that was really reaching. The math though. Numbers didn't lie.

To have a kid this age meant Ginny would have been with someone else shortly after Parker left. He'd never seen her as the type to do something like that, but then they hadn't known each other long. He hated to think it might have been a rebound mistake.

"I still don't know why you're here," Ginny said, just as he'd been about to ask Tilda her age.

"I forgot something."

"Ah, what a surprise." Ginny seemed jumpy, fisting the front of her shabby robe. Being caught in their semicompromising situation could account for her nerves. But her face should've been pink, not ashen.

Tilda's gaze settled on Ginny's hand, then lowered all the way down her robe. "Mom!" She moved closer to Ginny. "Are you serious?" she said, her hushed voice loud enough for Parker to hear.

He might've laughed if his mind hadn't been racing in several directions at once.

A horn honked.

They both glanced toward the window. Then Ginny gave her daughter a stern look. "Are Kaley and her mom waiting in the car for you?"

"Oops." Tilda backed up. "I need to get my phone charger, then I'm outta here." She sent her mom an eye signal that had something to do with the ugly robe, then she smiled at Parker. "Nice meeting you," she said and took off.

"I can't believe the time." Ginny's gaze lingered on the wall clock long enough for him to know she was avoiding him. "At the risk of sounding rude, I've got to get moving. I'm already late and I still need to get dressed."

"No problem. I didn't mean to keep you." He retrieved his cup from the table and took it to the sink.

"Oh, please, leave it. I feel terrible rushing you as it is. It's just that we have a few scheduled events and I haven't seen my old gang for ages. Anyway, I'm sure you're anxious to be on your way." She was rushing her words, clearly eager for him to leave, and that made him suspicious. "I don't know if you heard about the storm headed up the coast. You know how awful the winds can be this time of year. I'd hate to see you stranded because your flight was canceled."

Parker knew about the storm. If it hit land this far north, and that was a big if, the weather bureau predicted it wouldn't happen until next week.

"Thanks for your concern," he said, "but I'm in no hurry. Besides, what about having that drink we talked about?"

"Did we?"

Parker smiled. "Tell you what, your friends will only be here for…what…two more days? You go have fun with them. I'll entertain myself, visit some of my old haunts, then we can meet up after everyone's left. How does that sound?"

"I work for a living. It was hard squeezing in the reunion. I can't just—"

"That sounds like a great idea." Tilda stuck her head into the kitchen. "She never goes out. Ever. Okay, I've got my charger and we're off. See you on Monday."

Ginny's glare included both of them.

Parker waited until he heard the front door close. "Tilda's a smart kid. Very pretty too."

Avoiding his eyes, Ginny opened the dishwasher, forcing him to back up. She put both cups on the top rack and closed it.

"How old is she?"

After washing her hands and drying them, she muttered, "Thirteen."

He watched her hang up the towel, her hand trembling, and in that moment he knew. "Is she mine?"

Ginny straightened and faced him. Her eyes and voice clear as could be. "No. She isn't."

"You expect me to believe that?"

"What you believe is irrelevant. It's the truth."

If he hadn't seen the girl and then Ginny's reaction with his own eyes, he probably would've believed her. "Is she really thirteen?"

Ginny let out a sigh. "No. Fourteen. I lied because I knew you'd think exactly what you're thinking, which would turn into a big hassle for nothing." She shook her head. "I swear to you, Tilda isn't yours."

Parker frowned. They'd used protection, he'd made sure of that. But something wasn't adding up here. Before he could open his mouth, she walked past him toward the hallway.

She stopped, looked back. "By the way, this doesn't give you the right to ask any personal questions about my dating history after you left town. Now, I really do need to get going and so do you."

He had to admit, she was being calm now. But he sure hadn't imagined her nervousness earlier. "So I'm supposed to just take your word for it?"

"Yes."

"Mind if I see her birth certificate?"

She lifted a brow. "Yes, actually, I do."

"Why? You have nothing to hide, right?"

Staring at him, Ginny tilted her head slightly. "Even if you were her father, do you honestly think I'd name a man who'd suddenly disappeared without a word? No letter. No phone call. Nothing. A man who could've been dead for all I knew."

"Ah, so this is payback?"

"Not at all. I'm just pointing out the facts."

"I've already explained to you why I couldn't make contact at the time."

"And I answered your question. Tilda isn't your daughter." Ginny held his gaze without blinking or giving any indication she was lying. "But she is mine. And I won't allow you to disrupt her life in any way. Have I made myself clear?"

Parker studied her determined green eyes, the lush shape of her mouth, waiting for her to falter. She was a rock. Generally he was good at reading people, and rarely found reason to second-guess himself. But he was starting to do just that. Whatever had made Ginny nervous earlier might've had nothing to do with her daughter. Yet something still bothered him.

Finally he nodded. "I'm sure you understand why I had to ask."

"I do. Just as you must understand my first

duty is to protect Tilda. She's a sweet, compassionate girl and gifted student with a bright future ahead of her. The last thing she needs is an emotional upheaval that would only lead to disappointment."

"Does she know her father?" Parker saw the fire reignite in her eyes. "And yes, I know it's none of my business."

Ginny smiled a little. "No, it's not. And no, she doesn't know him. Now, I hope you have a safe trip back to wherever it is you live."

For a second he'd thought she might be softening. "I have to say, you sure are anxious to get rid of me." He walked toward her and she seemed to shrink back, into the hall. She didn't look all that confident now. He stopped short, not wanting to spook her further. Ironically, he'd been heading for the front door, about to give her what she wanted. "Do you hate me that much?"

"I don't hate you, Parker." Her voice dropped to a whisper. "Actually, I'm glad you came. The not knowing was hard. It's been a while since I've thought about you and that last night before you left, at least consciously, but it feels good to have some closure."

He put his hand out to her. She looked at it, hesitant, confusion swirling in her eyes, then she laid her palm on his. "I'm sorry I caused you any pain," he said, tugging her closer.

"I don't know what you're expecting but—"

"Expectations are for suckers." He'd learned that the hard way, but the lesson had stuck. "Just one drink, okay? I promise not to grill you, and I'd like to catch up before I leave. You name the time and place."

She gazed up at him, her confusion giving way to a flicker of excitement. He hoped it was more about the electricity that still arced between them than about him mentioning leaving. "Maybe," she said. "That's the best I can do."

Parker nodded. "It's more than I deserve." He lowered his head, and before she could protest, he planted a quick kiss on her forehead. Then he continued on to the front door before he did something stupid.

If anyone knew why he wanted to see her again he wished they'd explain it to him. He'd made his apology. Got his answer about her daughter. He should be relieved. His life was in Alaska. He was never going to leave there. The rest of the world revolved just fine without him. And luckily, he'd managed to find some peace in his life. Everything about living in his cabin, miles from civilization, suited him to a T. It was safe, free of emotional entanglements, less messy.

He and his business partner Mark Schwartz flew cargo, primarily to the outlying districts and small villages near waterways. They both flew out of Fairbanks, although they rarely ran into each other. Mark did most of the Anchorage deliveries. Parker liked delivering to the outliers.

He'd be a fool to allow anyone or anything to rob him of that life. Including the feelings building inside him. He'd felt the spark long before seeing it in Ginny's eyes seconds ago. He'd thought about her over the years, generally with a mixture of fondness and shame. But the ache to hold her in his arms again, that was unexpected. And dangerous. The last thing he wanted to do was hurt her again.

Ginny hadn't changed. She was a smart, compassionate, beautiful woman who deserved a good man, someone to share her life with and help raise her daughter. Someone a lot better than him.

GINNY STARED AT all the new cosmetics spread across her bathroom counter, defeat settling in every fiber of her being. Eyeliner pencils, a stupidly big eyeshadow palette, tubes of tinted moisturizers, highlighting sticks and a few other items she'd already forgotten how and where to apply. Did women really use all this stuff? Or did the saleswoman at the makeup counter know a sucker when she saw one?

It had been very expensive and now Ginny wondered how she was going to manage putting it to use when her hands were still shaking. She really needed to calm down.

Parker had left five minutes ago. And she honestly believed he no longer thought Tilda was his child. If he pressed, she had the consent to adoption Meg had given her. It was as good as a power of attorney, and had been witnessed by a social worker, who'd explained Meg needed it in order to give the baby up for adoption. The father's name had never been on any documents.

It wasn't until after several weeks—when Ginny had bonded completely with Tilda—that she considered adopting Tilda herself. She'd even spoken to an attorney about it, but the man had had concerns about the paperwork Meg had given her, and Ginny had been too nervous to move forward and have things blow up in her face.

By that time, Tilda had felt like her own daughter, and that hadn't changed in all these years. But she still had that paper in her safe, and she'd use it if she had to. She just hoped it wouldn't come to that.

If Ginny chose not to meet Parker for a drink and didn't bother to call, she was sure that would be the end of it. She'd never see him again. Which was her goal, despite the ache in her heart.

How could she still feel anything for him? Anything but disdain was nuts. He could've contacted her once he and his mom were in the clear. But he hadn't.

Determined to put all thoughts of Parker aside for her big night at the reunion, she faced the makeup once again. Unfortunately, her exuberance waned as she picked up the gray liner pencil that promised a sultry, smoky-eyed look. Ginny recalled it involved a lot of smudging. Not gonna happen—she was sure she'd end up looking like a racoon. Maybe she should just bag up the lot and return to the store for some help from the saleswoman. Before she could decide, the phone rang.

"Dad?"

"Ginny. I wasn't sure I'd catch you at home. Isn't this your big reunion weekend?"

She couldn't imagine how he knew that… certainly not from her. "It is."

"I hope you're enjoying yourself." He paused,

probably wondering what came next during a
normal parent-child phone call. "How's Tilda?"

Okay, this was getting weirder by the second. "Um, she's fine. She's gone camping with
a friend."

"By themselves?"

As if he cared. Ginny quashed the thought.
Lately he'd been trying to mend the rift between them. The least she could do was meet
him partway. "No, the whole family went."

"Well, good, I'm glad you have the weekend to yourself. Did your old gang show up?"

"Most of them, yes. It's fun seeing everyone. I've recognized quite a few people. One
charmer told me I could use a bit of Botox between my eyebrows."

Her dad barked out a laugh that had her head
spinning. When had she last heard that sound
come from him? Ten years? Fourteen? "Don't
listen to that nonsense," he said. "You're a
beautiful young woman just the way you are."

Ginny blinked. His words brought a lump
to her throat. What was going on? "Dad? Is
everything all right?"

"With me? Of course, I'm fine. Perhaps mel-
lowing with age, as they say," he said with a
trace of amusement. "By the way, I heard Tilda
made the dean's list."

Startled at first, Ginny quickly realized it

wasn't at all odd for him to know about the goings-on at Roger Williams Preparatory Academy. He and most of his cronies were alumni, including the current headmaster. Truly the "old boys club."

"Yes, she's doing very well."

"I must admit, I thought you were wrong in allowing her to skip the third grade. However, I imagine she would've been quite bored. It seems she has a head for science." He paused. "Honestly, Ginny, I wish you'd told me she was in an accelerated program. I'm very proud of that granddaughter of mine."

Ginny held her tongue. He should've been proud of her regardless. Ginny wasn't surprised though. This was a well-worn theme in his life. If she had stayed at Juilliard she would've been the apple of her father's eye. Not an outcast.

"Yes, I'm proud of her, as well. Funny you brought up her skipping a grade. At the rate she's going she'll graduate early and then be off to college. I'm sure going to miss her."

"Nonsense. You must do what's right for the child."

"I didn't say I would hold her back. Although if she wasn't at an appropriate maturity level, I wouldn't hesitate to do just that." Ginny's brusque tone was met with silence. She never spoke to her dad like that. She cleared her throat. "Tilda's SAT scores should get her a scholarship, especially now that we know MIT has her on their radar. So I don't think I'll have to worry about shelling out exorbitant tuition."

"Oh, for heaven's sake, you know I'll take care of my granddaughter's college expenses."

Ginny waited, holding her breath, half expecting him to give her a list of conditions. The offer was an amazing turnaround on his part, and she felt equal parts gratitude and resentment. If Tilda had been an average student, would they even be having this conversation? Would they be on speaking terms at all? Plus, she knew that if he were to pay Tilda's tuition he would insist on full input as to which university she attended.

"Thank you, Dad. That's very generous of you," Ginny said, choosing her words carefully. "We'll discuss it later. I'm running a little late here."

"All right, I didn't mean to keep you. Give my best to Tilda."

Out of pure selfishness, Ginny sometimes wished she hadn't let Tilda skip third grade. She couldn't imagine living in the house without her. They'd been through so much together. But she would never clip Tilda's wings, or do anything that would hinder her very bright future.

Anyway, if things went well with the Rhode Island Philharmonic, Ginny would have very little time to miss anyone. She'd have a second chance at a career—not the one she could have had. There'd be no Carnegie Hall in her future. Though if she did well, there was a good chance of steady work in smaller venues, which would be just fine with her.

But that presented another problem. At thirty-two, she still had time to have babies of her own. She'd been honest with Harlow… Ginny truly did want to have a bigger family. And she wanted to experience all of motherhood…the aches and pains of pregnancy, giving birth, all of it.

Oh, Tilda would always be hers. Ginny couldn't possibly love her more. But she knew Tilda would be thrilled with a little brother or sister, and Ginny longed for a partner to share her life, and the laughter of children to fill her house and her heart.

CHAPTER SIX

THE MOTEL MADE Parker's cabin feel like a palace—before he'd installed the indoor plumbing. But he'd stayed in worse. At least the TV worked, although it wasn't loud enough to compete with the *soothing* sound of the stone's-throw highway serenade keeping him from getting a nap at all. It wouldn't be so bad if he'd gotten some rest last night, but nope. He'd grown used to the calls of moose, bears, wolves, the squeal of hawks and higher calls of elk.

So he thought about Ginny. Not just Ginny from this morning, with her torn robe and half-done makeup, but Ginny from the night they'd come together for comfort.

He'd spent a lot of years regretting that he'd let things go so far, and just as many that he hadn't come back to find her, to explain why he'd left so suddenly. But he'd known she was headed for big things, and his own life plans had diminished to less than wishful thinking.

Nothing could have shocked him more than

finding out she'd stayed in Temptation Bay and taught piano from her family home. Except that she'd had a child.

Although Ginny had convinced him that Tilda wasn't his, he couldn't seem to shake the idea that Ginny was hiding something. It bothered him that he was making decisions based on a girl he'd known briefly years ago. Even though they'd been more than acquaintances, they hadn't been friends, not in the way he understood the concept. They'd shared a common loss. His sister running off had made Ginny doubt herself and what she'd meant to Meg. Finding his sister gone had made his father's absence so much harder for Parker to accept.

The idea that he believed he would have known if Ginny had lied to him was a conceit he had no business entertaining. Tilda could be his. What seemed clear was that whether he was the girl's father or not, Ginny had no interest in letting him into their lives.

Truthfully, he wasn't sure whether to be angry or grateful.

Maybe she had slept with some dark-eyed stranger the day after he and his mom had been forced to leave. Although that was as hard to believe as Meg wanting to come home.

Facing reality head-on was all that had

saved his sanity after his father's betrayal. And it was a lot easier to admit the truth when the nearest neighbor lived across three rivers.

He turned on his side and punched the pillow, although he felt certain the pillow had given up the fight hours ago. The ring of his cell phone was a welcome distraction. That it was Denali Wildrose screaming through his smartphone as if they were talking on two cans tied by a string made it a mixed blessing.

"Where you at?" Denali asked, his tone as gnarly as his calloused hands.

"I'm away. Mark is bringing your supplies."

"Who's that? Your partner?"

"Yep. You've met him."

Denali grunted. "He's late."

"I can't do anything about it from here."

"Anchorage?"

"Nope. Rhode Island."

"What? Who you got down there?" The old-timer didn't trust anyone who wasn't Native American. But Denali was a good man. Had six kids. Raised them all on his own after a boulder had killed his wife during an earthquake. But he was getting on in years and odder by the day.

"What else did you need, *Kaskae*?" Parker asked. "It takes time to get to Hoonah, and he's got double the work since I'm not there."

"That doesn't make my stomach stop grumbling. We can't cook nothing before we get that part for the oven."

"Light a fire. You've got a perfectly good camp stove right outside your back door."

"Okay, okay. You be back next week?"

"I hope so." Parker said, although he wouldn't swear to it. Not yet.

"What business you got in the Lower 48, anyway?"

"The none-of-your-business kind."

Denali snorted. "You ain't sick are ya?"

"No. It's family stuff, okay? I'll be back as soon as I can. And don't give Mark a hard time. He's doing me a favor."

"He's got shifty eyes, that one."

"Either deal with it or he can skip you this week," Parker said, imagining the old guy's eyes bugging out of his head. "Your choice."

"What's the matter with you? I gotta eat, don't I? So does Elmo," Denali sputtered. "By the way, he needs the other food. He won't eat the chunky kind."

"That cat eats better than I do. Call Mark and he'll get it out to you if I'm not there to do it myself."

"Don't stay out there too long. Too much noise'll rot your brain."

"Right."

"Now I have to call everybody and tell 'em you ain't coming."

"You do that. And tell them to be nice to Mark."

"If he's still shoppin', tell him to throw in some Tongass Forest cookies. The big box."

"I wouldn't count on it."

A grunt was the only response Parker got before Denali disconnected.

IT HAD TAKEN about an hour, but Ginny had finally relaxed. Catching up with her old friends felt like a tonic. Which was good, because the tea they were drinking hadn't done the trick.

Gosh, they all looked so beautiful and carefree in their colorful sundresses, and their laughter was a time machine, taking her back to the days when these girls had been her only real break from piano practice and study. Well, these girls plus Meg.

If only…

Harlow lifted her glass. "Old friends are the best."

Everyone nodded as they toasted, and Ginny couldn't help picturing Meg at the table. Although she hadn't been too tight with the others, they'd always made her feel welcome.

As Ginny lowered her glass, she did a quick sweep of the bar area, making sure Parker hadn't suddenly popped by. She had no business being distracted while she had the rare opportunity to be with her gang. From this moment forward, she wasn't going to do a thing but be present.

"Guess who's here this weekend," Harlow said, looking at Jade. "Fletcher Preston."

Jade winced. "So, what do I care?"

Cricket and Harlow laughed.

Ginny smiled, wishing being "present" made it easier to forget about Parker.

"You were into him all of junior year," Harlow said, as the waitress came to the table with a fresh pitcher of tea.

"At least you're not denying it," Ginny said, while Jade poured.

"No." Jade grunted. "Men are dopes."

Cricket and Harlow grinned. "Not all men."

"Most men."

Sipping her tea, Harlow looked around at the packed tables. "There's someone in LA that I've been kind of seeing. No one special though. Another teacher. Science and math. You'd like him, Jade."

"Just because I'm a chemist doesn't mean I instantly bond with all other science nerds. Especially the men—superior jerks."

"Now this is like old times," Ginny said. "Remember Tommy Zico? That creep? Is he here? I didn't see his name…" She gave in to the pull of scoping out the lobby again.

Harlow shuddered. "I hope not."

"Well, how about that?" Ginny said. "Cricket. Check out who's at the activity board."

Jade followed Cricket's gaze. "I'll take him to go, please."

It was Wyatt, the bartender from the local watering hole, Sam's Sugar Shack. She and Cricket had met him yesterday when she'd asked Cricket for legal advice regarding Tilda…without actually mentioning names or admitting the advice was for her. He looked even scruffier, wearing a sweat-stained T-shirt over running shorts, his stubble darker, his hair a mess. Ginny had to admit, he looked hot.

"Wait a minute," Jade said. "Cricket? He's so not your type."

"You don't even know what my type is."

"Uh, corporate. Silk tie. Penthouse apartment. Porsche."

"You're so wrong." Cricket quickly polished off her drink and dropped her napkin on the table. "Don't get into too much trouble while I'm gone."

"Why, you hogging him all for yourself?"

"Very possibly." She tugged her dress down, then headed his way.

Ginny's anxiety level rose at least two notches. Seeing Wyatt reminded her that Parker could be anywhere in the crowded lobby. She guessed there was no true break from reality. "Hey, I've got an idea," she leaned closer to the others. "How about we go to Sam's and get away from the reunion crowd for a bit?"

"I'm in," Jade said, still watching the action at the activity board. "That's probably where all the guys who aren't from Roger Williams are."

"Good point." Harlow put down her glass. "The mere idea of running into that blowhard Frank Geary gives me hives. I saw him yesterday, and he tried to talk my ear off."

"Well, that's a nightmare no one needs." Jade said.

Ginny laid some money on the table. "Do you guys think we should tell Cricket where we're going?"

"I don't think she'll care." Jade nodded toward the activity board. The two looked pretty cozy already. "Come on, I'd like to see Sam's now that I'm legal."

Harlow and Ginny both laughed.

"What?" Jade's voice was the epitome of innocence.

Harlow snorted. "As if being underage ever stopped you."

After they settled the check, Ginny led the way to the beach. Being outside was a relief. It was hot, yes, but the ocean breeze coming off the bay felt like heaven.

"I got dibs on anyone who remotely resembles the bartender," Jade said.

Harlow stopped so suddenly Ginny almost ran into her. "Are you nuts? You can't have dibs before we even walk in."

"Who says?"

Harlow towered over Jade, but there was fierceness in both their eyes. They'd had enough challenges in their lives that Ginny already knew they could hold their own against the rest of the world. She'd always envied their gumption. Cricket's too. Ginny had been more of a follower in the beginning. It was Meg who'd made her believe she could stand her ground. Always before, she'd been cowed by her father, who'd had a knack for finding her weak spots and exploiting them.

Meg had had his number from the first time she'd come over to Ginny's. If it hadn't been for her friend's unwavering belief in shy little Ginny, she'd never have had the courage to leave Juilliard and care for Tilda despite her father's vehement disapproval.

"Okay, fine," Jade said. "We get to the table and if we like the same guy, I'll arm wrestle you for him."

Harlow laughed. "You little pip-squeak. There's no way you'll win."

"Oh, really? We'll just see about that."

Ginny had clearly missed some of the conversation, but the two of them were now speed-walking to Sam's. Ginny had to hustle to catch up, anxious now to see the outcome of this World Wrestling Federation mash-up. She giggled as they went up the few stairs to the popular hangout, while Jade and Harlow egged each other on.

"Wow, this place hasn't changed a bit," Harlow said as she glanced around at the funky decor, with hanging piñatas and bikini tops dangling over the tables and wicker chairs, assorted bric-a-brac like Hula-Hoops and license plates hung on the walls and from the ceiling. Hula girls bobbled in the center of every table. Even the uniforms—short denim cutoffs and cropped T-shirts with the bar's logo—hadn't been updated…ever.

"Hey, you guys." Jade had already slipped into the thick of the crowd. "I've got a table. Come on."

The place was packed with tourists, and it

took Ginny a minute to get through the crowd but she finally took her seat.

Jade signaled the waitress. "This was a genius idea. We've hit the mother lode. Check out the guy by the jukebox."

"I'm pretty sure half the bar heard you." Ginny leaned in, keeping her voice low.

After Harlow ordered a pitcher of margaritas, Jade put her hand over Ginny's. "Sweetie, it's okay to loosen up every once in a while. You're not seeing anyone, am I right?"

"With Tilda around? I don't even remember the last guy who asked me out."

"Well, don't you worry. There are plenty of men here this weekend. We'll fix you up."

"I don't know. I think you guys are bad influences on me. I was always stuck behind a piano, remember?"

"And the night of the junior prom when you were out until one in the morning? Your father almost sent you to a nunnery."

Ginny groaned. "Jade, you know perfectly well we really did have a flat tire. It was you and Harlow who kept staying out past curfew."

"Oh, girl, what you've missed out on. Tonight's your chance to make up for lost time." Jade watched a far-too-cocky golfer sashay past their table. "I promise I'll find you someone decent."

"Oh, I don't need any help," she said, "I already have someone in mind."

Both women widened their eyes. "Who?"

Ginny was instantly sorry she'd teased them. She wasn't thinking clearly. Too much was going on, and she'd been completely caught off guard after Parker had shown up. Maybe she should meet up with him before the dinner. Get it over with. Send him on his way.

But something about him was making it hard to do the smart thing. It didn't seem possible that they could still have the chemistry they'd shared so long ago. Too much water under the bridge. Surely he had another woman in his life. Besides, nothing meaningful could come of the two of them. Not with Tilda in the picture.

"Ginny? You okay?" Harlow stared with concern.

"I'm fine. I've been thinking about Meg a lot, and it's distracting, you know? I haven't heard from her in a while, and I feel like we're losing touch." She'd never tell her friends anything about Meg's real situation. That even if she were alive, she must be in hiding, or under Danny's thumb. She knew Meg wouldn't want her to share that information.

"Yeah, you guys were close," Jade said. "I always liked her, even though she could be crazier than me. I kind of figured that we canceled each other out. It was that, or we'd end up driving each other nuts with our...eccentricities."

Harlow let out a laugh. "That's one way of saying you were a lunatic."

"Gee, thanks." Jade took a very large drink of her margarita, then dabbed her lips with a napkin. "You have to admit, the two of us made that uptight school a heck of a lot more interesting. Meg sure did have some great moves, aside from getting Miss Piano Practice out from behind the keyboard more than I could."

"Miss Piano Practice?" Ginny hadn't heard that one, and she didn't like it one bit. "Did you guys really call me that?"

"Not until today," Harlow said. "And that was all Jade."

"We love you, Ginny, you know that." Jade grinned. "We'd never diss you. Even when you had to cancel all the time."

"Well, yeah, I did. Which wasn't easy. But I might, and I stress the word *might*, be touring with the Rhode Island Philharmonic."

"What! Are you kidding?" Jade rushed on. "You waited this long to tell us?"

Harlow's mouth dropped open. Then she

started firing questions—when, where, how they could get tickets.

"It's not happening right away," Ginny said, shushing their exuberance. "I'm not going on tour while Tilda's still at Roger Williams. She still comes first."

"But that's fantastic. See? Who says you can't have your cake and eat it too?"

Ginny smiled, still carrying a bit of doubt about sharing the news. Normally, she preferred to remain cautiously optimistic, knowing all too well that the best-laid plans could turn on a dime. "I hope it turns out. I've been working with them, doing a couple of guest spots."

"Of course it'll turn out." Harlow lifted her glass. "To dreams coming true."

Ginny clicked her glass to theirs. "Maybe it's turning out that we're all getting what we need instead of what we wanted." Ginny smiled, even though she couldn't shake the feeling that Parker showing up out of the blue was the last thing she needed.

A few minutes later, Jade met a cute surfer who couldn't have been older than twenty-three, but Harlow quickly reminded her that they hadn't arm wrestled.

It felt as if everyone in the bar watched as the two women went for it. Ginny, safely staying in her chair through all the chaos, thought she heard a couple guys taking bets. Although Jade gave her a run for her money, Harlow won.

The whole thing brought them more attention than they wanted, or rather, than Ginny wanted. She didn't join in, but she did enjoy watching her friends flirt and act a little crazy, just like the old days.

When they finally settled, Jade lifted her almost empty glass. "I vote we all go back to our rooms and take naps before tonight's dinner. I'm wiped out, and a little drunk."

Ginny was grateful for the suggestion. She'd barely touched her drink, but she felt as if she'd been wrung dry. Time alone would give her a chance to decide what to do about Parker. She turned to grab her purse off the back of her chair and froze.

Parker was sitting at the table right next to theirs, his drink almost gone, as if he'd been there awhile. He gave her a nod and a slight smile as he stared straight into her eyes.

She turned back around, panic seeping into every nerve ending.

Harlow, who was on Ginny's right and had seen the interaction, didn't bother hiding her mischievous expression. "I don't think Ginny's distracted anymore."

"What? Who?" Jade scanned the room.

"Behind her," Harlow said, loud enough to be heard over the jukebox.

Ginny barely gave the girls a thought as she pulled herself together and shifted her chair so she could look at him again. "Parker. I didn't know you were here."

"I wasn't aware it was you before I sat down," he said.

Silence followed as Ginny wondered if that was true.

Jade cleared her throat. "Uh, hi."

He nodded, his gaze staying on Ginny for a beat too long, then he stood up and slapped a twenty on the table. "See you later, Ginny."

Before he walked out the door, he gave her a smile that made her heart clench. She wanted to sink into the floor, even though her stomach was fluttering.

Ginny explained Parker was Meg's brother, and no, she wasn't involved with him. Then they made their way back to the resort via the beach. Harlow was the first to peel off when Liam Tandy, wearing board shorts and carrying a six-pack, came trotting over.

Ginny and Jade edged away…until Liam's friend, who was almost as good-looking as Liam, joined his buddy. "You mind?" Jade whispered.

"Go for it," Ginny said. "I'll see you at the dinner."

Once alone, she felt nothing but relief as she changed course for the parking lot. Being home alone sounded wonderful at this point. Except for the part where she was so torn about seeing Parker again.

The drive gave her ten minutes to decide once and for all that she didn't want him showing up at her door again, and she didn't want to see him at the resort. And since he didn't have her phone number, that left her with only one viable option. She needed to call him.

By the time she'd parked in the garage and walked into the laundry room, her thoughts had filled with that little smile he'd given her at Sam's and the way he'd left so she wouldn't be uncomfortable. Which was just what the Parker she'd once fallen for would have done. She pulled out her phone but didn't call right away, deciding she'd get dressed for dinner beforehand, meet him somewhere. The Grind on Main Street would be perfect, and she'd have a credible time limit because of the dinner.

Sighing, she headed upstairs to take a twenty-minute nap, then she'd put on some Debussy and take her sweet time getting ready. Then she'd go and face the man who still made her heart race, just one more time.

CHAPTER SEVEN

PARKER WAS GETTING BORED. He'd been back at the nightmare motel for an hour, and all he was doing was thinking too much about Ginny. He never got bored at the cabin. He liked his own company—when he wasn't thinking foolish things about a woman who'd made it clear she wasn't interested.

What he should do was go out to dinner. He'd always liked Crazy Burger. Or maybe he'd splurge and go to Monahan's Clam Shack.

Who was he kidding? He'd probably pick the closest drive-through. It wasn't as if Ginny was going to call or anything.

Getting up, he went to the bathroom and splashed some cool water on his face. It was early for dinner and besides, he wasn't all that hungry. A walk on the beach might be nice... anywhere but near the Seaside on the Bluff resort.

His cell phone rang. Probably Denali again, complaining about Mark.

It wasn't Denali.

"Hello."

"Parker," Ginny said, her voice a little higher than normal. Nervous? Most likely. Probably had bad news to give him. Like she was leaving on the next plane to Somewhere Else. Or that she wanted him to leave sooner rather than later.

"If you're still free, I thought we could meet at The Grind on Main Street."

"The coffee bar?"

"Yes. I'm thinking I could make it in about half an hour and that would give us some time before I have to be back at the resort. If you'd like."

According to the activity board he'd seen at the resort, the dinner was two hours from now. "Sure. I can meet you there. I'll go a little early. Get us one of those outdoor tables."

"Whatever's available is fine with me."

He wasn't sure whether to be pleased or not. "Okay," he said. "I'll—" A drop of water hit the crown of his head. He looked up to see a small wet spot on the ceiling. Good thing it wasn't over the bed.

"Parker?"

"Sorry. Yeah, I'll see you there."

"Okay, see you soon." She disconnected.

It wasn't a good sign that his chest had tightened, his mood had lifted and he was picturing her so clearly it felt as if he could reach out and touch her.

But that was just him. It didn't matter that he felt the old chemistry. Tonight wasn't a date. It wasn't anything more than a coffee and a goodbye.

It also didn't matter that he kept wondering about Tilda. He had to take Ginny's word for it. Once he left Temptation Bay he'd have no connection to her, which was fine. There was no relationship in his future. Not here, not in Alaska, not anywhere. He wasn't about to count on anyone for anything. Or let anyone count on him.

When his phone rang his pulse started pounding again. "Hey," he said, without checking the caller ID.

"What's got you all excited," Mark asked. "Is it because I have to make all your deliveries?"

"As if I haven't pitched in for you. Just so you could go lose your money in Vegas."

"All right. Point taken."

"Listen, I'm not sure when I'll be back, but it most likely won't be till next weekend."

"What?"

"Now, just get out your board and take this down. I've got some changes to Denali's order."

"What do you mean next weekend?"

"What part didn't you understand?"

Mark cursed a blue streak, which Parker ignored out of his own surprise. A minute ago he'd decided tonight would be goodbye. So what was it about Ginny that called to him…

"You're never gone more than a couple days." Mark sounded cross.

"Well, I am this time. You got a pen ready?"

After a final curse from Mark, and a hit of static on the phone, Parker was glad now he'd extended his stay. Mark was getting lazy about taking the long flights. Except when he wanted to gamble.

"I'm ready," he said, his annoyance plain.

Just as Parker was about to give him the order, another drop of water hit him on the head.

A second later it was a full-on downpour.

GINNY FELT A LITTLE silly being as dressed up as she was. Her teal cocktail dress hugged her body in a way that was unfamiliar. Normally she wore classic styles that weren't formfitting. Now wasn't the time to feel self-conscious though. Besides, according to her daughter she was still a hottie. For a mom.

The thought made her smile. What actually had her concerned was walking in heels. She rarely wore anything higher than an inch or two, but these were four, and she wasn't exactly a graceful swan.

She checked her watch again. Parker wasn't late—she'd been early. Good thing too, since she'd gotten the last outside table at the very eclectic coffee bar. It was consistent with the newly renovated downtown and its Eurocentric crowd. She didn't come here often, but she did love their house-brewed lattes.

The umbrellas were large enough to bring shade to the hot afternoon, and the clientele was fun to watch. She'd sometimes come here alone in the afternoon and indulge in listening to music on discreet headphones while audaciously checking out the people from behind her sunglasses.

The second Parker arrived, her mood shifted. It was as if she'd been frothed like steamed milk, a heady mix of excitement, a dollop of fear and a hint of longing. He looked as if he'd just gotten out of the shower. His face was clean-shaven, and she kind of missed the scruff, though he looked more like the Parker who'd been hell-bent on Princeton. As he got closer, she could see that he didn't just have wet hair. Parts of his jeans looked damp too.

He sat down across from her with a sigh. His gaze traveled from her hair to her face, lingered on her cherry lipstick, then down her bodice. "You look beautiful."

"Thank you." She flushed with pleasure at the compliment. "You look...wet."

His eyes slowly closed before he opened them again, but his lips stayed pressed together as he shook his head. "Long story." After a quick glance around, he was all attentive again. "So, who's the lucky guy?"

"You already know I don't have a date. I think half of Temptation Bay knows I'm not with anyone, thanks to my *ex*-friends."

"As wing women go, they seemed pretty good."

The waiter's timing saved her from having to respond. Parker ordered hot black coffee. She wanted something cooler, and ordered an iced lemon ginger tea, something she'd never tried before but she hoped would soothe her nervous tummy.

"It's hard to believe you're not seeing anyone." Parker leaned closer with an almost smile. "You ever been married?"

"Nope. What about you?"

With an abrupt shake of his head that made her think he wasn't a big fan of the whole marriage idea, he said, "What is it you wanted to talk about?"

Surprised, Ginny sat up straighter. "You asked me to meet with you before you left."

Whatever might've been bothering him seemed to leave with his next exhale, replaced by a sly smile. "I would have been fine waiting till after the reunion. You suggested today, so I'm guessing you'd like to make sure I leave as soon as possible."

"I was trying to be nice. Once the reunion is over, I'm going to be ridiculously busy. You know, with work and a teenage daughter."

Her phone beeped with a text. She went to glance at the ID, but she hesitated.

"It's okay. Answer it. Could be reunion stuff."

"A mother of a teenager doesn't have the luxury of ignoring texts," she said, not proud of her tone, which was unnecessarily defensive. Ginny knew it wasn't her daughter because of the unfamiliar ringtone. But Parker didn't know that it wasn't Tilda.

The text turned out to be from Harlow.

I've run into an old boyfriend and might be a little late getting to the dinner.

Followed by a PS.

Jade thinks she's found you a hunk, and no one's heard from Cricket since she met up with that bartender.

Ginny sighed. Nothing with her friends had ever gone smoothly.

"Something wrong?" Parker asked.

"Nothing. You were right. Reunion stuff. I swear my friends haven't changed a bit since their teens."

"I gotta admit, I always thought it was interesting that you and Meg were friends. You two were like oil and water."

"I know." Ginny shrugged. It wasn't as if she hadn't wondered the same thing. "By the way, none of the others have heard from Meg since graduation."

"Not too surprising. I'm here only because my mother thought there might be a chance Meg would show up."

"And you didn't?"

"Nope. I figure there's a reason she hasn't been in touch with us. I have no idea what that might be, but it's her choice. Although, this is the last time I'm getting involved. I run a business. I can't be taking off, chasing after Meg, who obviously doesn't want to be found."

A shadow crossed his face. He could deny he'd lost all hope, but it wasn't true. She smiled. "What is it you do?"

Their drinks were delivered, and after a sip of coffee, he set the mug back on the table. "My partner and I run a cargo delivery service in

Alaska. We fly out of Fairbanks, but we serve pretty much the whole state. Mark covers south, I cover north. Sometimes we meet at the airport but not often. Mostly, though, we're surrounded by a lot of wilderness. It's beautiful, even though it's changing."

"It sounds lonely."

"Suits me just fine," he said, picking up his coffee and turning to study the crowded sidewalk.

He seemed ready to drop the subject, but there was still so much he hadn't said. Being a wilderness pilot was a far cry from being a lawyer. "What happened to becoming a lawyer for the people? You were so fired up about what you wanted to do. I thought that was your calling."

The shadow came back, this time shuttering his thoughts. "Life got complicated." His carefully casual shrug told her more than his words. "It took a long time for the dust to settle after my mother and I were forced to relocate following Meg's disappearance, and by then I'd changed my mind." He sipped his coffee once more and went back to avoiding her gaze.

Clearly he was hiding something. Probably a lot of things. But she understood more than most people that some things were better off left alone. And some were better off buried for good.

It was interesting, though, that he'd referred to just him and his mom. "What happened to your father?" she asked, knowing he'd been alive at the time.

The tension in Parker's jaw made her wonder just how big a part his father had played in Parker veering off his path. She would've remembered if Parker had mentioned flying or wanting to live in Alaska. Since she'd known Meg, he'd been determined to be the best lawyer in the country. And none of that defending the bad guys, not for Parker. He was all about truth and justice.

"He blamed himself, certain the job had something to do with her disappearance. So he buried himself in work." Parker's gaze briefly met hers. "Maybe he was right and that's what got him killed. His work put him in thick with some bad dudes."

She knew that had nothing to do with Meg taking off, and by now Ginny assumed Parker knew it, as well. "I'm sorry. It must have been so difficult for you and your mom."

Parker signaled the waiter, who came by quickly to refill his cup. When he looked at Ginny again, he gave her a halfhearted smile. "So, was Tilda the reason you left Juilliard?"

Although she should have expected him to turn the tables, the question still threw her for a loop. But she wasn't going to evade it and stir his suspicion. "Mostly. But after I was there a few months, I realized that being a world-class pianist and all the fancy trimmings that went with it might have been more my father's dream for me than my own. He'd loved that my mother was famous. At least in the world of classical music. Even though that meant spending time apart, he was enamored with the glamour. Actually, her glamour. She was, you know. I've seen so many videos of her, it's almost as if I knew her.

"The truth is, I'm not nearly as good as she was. It wasn't a matter of trying harder. She was exceptionally gifted. A rare jewel to my bauble."

"You believe that?"

"I know it. I'd never have been in her league and he would never have forgiven me for it. Once, when he was yelling at me over the phone about throwing away my life, he called me by my mother's name. But even that wasn't the worst of it. Not for me. It was how he was so dismissive of Tilda. He moved out a week after we came back to the house, and moved into his town house in Providence."

"Well, at least he didn't throw you and Tilda out."

"He couldn't have. The house has been in my mom's family forever. After she died, it automatically got passed down to me. Although he did have a right to stay if he'd chosen to do so. Anyway, it wasn't as if I would've tossed him out." Ginny sighed. "He's better off living in Providence. He's very good at what he does, which is getting rich people out of trouble."

"You don't think rich people should have good legal representation?"

She saw a faint smile lurking at the corners of his mouth. Probably because of her condescending tone. "I'm not thrilled by how much money talks. But you know that. I remember we talked about it a lot."

"Yeah." He nodded, the amusement gone. "Hard to think about how naively optimistic I was. Such a fool, thinking I could make a difference. I would never have made it in the real world."

She inhaled, wishing she could roll back the last few seconds. Whatever had changed Parker's mind still had a firm hold on him, whether he'd admit it or not. Best she could do was turn the conversation back to her own pitiful problems. "He's back in our lives," she said. "My father, I mean. Sort of."

Parker raised his right eyebrow, and for some unknown reason that little gesture hit her harder than any of his admissions. She used to dream about that move—his dark eyebrow raised in question. Or dare. Even now, she felt the shiver inside. Just like when she'd been eighteen.

"He called yesterday. All friendly, if not fatherly. But he tried. Primarily because he'd talked to someone at Roger Williams and found out that Tilda is scarily brilliant at science. Biology in particular. She's graduating early, and MIT already has their eyes on her after her team won the National Science Bowl. She was the youngest member."

"Wow. She must get that from you."

Ginny laughed. "As far as math and science were concerned, I was a good pianist."

He grinned. "Meg thought you were brilliant. That you could have done anything."

"Meg was sweet but wrong. Tilda is truly gifted. I was…am a very capable pianist, but I'm no Lang Lang, while she could be something extraordinary. Anyway, my father's delighted that she's so bright and he's offered to pay for her college expenses."

"That's great. I mean, considering where she'll be studying, it's still a very generous offer."

Ginny couldn't believe she'd said anything. Not even Cricket knew about her father's olive branch. Although, she couldn't afford to think it was a done deal. "It is great, but I doubt he would have been so generous had she been a B student."

"I hope he comes through. It sounds as though she's got a bright future ahead."

She nodded, her thoughts going back to a time when she'd offered him so many of her fears, aside from the worry she had about Meg. But she'd also offered him her heart. They'd both been blindsided by Meg's disappearance, and somehow, they'd become very close, very quickly. Before that Ginny had mostly known about him through Meg. He was older, wiser, enigmatic and too handsome by half. When she'd lowered her guard, he'd dropped his, as well.

Maybe he knew, somehow, that he'd only be in her life for a short time. That he'd disappear like a dream one can't quite remember after waking.

He put his hand over hers, just long enough for her to snap back to the present. "Believe me, I understand what an impact a parent can have. It doesn't matter how old you are, disappointments always cut deep." He leaned back, ran a hand through his thick dark hair. "So, what are your plans after Tilda's off to school? Resuming your career, perhaps?"

"It's crossed my mind," she said, wondering if he'd heard something about the philharmonic tour, although she couldn't imagine how. Maybe the mysterious Jane Winthrop had told him. "Now, are you going to tell me how you got so wet, or am I going to just assume you went for an impromptu dip in the bay?"

He chuckled, a deep, resonant sound that made her hold her breath.

"You remember that old motel on Highway 1? The Pelican's Nest?"

"That turquoise monstrosity?" She laughed, tried to get serious, but cracked up again. "Tell me you're not staying there."

"I didn't have a lot of choices. Everything's booked for the reunion and the golfing and who knows what else. Anyway, I'm not staying there anymore."

"Because…?"

"Aside from the ceiling practically crashing down on me and flooding my room, no reason."

"Oh, no. A busted pipe?"

"Something like that. Almost everything, including me, got soaked. Luckily I managed to salvage a few things. Have any suggestions for another motel in the area? Something a little more sturdy?"

"Sorry, I don't. That's awful. What have you done with your clothes?"

"I didn't have many, but they're all in the trunk of the rental car. Probably growing bio-organisms as we speak. Tilda would have a field day."

Ginny bit her lip to stop from laughing even more, but she was a lost cause. Until Jade sent her another text, telling her that they'd found the perfect guy for her. *Good grief.*

Ginny's gaze moved to Parker, who was pulling out his wallet. She could still see the college guy, with his tidy hair and his polo shirts. He might be a bush pilot, flying the last frontier, but he was also the man who'd held her as she'd cried buckets, feeling so lost when she had no idea where her best friend had gone. He'd never tried to fix her or change her or make her get over it. He'd been great that way.

"Are you in a hurry?" she asked.

"No, but I figured your friends are worried you won't make it to your dinner."

"Oh, it's fine. I have plenty of time." She hesitated. "I also have a guest room that's yours for two nights if you want it. There's a shower, a queen-size bed, no leaks in the ceiling and there's even a washer and dryer you could use."

Parker's eyes narrowed. "You sure?"

Not even close. "Absolutely." She hoped like crazy she wasn't making a mistake, but the invitation felt right. "Yes, I'm sure. But you'll have to leave before Tilda gets home Monday afternoon. And all I'm offering is a guest room."

"I never thought anything else. And I'll happily accept. But what about your dinner?"

"I still have time. Why don't you follow me to the house and I'll get you settled, and you'll have the place to yourself for a few hours."

His smile changed his face. It was as if a spotlight had turned on, showing off his very white, even teeth. He was still one of the most handsome men she'd ever met.

As the waiter came by and put down the check, it occurred to Ginny that she might have just made a colossal error. If he hadn't had a place to stay, he might've flown back to Alaska, never to be of concern again.

On the other hand, the idea of him leaving wasn't as appealing as it had been earlier. As long as Tilda wasn't around, what could be the harm? She'd liked talking to him. Laughing. It felt good, and normal. She felt pretty and the way he looked at her was very flattering.

Maybe she could even take him to the dinner with her. None of her friends knew the situation with Meg or Tilda. But...

She'd have to think that one through. After swallowing the last of her ginger tea, she put the glass down and said, "You ready?"

CHAPTER EIGHT

PARKER ENTERED the downstairs guest room as Ginny moved nearer to the wall to give him space. It reminded him of a higher-end hotel room. Not as overblown as the resort or anything but classy, like the rest of the house. The comforter was plush and white, as were most of the pillows. A few were in purple and red, bright spots against the headboard, that went with the lampshade, the curtains and the reading chair. No surprise that there was a small bookcase with different offerings he'd have to investigate later. He felt pretty sure there would be at least a few of the mystery stories Ginny had favored as a teen.

"This is great, thanks." He went to the en suite bathroom, reluctant to put his duffel bag down on the clean tile floor. His gaze stalled on the stand-alone shower though. He itched to wash that motel feel off his body.

When he stepped back, Ginny was staring at him, and he wondered what she'd think of his cabin in the woods. His whole place would fit in her living room, which was how he liked it. Not much to heat or clean. Nothing color coordinated. Practical. It had everything he needed.

"There are extra towels underneath the vanity and extra pillows in the closet."

"Extra? I count seven, including that little guy."

Her smile was accompanied by a little blush on her cheeks. She looked more beautiful than ever. He'd always thought she was pretty, but she'd grown into an elegant, graceful woman who made him want to step closer. Lean in. Explore her lips.

Not that it was going to happen. She'd made the rules clear, and he didn't want to break her trust, especially not after her generosity in offering him a place to stay. But he couldn't help thinking about how it had been so long ago. What it felt like to hold her. It was as if the memory of holding her in his arms had stayed in his head, just waiting to be awakened.

Things could have been so different. If his father had been the man he'd pretended to be. If Parker had been able to finish his undergraduate work at Princeton and go on to Yale Law. He could have given Ginny a life like this. Although he'd have liked it if she'd kept that ratty old robe she'd had on yesterday.

"I'll show you the laundry room," she said, leading him to the hallway where she made a right that led them through the kitchen. "Make yourself at home. Feel free to make coffee, have whatever you want from the fridge." She pointed to a side drawer. "There are take-out menus in there if you'd rather not cook."

He couldn't help noticing that her patter had sped up along with her quick step in those high heels. "I can still find a motel if you've changed your mind. I completely understand if leaving me alone here feels too weird."

"Don't be silly. I trust you. Why wouldn't I?"

"As long as you're sure…" He looked into her big green eyes, wondering if he could trust himself. "Uh, shouldn't you be going? They're probably serving dinner already. I know my way around washing machines, so don't worry about that. I've even fixed a few."

"Oh, really?"

"It's not like most of my customers live near a Home Depot or anything."

"So they ask the pilot who delivers their supplies?"

Parker shook his head. "They're pretty self-sufficient, but I made the terrible mistake of fixing one old man's snowplow, and everything went downhill from there."

She laughed, the sweet sound lingering well after she'd shown him the washer and dryer, both with more buttons than his cockpit. There was even a bench where he could put down his rank duffel bag without fear of messing things up. After she'd given him a quick tutorial that he'd absolutely needed, she looked at the silver watch on her wrist, and frowned.

"Go," he said. "I'll order a pizza from Antonio's. I'll even save you a couple of slices."

"I haven't had a pizza from there for ages. They used to be so—"

His cell phone went off. It was Lily, one of his regulars. Man, he wished they'd all learn to text. He let it go to voice mail.

"Don't mind me," Ginny said. "Go ahead, take the call. I have something to do before I leave."

"Nah, it's fine. I'll call her back later."

"Her?" Ginny's eyes widened as color filled her cheeks. "I didn't mean anything by that."

Parker grinned, tempted to tease her. Tempted to read too much into her reaction. Whatever she was feeling, he doubted it was jealousy. "Lily's around eighty, has a bum leg, and three husky sons who are there to fetch and carry for her. She can wait."

Just as Ginny stepped out of the laundry room, her own cell phone rang. A text message from one of her friends from the look of it. But she just frowned again. And sighed. Then she texted a reply. He thought he heard her mutter the name *Jade*.

As if some cosmic signal had gone off, his phone rang. It was Lily. Again. Now it was his turn to grumble as he answered. "Hey, Lily. What's going on? I'm sure by now you know I'm away."

"I do. I got my order today, but your friend was surly as all heck. He practically snarled at me when I asked him to put the flour and the oats in the big pantry, and then he just dumped all the bags on the porch."

"Mark's an okay guy. But he's covering all my customers as well as his own, so he's pretty busy."

"Doesn't mean he can't be civil. When are you coming back? I heard you were in Florida. You're not planning to move south are you?"

Parker rubbed the knot at the back of his neck. Their customers were all over the map, from one end of Alaska to the other, yet they all seemed to know his business almost before he did. "I'm not in Florida. And I'm not moving. But I'll be back soon enough. In the meantime, get Bobby or Jacobi to lift those heavy bags."

"Well, can you just pick up some gator jerky

while you're out there? You can get that at any drugstore or gas station."

"I'm not in Florida. I'm in Rhode Island. No gators."

"Oh, right. Okay, but I think Rhode Island has those big clams. How about bringing a few bags in the cooler? I'll cook 'em up and we'll have a real nice supper and a visit."

"I'm not running a take-out service." Parker thought for a moment, not liking the route his mind had taken. "What's going on? Is something wrong?"

"With me?"

"Yeah, you."

"Good grief. Better get on back here. Your brain's already turning to mush from the smog."

"You'd tell me," he said, lowering his voice. "Wouldn't you, Lily?"

"What would be wrong? I'm stronger than all three of my boys put together."

"I know that. But it's also not like you to call me twice." Or suggest they have a visit over supper. "What gives?"

"I don't know. I can't shake a bad feelin' I got when I heard you were gone. You know I got the gift."

"I know you have a great imagination." He shook his head, but no denying he was relieved. She tended to push herself. "Everything's fine, Lily. I'll be back before you know it. Just don't go trying to lift the heavy stuff by yourself. You know what happened last time."

"Hush, you. It was just once."

"Look, if I can, I'll bring you some clams, all right? Take care of yourself, *pinnariyauyok*. And watch your step."

"You too."

He disconnected and put the phone back in his pocket. When he turned, Ginny was still standing there, smiling at him.

"You old softy."

Parker snorted. "Not likely. I just know that wily old woman, and she'd talk my ear off, if I let her. Considers herself an *angakok*, or shaman, and thinks she has visions of people's future."

"And what was her vision about you?"

"Yeah, like I'd ask. She sees only one thing. Disaster. I learned a long time ago to ignore her. And what are you still doing here? Your friends are gonna send out the cavalry."

"I'm skipping the dinner."

"Why? Look, I can find another motel. I don't want you to miss out on your friends. And I sure don't want to make you feel like you have to stay." He turned and grabbed his bag, ready to walk.

Ginny stopped him with her hand over the one holding the duffel. "I'm not staying because of you. It has nothing at all to do with you."

He couldn't seem to look away from that delicate hand, the soft warmth of her silken skin covering his, scars and all. When he dragged his gaze up to meet her soft green eyes, emotion flared inside him, a longing so strong he had to look away before he did something foolish. "I don't believe you. You probably think I'll run off with the good silver."

"Nope," she said, moving her hand away. "But I'm a little worried about the antique tea set."

"You got me," he said, finally ready to look up again. "It would go so well with the decor in my cabin."

She laughed, and that made him grin.

"Why aren't you going, Ginny?"

She drifted over to the kitchen and opened an upper cabinet, from which she brought out a coffee press. "It's just that they've all got dates for tonight, which I don't blame them for, honestly. What I'd looked forward to was being with them—you know, just the girls, but that's not in the cards. Even worse, they found someone for me." She faked a shiver. "A stranger. At least I assume he would be, but I'm not interested in a blind date. That's not my style. Never has been. I'd like to know someone before I invest any time in a date."

Parker believed her. That's why it didn't add up that she would've been intimate with another guy so soon after he left.

"I know they just want me to let loose, have some fun. But they forget that I have a child. None of them do." Ginny shrugged. "They mean well, but frankly, I'm more interested in sharing a pizza with you than going to the dinner. If I won't be spoiling your plans."

"I hope you're not just saying that."

She shook her head. "The other thing they forget is I still live here. I don't need the whole town talking about who I'm seeing."

"They do that here?"

She laughed, then frowned at the coffee press as if she'd just realized it was there. "How about I open a bottle of red while you go shower? I'll get changed, and by the time the pizza gets here, we can sit out on the terrace. Have a civilized meal."

"You mean with plates and napkins?"

"And wineglasses too."

"You still like the half pepperoni, half veggie?"

"You remember that?"

He tapped his temple. "Memory like an elephant."

"And from what I remember, an appetite like an elephant too. Better make it an extra large."

"Will do," he said.

As she got a bottle from the very nice wine rack that sat in the corner of the kitchen, he wondered if she really wasn't interested in going on a blind date while the kid was away, or if she just didn't want the rumors that came with it. Could it be that she already had her sights set on someone who wasn't a stranger?

He headed to the guest room, ready to climb into that shower and wash more than the motel off his skin. It was time to get that idea clean out of his brain.

If only he hadn't seen the look of longing in her eyes just after she'd touched him.

CHAPTER NINE

GINNY WANTED ONE more slice of pizza. And another glass of wine. But since she'd had two of the former and one of the latter, she didn't dare. Not when Parker was being so charming. He looked refreshed in a clean pair of jeans and a white T-shirt that hugged his body like a second skin. She'd changed into a pair of silky lounging pants that were forgiving, and a cropped shirt. Plus, wonderfully, some comfy summer sandals.

"If I lived here," he said, after taking a sip of the merlot, "I'd put out a hammock and sleep on this patio all summer long."

"With or without clothes on?"

Parker nearly spit out his wine.

"I was just wondering how much of a scandal you'd cause. Arianna, the head of the homeowners' association, is not a woman to be trifled with. She's hauled people into court for less."

He smirked. "She wouldn't dare."

"Hmm…" Ginny murmured, looking him

over. "You're probably right. She'd have other plans for you."

Parker laughed. "Should I be flattered, or hide the wine?"

"Both. Here I thought staying home would keep me out of trouble."

Their gazes met and held, until Ginny looked away. Focusing on how the moonlight glinted off the water didn't help at all. This was a mistake. Him here. The two of them alone.

Parker cleared his throat. "Okay, I've got a real dilemma," he said. "If I eat another piece of pizza, I'm going to regret it. But if I don't, I'll regret that."

She smiled. "Life is full of difficult choices."

His mood shifted, but only for a moment. If Ginny hadn't been watching him so carefully she would have missed it. Had she been able to she read him this well in the past? Or was she misreading things in his expression now?

"Don't I know it." Leaning back in his chair, he looked out at the smooth, glassy ocean, the sailboats gliding like clouds.

"The calm before the storm." She folded her napkin, put it on her place mat and went for the age-old safe topic. "Literally. The news forecasts are talking more and more about the hurricane."

"I don't think it'll end up being too bad this far north. Although, nowadays it's hard to predict anything. But since you're not on the beach, you shouldn't have to worry too much."

"I'm not concerned yet. However, up here on the bluff we have high winds to consider. But the bay has mostly protected us, and we have a generator in the garage, which is handy when the lights go out."

"If there's anything I can do to help prepare, just let me know. Water, storm shutters, whatever."

His offer warmed her. Probably too much. The night was magical, with the sweet breeze that carried the scent of sea and sand, the great food, and the ease she felt with Parker. She wanted it to last forever. But Tilda would be back in two days and the spell would be over before her return. Even the thought of keeping him around longer than Monday morning made her nervous. So much was at stake.

Still, it was difficult to think of anything in the future when her thoughts kept sending her back to another evening on this very terrace. Fifteen years was a long time, but time was a slippery thing. They'd been watching the sailboats that night as well, although the sun had been lower in the western sky. Naturally, the topic of conversation had been Meg.

He'd come to the house to question Ginny. To compare notes, to find something. Anything. After Meg had gone, he'd taken a leave from his job in a law firm near Princeton. His father hadn't returned from his assignment yet, and Parker had tried to be there for his mother. To fix the Meg situation, since he had no hope of fixing anything about his father's long absences.

Ginny had been frantic herself. Since her own father had been on a case, staying at his apartment in Providence, she and Parker had been alone. She'd explained that Meg had met a boy, someone Ginny had never seen. He was older, somewhere in his early twenties. He lived in New York. Where, Meg had never said, if she'd even known. She'd asked Ginny to join her on the tantalizing adventure, ditching school and taking the train to the city to meet him. But Ginny hadn't gone. There'd been a test that day, and she'd needed her grades to be top-notch.

If only she hadn't been so stupidly eager to please her father and had gone with Meg, things might've turned out differently.

The guilt had brought her to tears, and Parker had held her close, assuring her she wasn't at fault in any way—although she hadn't really believed him.

And then they'd kissed. She wasn't sure how comfort had turned so quickly to escape in each other's arms, but it had.

"You know," he said, his voice low and careful. "I had no idea you were such an innocent back then, or I'd never have kissed you."

She blinked at him. Had something on her face given her thoughts away? "I don't believe that for a minute."

"Okay, I might have kissed you, but I wouldn't have coaxed you into doing anything more."

"Coaxed? You're mixing me up with someone else, because I wasn't exactly fighting you off. I'd already had a crush on you."

"Since when?"

"Since your family moved to Temptation Bay. It didn't stop when you left for college either."

"Huh." He looked so handsome in the light of the setting sun. Young. His hair was longer and shaggier than it had been back then, but with his jaw clean-shaven it was as if he hadn't changed at all. "You were always so reserved. I had no idea, and Meg never said. Which was odd, considering she delighted in tormenting me about everything from my clothes to my taste in girlfriends."

"I didn't confess to her about that. We were

mostly open books with each other, but you were off-limits. At least for me."

"Huh. What else didn't I know back then?"

"Let's see. You probably didn't know that Meg and I were responsible for that little explosion in the chemistry lab."

"Little explosion?" He laughed. "They had to practically replace two walls. My mother wanted to sue the school for endangering her baby."

"Wouldn't that have been something? I'm sure Meg talked her out of that because no one ever knew we were the culprits."

"It was Meg's idea though, wasn't it?"

"Wait. First, we didn't do it on purpose. Second, I was a willing accomplice." Ginny decided not to mention she'd almost had a heart attack when their little experiment had gone wrong. She'd felt so guilty she'd almost confessed. "Whatever Meg's faults, she was daring and brave, and she showed me that I could be too. Not that I went on to have a career in vandalism, but I'd always been so obedient. Never skipped practice, did my homework, obeyed all the rules. Jade and Harlow and Cricket were all excellent students, but they weren't innocent little lambs like me. But it was Meg who truly made the difference. If I hadn't met her, I doubt I would have ever thought twice about my future. I never would have considered leaving Juilliard."

"Wow. I just thought Meg was a pain in the butt and determined to test the limits of my mother's patience."

"Actually, I think it was your father's attention she was trying to get," Ginny said, and wished she hadn't when Parker turned a solemn gaze toward the ocean.

"I remember you guys spent a lot of time at the beach," he said after a moment. "You even got her surfing."

"No, that was Cricket. She was the instigator of our beach adventures."

"Like taking out her father's boat for an unsanctioned trip to Nantucket?"

"You knew about that?"

"Who didn't? You were the talk of the town. Remember, I was home for that little stunt."

"I know," Ginny said, feeling her cheeks heat up. She hadn't stalked him or anything, but she'd always made it a point to know when he was in town. "You used to go down to the fish market a lot."

"Oh, man, that's right. Meg had gotten that job with the fish people. That's when she started swearing like a sailor."

"That's true. I'd forgotten."

"It always sounded weird calling them the fish people."

"They like it. It's what they call themselves. Probably to annoy the tourists." Ginny picked up her glass, thought again about refilling it.

"So, did you pick up their salty language too?"

"Salty? Very good." They locked eyes for a second. Again, it was Ginny who looked away first. "No. I was too scared to cuss. I think my father would have disowned me. But we did hear some wild stories back then. I used to try to pretend I wasn't one of the wealthy Waverly Hills crowd. The fish people were so much cooler."

"Yeah. I learned a thing or two from that crowd when I was in my senior year at Bay High School."

"Like?"

"Knowing where along the beach we could drink beer without the cops busting us. And how to sneak into the movies at the Rialto."

"No."

"Only twice. I hated it."

"What else?" she asked surprised at this new side to him.

"Shoplifting."

"You did not." Her voice sounded much

louder than she'd intended. "You were a poster child for the letter of the law."

"It was a six-pack. I was scared spitless and never did it again." He shook his head as he focused on his wineglass. "It's actually a shame we couldn't stay in Rhode Island. My mother liked it a lot, and I did too. I have some great memories of this place. And of you."

Me? That couldn't be true. He'd barely known she was alive... Although he had teased her a lot the odd times he'd been at home when she'd been invited to stay for dinner.

She sipped her wine, forbidding herself from thinking about what might have happened if they'd gotten together earlier. Knowing her, probably not much. Not back then, although it would have been a terrible shame. Perhaps they could have gotten to really know each other. She was tempted to tell him how often she'd dreamed about him, both awake and asleep, but sadly, she could see he regretted the admission.

After struggling for a moment to remember what they'd been talking about, somehow she managed to get back on track. "Meg told me you guys were very upset about having to leave San Diego."

"We were. It was our second move in two years, but it was for my dad's job. We just didn't know what his real job was. He'd get transferred when his undercover work got too dicey. It was for our protection, apparently," he said with that ever-present trace of bitterness. "Not that we'd ever been aware we needed any."

"Is that why you had to leave Princeton?"

Even with the twilight sky, she could see Parker deflate. As if all the joy was leaching out of him. She'd crossed a line, and she hadn't meant to. "It doesn't matter," she said, trying her best to take it back. "Forget I asked."

"Nah, it's okay," he said, his shrug hardly convincing.

He no longer looked like the boy he'd been, and in his eyes there was a world of hurt. She cursed her big mouth but couldn't think of a thing that would make it better. After a long silence, his lips parted, and she winced, waiting for him to make up some excuse to leave her house and forget about her forever.

"There was more than one reason why I left Princeton," Parker said finally, his voice and expression devoid of emotion. "Although, I suppose you could say my father was the common denominator. At the time Meg disappeared he'd just infiltrated a very dangerous drug distribution ring, so he had no contact with my mom or even his boss."

"But he knew about Meg."

"No. He didn't. Not for quite a while."

"You told me yourself that he was on his way back from… I think it was Texas?"

"I lied."

Ginny stared in confusion. "Why?"

"Because I couldn't believe the bastard wouldn't drop everything to go find his daughter or be with his wife." Parker scrubbed at his face and exhaled. "Remember, at that point I didn't know he worked for the DEA. I thought he was in Texas investigating a fraud case and got caught when a hurricane hit."

Pressing her lips together, Ginny suppressed a whimper. Her stupid curiosity was making Parker relive that horrible time and now she didn't know how to stop it.

"We'd already been relocated to Indiana before he caught up with us. A month had gone by, and still nothing from Meg. I think he was in shock at first, then the guilt sank in. But the rage that came after…" He shook his head. "I'd never seen him like that before. Neither had my mom. It scared her badly."

Ginny practically stopped breathing. Her chest was so tight, she could barely move at all. She'd kept something from Parker, from everyone. Something that might've mattered…

"Obviously, by then I'd learned he'd been

working for the DEA but when the two of them sat me down and told me the whole truth about his job, I actually felt relieved. Even knowing that someday he'd return to undercover work, put himself right back in danger, and that it was possible we might never see him again, as well." He huffed a laugh. "What I didn't know then... A week later he returned to Mexico under his alias. Can you believe that? Meg was still missing and he left.

"He said he wanted to go find her. He blamed himself and thought her disappearance was connected to his job. That's why they'd initially relocated us. But too much time had passed. Even his boss was certain the organization they'd infiltrated had nothing to do with it."

Parker stopped and poured them each more wine, staying focused on the bottle so she couldn't see his eyes. His jaw was still clenched.

"Did he— Did you—" She cut herself short. Hadn't she done enough, said too much? Not said enough?

"Did we see him again?" Parker asked. "Yep. For a few days. A couple months after that he was killed while undercover. Hard to tell if and when his cover was blown."

Ginny felt moisture on her arm, but it wasn't

raining. She hadn't realized she was crying. When she raised her hand to wipe the tears, it was trembling.

Then Parker was urging her to stand, and she snapped back to herself. She promptly moved away from him and picked up the plates and the napkins, before heading into the house. She should have brought the glasses too, and the wine bottle. When she turned around, she saw that Parker had carried them into the kitchen behind her.

"Ginny—" He took a step closer, but she scooted back until she met the counter.

"There's something I need to tell you. Something you don't know."

"What's that?" he asked, putting the wine down carefully.

"Meg came back two days after you and your mom disappeared."

Parker froze except for a narrowing of his eyes. Ginny felt his stare like a laser burning straight through to her heart.

"She didn't understand where you all had gone. She'd lost her cell phone after she'd left the train, and she'd let Danny talk her into going down to Florida with him. To run an errand for his boss. She'd been excited about riding in his fancy sports car. I think he might've kept her down there too long, but she didn't say. She was too upset about your house being empty.

"I couldn't tell her anything—I had no idea what was going on. In fact, I'd hoped that she'd tell me where *you* had gone.

"When I told her you and your mom had disappeared overnight, she was inconsolable. Devastated. I begged her to stay here until we found out where you were…" Ginny took a shuddering breath as her vision started to narrow. Finally, she closed her eyes. "Meg was convinced that your father had run off with another woman. I had nothing but her word to go on, but I still tried to tell her there could be another explanation. Meg wasn't buying it. And I was so upset about you vanishing, I'm not sure I did everything possible to get her to stay.

"She didn't even spend the night," Ginny said, the confession far more difficult than she'd expected. But with the truth out there, she was able to look at him again.

His bleak expression made her want to cry. Scream. Run. She'd done it again. Messed everything up. Sure, it had helped assuage her guilty conscience, but he looked as if he'd been run over by a train. "Did she mention his last name?"

Ginny had to think for a minute, feeling

horrible about having told him anything at all at this point. "No. She didn't. I only knew his name was Danny. And that he was ambitious, trying hard to curry favor with the big boss. She honestly didn't say much more before she bolted."

He swore quietly, vividly. But it was the helpless look in his eyes that got to her, as if she'd ripped open an old wound. She had no idea what he was thinking. Other than how much he must hate her.

If only she'd stopped a second to think, to consider what the truth would do to him. She was an utter fool. "I'm sorry," she said, her voice shaky and too soft. Trying again, she focused only on his pain. "I'm sorry. Truly. I should never have told you. That was a horrible thing to burden you with. I didn't give it enough thought—"

The shaking had returned, only now it was her whole body, not just her voice. Against her will, hot tears escaped down her cheeks.

His warmth hit her first, then his nearness. By the time his arms had come around her, and he'd pulled her closer, she was drowning in confusion. The moment felt so surreal. Was this really happening, or had she entered some kind of fugue state?

"Shhh," he whispered. "You're wrong. I'm

relieved to know Meg came back. My mom will be glad to know too. At least we know she cared. That she didn't run away from us."

"But I should have tried harder to get through to her," she said, mostly into the safety of his chest as he gently rocked her. And while his kindness soothed her, it deepened her guilt at the same time.

She hadn't told him the whole truth, not even close. He still knew nothing about Tilda, about her own devil's bargain.

When he pulled back and lifted her chin with his fingers, she didn't try to stop him. And when he lowered his lips to hers, she met him halfway.

His kiss was careful, gentle. For a moment, her body stilled, the tremors replaced by memories and longing. It was her hand that moved up to his nape while she pressed her mouth a little harder against his. The kiss remained chaste. Nothing more, but when she heard a faint moan coming from the back of his throat, she parted her lips slightly.

Except he didn't do anything. His lips had firmed, they weren't moving at all. Embarrassed, she broke contact and stepped back.

They just stood there, staring at each other as if they'd never met before.

His eyes had darkened, his face was strained.

Of course. He was being smart.

Or he simply wasn't attracted to her anymore. Now twice as flustered, Ginny inched back, putting more distance between them.

Only Parker's hands tightened around her, and he kissed her until she parted her lips again. She tasted him; the wine, the spice and the scent of him stirring a visceral sensation inside her, something long buried and kept separate from her real life.

When she felt how hard her heart was pounding, and that his was racing just as fast, her good sense kicked in—not without a fight though. But she pulled back, caught her breath, then stepped away from the circle of his arms.

She knew she was flushed, knew he had felt her excitement, but she hadn't expected him to look so wrecked. And she didn't know what it meant, exactly.

"I think I should go upstairs," she said, barely able to maintain eye contact. "You going to be all right? You know where everything is?"

His nod came slowly. He cleared his throat. It took a few seconds after that for him to speak. "I'll be fine. Thanks again for letting me stay here."

"You're welcome," she said, giving herself a little more distance, just to be safe.

He turned and walked out of the kitchen but then he paused and looked at her. "I had a really nice time tonight."

She smiled, couldn't help it. It wasn't even nine o'clock yet. "Me too. Sleep well."

He looked down at the floor, then back at her. All he did was smile before he left, and it was just perfect.

CHAPTER TEN

THE NEXT MORNING Ginny was in the kitchen scooping coffee grounds. She was wearing a different robe this time. It was pastel blue with a belt and thick lapels. It looked soft. So did she.

He lingered in the doorway, not saying anything, but something made her turn around. When she saw him, she tugged the lapels closer together.

"Morning," he said.

Her gaze ran down his black T-shirt to his jeans, which were a little snug from the dryer. His feet were bare because he hadn't found a matching pair of socks. Her inspection stalled there. He wondered if she had a thing about feet.

With very pink cheeks, she asked, "How'd you sleep?"

"Great," he lied. "Terrific. Best night I've had in ages." Actually, she'd kept him awake for hours. They'd gone their separate ways after the kiss, but that hadn't stopped the memory from making him nuts. He'd stared intermittently at the ceiling for hours, knowing her bedroom was right above him. "How about you?"

"Great. I thought I might be worried about Tilda being away, but I crashed hard. I didn't wake once until a few minutes ago..." She changed the subject to the weather, and he smiled, feeling a whole lot better knowing that her night hadn't been a cakewalk either.

The way she'd turned didn't hide how her blush had reheated, or that she'd spilled almost a whole scoop of coffee grounds. If that wasn't a giveaway, her chattering would've done the trick. She did that when she was nervous. Her "tells" were the same now as they'd been fifteen years ago.

After she wiped up the coffee, she got out the milk and put it on the counter, then went back to the fridge and pulled out a carton of eggs.

"Am I making you nervous? Do you want me to leave?"

"What? No."

"I don't mind. The hotels should have some vacancies once the reunion activities are over."

"How long are you staying?"

"Here? Till tomorrow morning, or whenever you say the word."

"No, I mean…how long are you staying in Temptation Bay?"

He shrugged. "I'm not sure yet. Told my business partner I'd get back by next weekend, but there's nothing written in stone." He watched her cinch the belt of her robe for the second time. "You sure I'm not making you nervous?"

"Yes, I'm sure. I just need to get ready to meet the girls for brunch. I haven't showered yet and I'm not sure what to wear. According to Harlow I've got some explaining to do about being AWOL last night. Anyway, I need to get ready."

Parker held back a grin. "I'll finish up with the coffee if you like."

"That's okay—I have to dump it all out and start counting again." At that, she spun around facing away from him. "I have no idea when I'll be back from whatever else they have us doing this afternoon. You'll be on your own most of the day. It's probably going to bore you to death."

"I can amuse myself while you're gone," he said, walking slowly toward her. "I might even take a drive up the coast. See it before the storm hits. Maybe check out the fish market. I assume most of your friends are leaving today.

I could grill us something for dinner. That is, if you don't have other plans."

"Nope. None at all."

"You might want to reconsider me putting up the storm windows. Or boarding up the ones in the front of the house. According to the latest news, the hurricane is swinging back to the east, so the winds will be picking up again. Which is why leaving at the end of the week is sounding better and better."

Ginny sighed, and it wasn't the sound of her being thrilled he was going to stick around. She probably wouldn't have let it be that obvious if she'd realized how close he was to her. Before he scared the daylights out of her, he cleared his throat.

She whirled around so fast, it was lucky she wasn't holding a knife. He wrapped his hands around her upper arms to avoid a collision.

Her inhale was sharp, her pupils getting darker by the second. Loosening his grip, he thought about stepping back.

Or not.

He sure hadn't expected her to lean into him. Not enough that it made him too cocky though. She was staring at him as if she didn't know whether to smile or run for cover.

"It's nice of you to offer. About the storm shutters. But I have someone. A local handyman. Lee. If he thinks I need any preparations, he'll come and do them. He's been a real godsend."

She'd moved so she was no longer pressing against him, but her pupils were still dark. Probably due to the fright he'd given her. Nothing else.

So why hadn't he lowered his hands?

Ginny didn't seem too bothered by their current status, and the deeper he looked into her eyes, the further he seemed to fall into whatever this was. Thoughts flooded his brain, thoughts of holding her in his arms, tasting her lips, trailing kisses down her throat…

That kind of thinking was going to land him on his ass outside her front door. He needed to change that up real quick. Trying to distract himself, he looked around the kitchen. His gaze landed on an old photo of Ginny with a baby Tilda in her arms. Ginny had practically been a child herself, he realized. He couldn't understand how her father had left her to live on her own, a young single mother with a child to support. And the man was just now paying attention because he wanted the kudos of a bright, inquisitive and potentially successful granddaughter? What kind of despicable person would sit back and let his own motherless child fend for herself?

And where was Tilda's father, anyway? He must have been a moron for walking away from Ginny, let alone her being pregnant.

At least Parker knew he wasn't good father material. That was another reason he didn't get serious with anyone. Wouldn't go there. He'd had a lousy teacher, and the last thing he wanted to do was mess up an innocent kid.

"Parker?" She leaned back. "What's wrong? Why do you look so…angry."

"Not at you. Sorry. In fact, just the opposite. I admire you, Ginny, your strength and determination to live your own life. And how you've dedicated so much of yourself to raising your child. I always thought you were wise beyond your years, but the way you've handled everything that's happened is pretty extraordinary."

"Oh, no," she said, laughing. "I'm in no way extraordinary. Trust me on that. We barely know each other. I'm just showing you the good parts."

Oh, how he'd grown to love those bursts of pink on her cheeks. He'd have liked nothing better than to give her reasons to blush every hour on the hour.

"Talking about good parts," he said. "I had a tough time staying in that guest bed last night."

"Seriously? I don't have many guests, but everyone always says it's comfortable."

"That wasn't the problem. It wasn't easy walking away after that kiss."

Her lips parted, her hand going to her hip. "So, you lied. Didn't you say you had a great night's sleep?"

"Ah, you caught me."

"Yeah. I didn't like it either." She blinked and looked away. "Although it was for the best…right?"

Inside, he was vehemently expressing his disagreement. And from the way she bit her lower lip, he gathered his true thoughts had bled through. It didn't matter, though, what he thought. He wouldn't cause Ginny any more pain, and that was all this could lead to.

He realized he was still holding on to her and released her arms, then moved back a few steps.

"I'll let you finish making the coffee after all. I need to shower and get ready. I really want to make it to the brunch. I do miss those crazy women. So go ahead and raid the fridge. The milk and eggs are on the counter," she said, glancing in that direction. "I'm sure you'll find the bacon. The oatmeal is in the pantry, so whatever you want…"

"Thanks. Want me to bring you some coffee when it's finished?"

"Um…" She let out a slow breath. "We probably better not."

"Okay," he said, nodding and fighting a grin. Clearly she was just as affected as he was. Nothing had changed though. It was still hands-off. No point in getting grumpy about it either.

After she went upstairs, he got the coffee started, then stole a mug of it while it was still brewing. Sipping the hot brew, he wandered into the living room to look out at the ocean. Fate certainly hadn't been kind to either of them. It did hurt to know that Meg had come back so soon after they'd been forced from their home. Missing her by two days had cost all of them fifteen years. It wasn't fair. But he'd given up on fair a long time ago.

He wasn't sure how long he'd been staring out at the water when he heard a noise at the front door. It wasn't a knock. The knob jiggled, and then the door opened.

It was Tilda.

Who wasn't supposed to be home until tomorrow afternoon.

All her camping gear was piled in front of the door, but she seemed to have forgotten about it in favor of staring wide-eyed at him.

In his jeans, his too-snug T-shirt and his bare feet. He knew exactly the conclusion she'd jumped to. He just wasn't going to acknowledge it. "Your mom's getting ready for her reunion brunch. You need some help with your gear?"

Shc didn't say anything. Nor did she close her mouth. Her gaze moved from his face to his jeans to his feet, then went back up again.

He put his mug down on a coaster and went to the door, lifting up her sleeping bag and backpack. "Your mom is letting me stay in the guest room. But if any of this gear needs to be stored in there, no problem."

Tilda nodded, but her eyes had narrowed. Was it that she didn't believe the part about the guest room or... No, it was definitely about the guest room.

Halfway to the stairs he stopped. He needed her to either invite him up or tell him to put her things down. "Was it the storm that made you cut your trip short? It seems the wind has pickcd up."

"The water was getting choppy, but we left because my friend's little brother had some kind of allergic reaction to the medication they'd given him the day before. So it was Urgent Care Part Two, which sucked."

Finally she entered the foyer, put her tote

bag on the hardwood floor and kicked her shoes off, which sent sand flying. "Oh, no. Don't tell my mom, okay? I'm not supposed to…"

He didn't hear the rest as she'd already scurried to the kitchen. But not before he saw her feet. Her bare feet.

Tilda had webbed toes.

Everything slowed, especially his thoughts. He knew a lot about webbed toes. It wasn't a rare condition, except in certain cases. His grandmother had explained all about it, made him look it up. She'd told him she could have had surgery to separate the toes, make them look normal, but she'd been too afraid to go "under the knife."

Her father had had webbed toes of the same type, along with his father's second cousin. The fingers weren't involved, which was the rare part. Just the second and third toes of the left foot.

Exactly what Tilda had.

Parker's mom had warned him he'd probably have at least one child with the hereditary condition.

Dammit. Ginny had sworn Tilda wasn't his. But the odds of her having that phenotype were off the charts. How could Ginny have lied to his face?

"It's called syndactyly," Tilda said, broom in hand. "I could have had an operation, but I think my left foot is cool. When I was a kid I used to pretend I was a mermaid. Anyway, that's why I got into biology. I think I'm going to end up focusing on genetics. Did you know there are some types of webbed toes that science can't quite explain?"

"No, I didn't know that," he said, although he had known for a long time. But Tilda was obviously enjoying teaching him about her condition. She'd clearly taken ownership of the trait and had made it her thing. Although he already knew she had a lot more going for her than webbed toes.

He wanted her to keep talking. To tell him everything she knew. It would help him hide his growing anger, his disappointment over Ginny. She'd flat-out lied and he'd believed her, hook, line and sinker. What an idiot. He should have known better. Guess he was an easy mark.

The only thing he knew for sure was that he'd been right to move as far away from civilization as he could get without having to give up his citizenship.

He had his own world, out in the wilderness. He and his dogs and the wild creatures.

At least if you got your heart torn out by one of them, it was honest.

"What do your friends think?" he asked.

"They're okay. Everyone but the idiots. I get more shade for my science kink than my webbed toes. Although last year one of the football players, not even a good one, went as my left foot for Halloween."

"What a jerk." Parker had almost let something worse slip out.

"I had to hand it to him, he did a pretty good job. Except for the crap about syndactyly meaning that I'm a witch or something. Moron."

Parker smiled at that. "Have you ever seen anyone else that has it?"

"Only in pictures, but I'm sort of friends with this guy in New Zealand who has Haas type IV. That's when all the fingers are completely fused together. They call that cup hands, which is very rare. He's had a lot of operations, and now he can do a lot. He's nice. Smart too."

"Isn't your type rare too? Because it's not in your hands?"

She looked surprised. "Yeah, it is. You know about this stuff?"

"Not a lot, not nearly as much as you do." He backtracked as quickly as he could, not wanting her to freak out. It wasn't time to tell her about her grandmother and all the others in her family who had the same condition. Not yet, at least.

CHAPTER ELEVEN

AFTER STEPPING OUT of the shower, Ginny wrapped her head in a towel, her mind running circles around her good sense. She knew she shouldn't want to kiss Parker again, to feel his strong arms around her, but last night she'd had difficulty keeping herself locked in her room. Well, she hadn't gone so far as to lock the door. But really, how could he be so difficult to resist? Maybe it had been the way he looked at her. Or that smile that stirred the butterflies in her tummy into a frenzy. Ridiculous. She knew better but he—

Voices. Coming from downstairs. Quickly slipping on her robe, she moved to the hall. That was Tilda. Tilda, who wasn't supposed to be home until tomorrow.

She moved closer to the edge of the hall, nearer the stairs. They shouldn't be able to see her, but she could make out what her daughter was saying. "…a pretty good job. Except for the crap about syndactyly meaning that I'm a witch or something. Moron."

Every molecule in Ginny's body froze. A second later it felt as if she'd been given electroshock treatments. She wanted to race down the stairs, stop this fiasco in its tracks. How on earth had the subject come up? It wasn't as if Tilda went around bragging about it.

"…you ever seen anyone else that has it?" Parker asked.

While Tilda went on to describe a young man from New Zealand she'd met on her Facebook group, Ginny prayed as hard as she could that Parker would leave. Vanish. Or that Tilda would cut him off and come upstairs. Anything but continue to talk about her revealing condition. An issue that had never occurred to Ginny. If it had, she wouldn't have risked inviting Parker to stay in the first place, regardless of Tilda being away.

"Isn't your type rare too?" he asked.

Ginny could barely breathe. Her prayers had fallen on deaf ears, and it was too much to hope that Parker wouldn't think she'd lied to him. The irony was, she truly hadn't. But that wouldn't be the way he'd see it.

"You know about this stuff?" Tilda's voice was higher. Louder.

"Not a lot, not nearly as much as you do."

Ginny's thoughts careened. Why was Tilda

even home? Had something bad happened? How long had this conversation been going on?

Giving up all hope of getting out of this unscathed, she hurried down the stairs. They were both still in the foyer, Parker holding her sleeping bag and backpack. Tilda with a broom, her feet bare.

Ginny remembered the conversation she'd had with Meg about her family's particular variant of the condition. Of course, Parker knew everything about it.

She took another step, only stopping when Tilda said, "Don't worry, Mom. Everything's fine. I just got some sand on the floor."

Not daring to look at Parker, Ginny checked out her daughter from head to toe. "I don't care about the floor. What happened?"

Tilda started telling her about having to cut the weekend short, but as long as Ginny knew her daughter was fine, she didn't particularly care. Or hear the words. It was as if she'd stumbled into the center of a tornado swirling with everything she'd ever known about Meg, everything that she'd said to or heard from Parker, and at the eye of the storm was a fear greater than anything she'd experienced before. The thought of losing Tilda was paralyzing. Ginny needed her wits about her, to be calm and collected. Tilda was not Parker's daughter. That was her most formidable fortress. It was the truth.

When she realized Tilda had stopped talking, she finally met Parker's eyes. The scorn and feelings of betrayal there were obvious. But not to Tilda, Ginny felt sure. At least she had that to be grateful for. Still, the man Ginny had kissed last night was definitely gone.

"Uh, I'm just gonna take my stuff up to my room," Tilda said, her gaze moving from Ginny to Parker and back again.

"I'll help you." Parker shifted her sleeping bag in his arms.

"That's okay. I've got it." She pushed the broom and the dustpan into Ginny's hands, then shouldered her backpack before she took the rolled-up sleeping bag. "I've got some calls to make," she said, heading for the stairs. "Hope there's still some hot water left."

Ginny didn't smile or even watch Tilda as she made her escape. The tension was far too thick in the room. Parker took a step closer to her and used his voice like a whip. "You lied to me."

"Tilda is not your daughter."

"Right. As if I'm going to believe a word that comes out of your mouth."

"It doesn't matter what you think. She's not yours. I can understand why you might believe that, but you don't have the only family in the world with a history of webbed toes. Meg told me about your grandmother and the rest of your family a long time ago."

"So it's just a coincidence? That she's fourteen. Which would mean you got pregnant right around the time we were together. And it's completely random that she's got that variant of webbing?"

"As it happens, it runs on my mother's side of the family. Meg and I spoke about how weird that was. I mean, what are the odds?" she said, lying through her teeth. The instant it was out of her mouth, she regretted it though. She'd never been a liar before, and now it was the first thing that came to mind.

Parker shook his head, looked at her, shook it again. "Funny, Tilda never mentioned that. Seems like a pretty big thing to omit."

Naturally she would've said something about it to Tilda before now. God help her, she was only digging herself in deeper.

"I really underestimated how good a liar you are. Makes me wonder what else you've spoon-fed me. Have you been in touch with Meg all this time? Have you been encouraging her to stay away? I know you had to be pissed when you were left in the lurch with a kid on the way, but I've explained everything."

Even though he was hitting her so far below the belt she almost crumbled, she kept thinking about Tilda as guilt threatened to overrun her sanity. "Everything? Really?"

That he looked away startled her. He made a show of checking the staircase, giving her a precious moment to collect herself. And to wonder what *he* was hiding. She'd been reaching, going on the offensive because she didn't know what else to do. But she had no doubt he'd come at her again. What she had to remember was that, ultimately, she was doing all of this for Tilda. As she'd done from the very beginning.

Meg had asked her to find a good home for Tilda. Ginny had done exactly that. Given up school, a career, a whole different life to make sure that child was cared for. So now was not the time to fold. Making a point to look as if his words had had no effect at all, she said, "It doesn't matter how many times you ask, or what terrible things you have to say about me. It won't change the fact that Tilda is not your daughter. So, you're free to make up whatever scenarios you like, but you'll need to do them somewhere else. The deal was, you'd leave before Tilda got home. I know it's cutting things short, but…" She just shrugged, but his attention had turned to the window.

The water was choppy, the waves crashing against the rocks. She thought of the upcoming storm and prayed it was about to hit with enough force that he'd fly out of the area while he had the chance.

Parker smiled. It didn't reach his eyes, which was worse than everything he'd said. "You're right. I should leave. This isn't getting us anywhere…but a paternity test will." He lingered for a moment, probably hoping she'd collapse into a sobbing heap.

She just smiled back, using every ounce of strength she could muster. Despite being barely able to breathe, she looked at the clock over the mantle, then glanced toward the hall that led to the guest room.

He didn't take the hint. Just continued to stare at her.

"I don't mean to be rude, but I'm going to be late for the brunch."

"Go ahead and get ready. Tilda already knows I'm here. You don't have to babysit me while I pack up my things."

There was no way she'd leave him alone with Tilda, not for a minute. Even if it meant missing the brunch, which she didn't want to do. Although it wasn't as if she had any hope of having a good time with her friends. But maybe she could talk to Cricket again. Explain enough for her to recommend an attorney. Ginny couldn't let her father get wind of this. It was tricky though. She couldn't afford to let anyone know the truth. Especially not Tilda. Not if it came from someone else.

The thought of her daughter finding out from Parker made her feel sick to her stomach. Would it be better to let Tilda think Parker was her father? Everyone, including Tilda, already thought Ginny was her biological mother. Parker's assumptions were a lot easier to explain. She hadn't been able to get in touch with him. No one needed to know she'd never tried. At the worst, she might have to share custody with him. Which was better than having Tilda cut out of her life forever. But could Ginny live with that? It wasn't as if she hadn't planned on telling Tilda. Someday. When she was older. When the time was right.

"You're not dressed."

Parker's voice made her jump. She hadn't even realized she still had a towel around her hair and wore nothing but a robe.

"And you're not looking too good," he continued. "Maybe you ought to sit down. Have a glass of water."

Ginny refused to react again. He was trying to provoke her into admitting guilt. And being incredibly smug about it.

"I'm fine. The only thing I need is for you to leave."

Behind her, the window that had been letting in warm breezes all morning suddenly rattled with a strong gust of wind that swept through the living room. She inhaled sharply when it occurred to her that maybe this was exactly what she'd been praying for. She didn't even have to say a thing about the storm.

Her hope was dashed far too quickly by the expression on Parker's face. From the smirk, it was obvious he'd read her like a comic book. It was also obvious that he had no intention of leaving this situation alone.

What she didn't understand was what he was actually after. Even if he had been Tilda's father, would he want to be a part of her life? He'd been unequivocal in his choices. He'd said he wanted the wilderness. A solitary life. He'd sought out the isolation. As much as she'd like to think he was the same compassionate man she'd known all those years ago, he simply wasn't. Despite the conversation he'd had with his customer in Alaska. Perhaps he was fooling himself, but she'd learned a long time ago that when someone tells you who they are, you should believe them.

"I'm going to get myself a cup of coffee, and

then I'm going to get dressed. I expect you to be gone by the time I come back downstairs."

Instead of replying, he kept that smug smile going. Oddly, she wasn't willing to disregard the honest pleasure of spending time with him last night. Quite possibly the best evening she'd had in fifteen years. A lump formed in her throat and she turned for the kitchen. Fate could be incredibly cruel.

PARKER THREW HIS duffel bag into the backseat of the Jeep and climbed behind the wheel. The sky had some nerve being clear blue and perfect for flying. Not that it couldn't change in a moment. That gust of wind had been a harbinger, and not simply about his life taking a turn for the worse. Actually, whatever storm hit the bay would work in his favor. So many guests were leaving, and they'd all try to move up their flights. Which meant he shouldn't have any trouble finding a room for the rest of the week.

After turning on the ignition, he looked back at the house. He couldn't see Ginny, but he was certain she was watching. Making sure he left. Weirdly, he was more disappointed than angry.

The idea of Tilda's webbed toes being a co-incidence was ludicrous. And it wasn't as if he was some slacker who'd come prepared to blackmail Ginny based on the assumption of paternity. He'd never imagined she'd have his child. He had even believed her when she'd sworn Tilda wasn't his. But she acted as if his being the father was the worst thing that could happen. He was reasonably intelligent, owned a business and made a decent living. She wouldn't even have to see him very often…

He drove down the winding streets of Waverly Hills, full of multimillion-dollar homes, polished lawns, luxury cars and boats. All the trappings of a happiness that didn't exist.

Okay, so he could understand why Ginny might have lied when he'd first shown up. Given her circumstances, she'd be very protective of Tilda. But why not tell him now? After he'd explained why he'd been forced to leave town, and no, he hadn't contacted her later, but she hadn't mentioned trying to look for him either. It wasn't as if he was trying to steal the girl away.

Even if Ginny never told him the truth, Tilda was a bright girl. Someday she'd go looking for her father. How would Ginny explain that Tilda had met him when she was fourteen, only her mother had decided not to tell her who he was?

Tilda would be even more confused and

rightfully angry. Ginny's secrecy made no sense. If nothing else, she could be getting some financial support, even if nothing was done through the courts. Whether she felt she needed it or not, Tilda shouldn't be denied the extras he could provide.

He stopped at the red light on the road that separated Waverly Hills from the town proper, thinking about Tilda. Bright, funny, well-spoken—she was a daughter any man would be proud of.

But he wasn't about to pretend that suddenly knowing he had a kid wouldn't turn his life upside down. It would be simpler all the way around if he got in his plane and never looked back. That would make Ginny happy. But the truth was, he couldn't leave without knowing the truth. And he'd like to know Tilda better. The last thing he wanted was to end up like his father.

Just as the light turned green, his cell phone went off. It was Mark. Probably to complain about another customer of Parker's. He pulled into a parking lot that was jam-packed, but he wouldn't be long. Accepting the call, he said, "What?"

"What the hell is it with your people? Lonny Atuat wants me to fly a baby moose up to his place so it can be nursed in the wild. You know what a baby moose is going to do to my plane?"

"Yeah, because we've never had anything make a mess in the planes."

"We usually charge accordingly, but Lonny claims you said he didn't have to pay anything over his regular delivery fee. I swear, the way you coddle your customers is turning them into a bunch of crybabies. Cheap ones."

Parker cursed. "They're the crybabies?"

"Yeah, they are. Are you aware that storm heading your way is expected to hit early and hard. You should probably get out of there ASAP and get ahead of it."

"Can't you do one week of deliveries without complaining about it? Maybe I should look for a partner who understands what it means to have my back." The silence that followed was time enough for him to regret his hasty words. But he was too irritated.

"Now that was uncalled-for." Mark sounded as pissed off as Parker felt. "At least you don't have to handhold my customers. They aren't spoiled rotten. What's with you, anyway?"

"Nothing."

"Family, huh? Everyone in your face?"

"None of your business. I'm hanging up now."

"Ah," Mark drawled in a tone guaranteed

to make Parker want to strangle him. "This is about a woman."

"It's none of your—"

"It is. A woman. And from the mainland? I never would have thought—"

"Shut up, Schwartz."

"Don't be like that, Parker. You can tell Uncle Mark everything, you know that. With my vast experience with women, I'm sure I'll have all the advice you need."

Parker took great pleasure in disconnecting the call. *Uncle Mark* knew exactly what he could do with his advice.

CHAPTER TWELVE

GINNY LOOKED AT HERSELF one last time in the mirror before she headed downstairs and off to the brunch. Her hair had refused to cooperate, her outfit felt awkward and too flimsy even though it had been one of her favorites. But all she really cared about was making sure Parker and Tilda wouldn't meet again.

Kaley had arrived a few minutes ago, and the plan was that the girls would stay in and watch a movie they'd missed when it had hit the theaters. While Ginny was reasonably sure Parker wouldn't return, at least not this soon, that wasn't good enough.

Stopping at her bed, she opened her purse and checked to see what cash she had in her wallet. It was more than she'd remembered, which was great. Her steps got quicker as she went down the stairs, but she slowed herself when Tilda gave her a worried glance.

"Hey, girls. Change of plan."

Tilda groaned, but Kaley kept her opinion to herself.

"All right," Ginny said, as if it didn't matter a whit to her. "Then I won't give you money to go to the mall."

The girls were on their feet and in front of Ginny in two seconds. "Wait, wait, wait," Tilda said, her brown eyes wide and hopeful. "You want us to go to the mall? To shop? By ourselves?"

"Since you got the raw end of the deal on camping, I was going to suggest a little treat."

"Treat?" Kaley sort of hopped at the mere suggestion.

"I was thinking you could go to the cosmetic counter and have a lesson on makeup by Angela. You remember her, don't you, Tilda?"

"She's the one who got you to buy a year's worth of face stuff."

"Maybe not a year's worth." Ginny was beginning to think she was making a mistake.

"That would be great," Kaley said. "Thank you."

But Tilda wasn't quite so ready to bite. "What's the catch? I'm not fifteen yet. You're the one who only lets me wear lip gloss and mascara on special occasions."

"You're going to be fifteen soon enough and you should learn about your colors and skin tone."

Kaley gave Tilda a look that could singe her

lashes, then smiled brightly at Ginny. "I know I want to learn about my colors. And my tones. It's such a smart idea to start now."

"This is about Parker, isn't it? You're not going to brunch. You want to hook up with him again."

"What are you talking about?" Ginny said, the alarm in her voice 100 percent genuine.

"I approve." Tilda's mischievous little grin was almost more than Ginny could take. "He's completely hot, and he knows about syndactyly."

"You're to go to the mall, and after you have your makeup done, you can go to the food court, and maybe catch a movie but don't go crazy. Also, I'll be speaking to Angela and she'll give me a rundown on both of you, so watch yourselves. Don't go getting anything pierced or trying any wild colors in your hair."

Just as Tilda opened her mouth, Kaley jabbed her in the ribs with her elbow. "Yes, Ms. Landry," she said, holding out her hand. "Thank you. This is so cool."

Tilda looked at her friend as if the world had gone wonky, but then she shook her head and held out her hand too. "Thanks, Mom."

Ginny gave them each far too much cash, but she was running ridiculously late, and even though she understood it was guilt pushing her along, she couldn't seem to hold back. "I'll call you after brunch."

GINNY WAS THE LAST to arrive at the hotel restaurant. One of her friends must have gotten there early because the place was filled to the rafters with golfers and other reunion attendees. Still, they had a nice table that was relatively private. Although she could hear Jade's laughter from the entrance, and all the way until she took her seat to complete the foursome.

"How's Tilda?" Harlow asked.

"She's fine…" Another wave of guilt—evidently that was the way her body worked now—swept through her. She'd used Tilda as her excuse for getting out of the dinner last night.

"Tilda, huh?" Jade said, sipping her Bloody Mary. "That blush on your cheeks is quite telling. So, was it the guy from the bar? Meg's brother? Or was it someone else?"

"It wasn't anyone," she said, sticking with her story. For heaven's sake, she'd kept a monster secret from everyone she knew for years, and yet this little white lie nearly did her in. "Why does it always have to be about a guy?

Although from what I gathered, you two both had dates last night."

"So did Cricket," Harlow said with a grin that showed off her perfectly straightened teeth.

Ginny stared at her friend. "You were with Wyatt?"

"Nothing happened," Cricket said. "But it was very nice. We walked on the beach."

"Fine, well, what both of you missed while off doing whatever was Nia Quail falling on her bountiful behind smack-dab in the middle of the dance floor. Her cocktail dress rode up all the way over her Spanx."

"You're evil," Ginny said, trying hard to be seriously disapproving while also wishing like crazy she'd been there to see it. Nia had been a horror during their school years. Talk about a mean girl. She'd been especially rude to Jade and Cricket because they belonged to the fish people. Generations of their families had made their living fishing off the shore from their large trawlers. Ginny and Harlow had lived in Waverly Hills where the summer folk had landed, jacking up real estate prices by buying second homes on the bluff overlooking the ocean. Everyone complained about the tourists, which was ironic since that's how Temptation Bay residents made most of their income.

"I got it all on my iPhone," Jade said. "I'll send you a copy."

"Thank you," Ginny said, far too enthusiastically. Who was she trying to fool, anyway. Their group had always been regular gossips, and they sort of competed to outdo each other in the witty banter department. Jade was the acknowledged champion, but Meg had given her a run for her money.

The thought brought Ginny's good humor to a halt, and she ended up ordering a very fattening eggs Benedict and hash browns along with her coffee. The other girls had no trouble carb-loading even while they complained about having indulged too much.

"Before I forget, you all have to promise to come to the yacht club mixer at four," Harlow said. Three distinct whines followed, but she didn't pay them any mind. "I won't take no for an answer. Last night I met the most amazing guy—tall, handsome, a former football player. He was a dream. And he manages the club now."

"Go ahead and tell them the rest," Jade said.

"Fine. I changed my flight out from tonight to tomorrow morning."

"Wow, that's impressive," Ginny said. "What about your dream date, Jade?"

She shrugged. "He was perfect in every

way. Especially the part where I won't ever see him again. But I'm not leaving until after I see my family, and then I'm hoping the storm doesn't cripple air travel. But I need to make an appearance, no matter what."

"You don't want to see them?" Cricket asked. "You like your family."

"I do, but it's not like I have much time. What about you? Have you seen your dad?"

"Yeah, I did." Cricket inhaled deeply, and her eyes were so sad, Ginny forgot about her own troubles.

"What's going on, Cricket? Is Ronny all right?"

"I'm not sure. He's had a couple of mishaps. I think he might be having dizzy spells, but he won't say." Then, as if shedding a hair shirt, Cricket confessed that her position at her Chicago law firm was in jeopardy because her bosses wanted her to participate in getting their wealthiest client's son off the hook for a rape charge.

"But you're a contract lawyer," Ginny said.

Cricket nodded. "It's insane, every bit of it. Some jury expert convinced the client I'd be nice window dressing at the table." She shook her head. "It doesn't matter. Except now that I know something's off with Ronny, I need to stay and make sure he's checked out by his doctor. He won't go if I leave it up to him. It's all right though. I'm sure Ronny will be fine, and I'll come up with some logical way to get out of that case. So, yes, Harlow, I will join you at the yacht club. But I can only stay for an hour. I'm meeting Wyatt at the bar at five."

Ginny set aside any plans she'd had to ask for Cricket's help with Parker. Her friend had a very full plate, and she didn't need another burden. But she did want to give Cricket the opportunity to unload on her, so she agreed to go to the yacht club, as well. It helped that she knew Tilda would still be at the mall, catching a movie with Kaley. After that, Ginny felt fairly confident Wyatt would distract Cricket from thinking about work.

Their meals were served, and while Ginny ate like a starving waif, she mostly listened to other tales of her friend's lives. She was even able to slow down her feeding frenzy as she relaxed into their stories and realized what a gift it was to see them.

Two hours flew by quickly, and after the others finished the last round of mimosas, they left the table and walked to the lobby. As usual it was crowded, but mostly with people checking out and saying their goodbyes. She glanced at the reception desk. Parker was standing in line, his duffel bag in hand.

For a moment, she froze as her heart sank to the pit of her stomach. Although, she shouldn't be too surprised that he wasn't going to leave before the storm. That was wishful thinking on her part. And it left her with only one option: she and Tilda would leave first thing tomorrow morning.

BY TEN THE NEXT MORNING, Parker still couldn't shake his sour mood. For the second night in a row, he'd had a lousy night's sleep. Despite being in a great room with a great bed, thoughts of Ginny had kept his mind spinning. Even more troubling were the many instances of pretending that the lies had been explained away to his satisfaction—which he doubted could ever happen.

At one point, when he'd been on the verge of sleep and not in complete control of his faculties, he'd tried picturing Ginny and Tilda in his cabin. But that had fallen apart quickly. The unbidden image was ludicrous. Then he'd imagined the three of them living in his old house in Temptation Bay. That little nugget had gotten him completely out of bed at three-something. He'd paced, he'd showered again and then he'd eaten two candy bars from the minibar.

He'd called her twice since breakfast, leaving voice mails each time, but there'd been no response. Now that he was in his car, instead of going straight to the airfield to check that his plane was safely tucked away in the hangar space he'd rented, he was on his way to Ginny's house. The odds of her actually talking to him, or even letting him inside were slim.

Didn't matter. He had to try.

A lot of people had been checking out of the resort, which was understandable. And the docks would be utter chaos as the storm headed toward the bay. Not to mention traffic was terrible—what should have been a ten-minute drive had taken twenty.

Once he was in the driveway, he saw a middle-aged man boarding up the windows on the main level. Parker jogged to the porch, and the man looked over at him. She'd called him Lee... "Do you happen to know if Ginny and Tilda are up and about?" Parker asked.

"They're not here," he said, holding up one of the shutters. "Left to keep ahead of the storm."

"Huh. It's early, and I was under the impression it wasn't going to do much damage this far away from the shore."

"Could be, but Ginny wanted them to miss the worst of the tourist panic. The roads will be a mess."

Parker nodded agreeably. "They already are. Do you know where they were headed?"

The man squinted at him, warier now. "I've never seen you around here before."

"Oh, right. Sorry." Parker extended his hand. "You're Lee, aren't you?"

Looking surprised, the man nodded as they shook.

"I'm Parker, an old friend. I used to live on Peacock Street, across from the school. I came for the reunion, and I seem to keep missing her. We were supposed to connect last night but things got in the way." He sighed and looked distractedly toward the bay. "Well, I know she's not headed to her dad's place."

At his mocking tone, Lee snorted. "For a smart man, Robert Landry is a damn fool. Not that it's any of my business."

Parker had watched him relax in stages. "I know what you mean. Poor Ginny." He smiled, pretended to head back to the Jeep. "Thanks. Maybe I'll give her a call after I fly home."

"I think they're headed for the Marriott Suites in Providence, but with all the traffic I imagine they're still on the road."

Parker tamped down a smile. "How long ago did they leave?"

"About thirty minutes. But she said she had to fill up the car. Can't expect to get anywhere ure, but knew it would make him worry, and he hadn't wanted to do that.

Sure enough, Parker found her easily, and he parked directly behind her, cutting off her escape route. At least Tilda wouldn't see them.

He hopped out of the Jeep like a man on a mission. She got out, just so he wouldn't be able to hover over her, and made the first move. "Are you following me? There are laws against that you know."

"Why are you running away if you've got nothing to hide?"

"Running? We're leaving because of the storm. Heard of it? Most private pilots have already cleared out before the worst hits. I'd assumed you would be smart enough to do the same."

The door to the mini-mart opened, and Ginny held her breath as someone walked out. Thank goodness it wasn't Tilda. If it had been, she'd have spotted them. The fear that gripped her was her own personal storm surge, and she had to make a decision. Quickly.

Her cell rang. She saw it was her father again and she turned it to Silent. She had no time to think about him at the moment. "Look, Tilda is inside the store. She can't hear us arguing about this. It's confusing enough being fourteen-year-old. Please, I'm begging you

fast with all the tourists around here. The curse of the summer season."

"Too true. I don't miss the seasonal traffic. Even at the best of times, those roads to the highway are a mess."

"You don't have to tell me," Lee said, after he finished with the last nail. "I'm on the committee to get the roads widened to at least two lanes. But a lot of the locals, you know how they can be so nostalgic…"

Parker caught most of what Lee said, but he was thinking that if Ginny had only been gone for half an hour he might be able to catch up to her. "Thanks a lot. For helping Ginny out. She said she can always count on you."

"That's true. She's a good'n, that Ginny."

Parker nodded. As he hurried to the Jeep, he heard Lee shout, "You should try her cell."

With a wave, he got in the car. Oh, no, he wasn't going to try to call her again. He wasn't about to give her a single minute's warning.

CHAPTER THIRTEEN

GINNY PUT the gas nozzle back in the cradle, grimacing at the traffic buildup. The tourists were leaving in droves, scared of being swept away by the tropical storm. Or worse, being without air-conditioning. Her cell rang and she pulled the phone from her bag. It was her father calling, but she'd have to call him back later.

The passenger door slammed and Tilda, still looking disgruntled at being woken up so early, sighed mightily. "Can I go get some snacks? It's going to take forever to get to the hotel."

Ginny grabbed the receipt. "Now? You couldn't have thought of that when we first got here?"

Tilda sighed again. "I still don't understand why we have to go anywhere. The storm's probably not even going to reach our house, and we have the generator. It's so stupid that we're leaving. I'm supposed to go with Kaley to the community center. Now she doesn't

have a doubles partner for the Ping-Po nament."

"I'm sure she'll find someone to fill really so terrible that I wanted to spend time away from the house and the pia a few days before the students come po back? Just us? I don't think it's too mu ask."

"Fine. Do you want anything?"

"Coffee. A big one. You know how I like

"Can I have one too?"

"Really?"

Rolling her eyes, Tilda went inside the minimart, most likely to pick out a varied range of unhealthy snacks that Ginny would find revolting.

Getting back in the car, she thought she might run in after all. She started the car move closer to the door and to free up the b when a very familiar Jeep turned into the l

She ducked her head, and did her best hide behind the wheel, then changed cou to find a space at the far end of the lot, tween a couple of big trucks. Not that it w help. It wasn't a coincidence, Parker sho up here. He must have gone to the hous spoken to Lee. She'd considered tellin not to say anything about their abrupt not to say anything that will upset her. She's completely innocent in all of this."

Parker's nostrils flared as he pressed his lips together. "You really think I'm that cruel?"

Shame joined the mix of emotions causing her turmoil. "No. I don't."

"Although she's going to ask at some point. You know that, right?"

Trapped, panicked and knowing Tilda would be out any second, Ginny looked at Parker, making sure she met his gaze squarely. "Look, I'll tell you everything, all right? Just not here."

"How do I know you're not going to make a run for it?"

"Oh, please. There's no chance of running anywhere with this traffic. Why don't you meet me at my place in an hour. I'm going to drop Tilda off at her friend's house, at least until the storm gets closer. That should leave us enough time to talk."

"I don't know why I'm even considering believing you. It's not as if you've given me reason to. But fine. Just know, I'm not going anywhere until you tell me the truth. All of it."

"I will. Not for your benefit, I assure you. But I won't let Tilda be hurt. Not for anyone or anything. Now, please, go before she sees you."

He hesitated for a second as if he had more to say, but then he got back into the Jeep and backed out with the speed and finesse of a stunt driver. He'd just gotten on the road when Tilda walked out with a large plastic bag in one hand and Ginny's coffee in the other.

"Was that Parker?"

There was no use prevaricating. Ginny nodded. "He wanted to make sure we were okay."

After tossing the bag onto the floorboard of the passenger side, Tilda made what Ginny thought might be an attempt at a Victorian swoon.

"So romantic," she said. "Chasing us down like that. He must really like you."

"It wasn't like that," Ginny said, although she couldn't offer an alternate explanation.

"Seriously, Mom. You shouldn't be leaving with me for a few days away. He seems like a really nice guy, and honestly, it's time you had a life of your own. You're not getting any younger."

Ginny wanted to cry. Instead, she made a face at her daughter which she hoped looked cynical and mother-like before she got into the car.

Tilda got in beside her and handed the coffee over.

"I'll have you know I'm going to grant you

a reprieve for the day, unless the weather changes drastically. First, I'll call Kaley's mom, and if it's okay, I'll drop you off at their place."

"Oh, does this mean you and Parker are gonna—" Tilda made kissing sounds.

"No. We're going to have a talk. Despite what you think it has nothing to do with romance. He wants to speak to me about Meg."

Tilda settled, looking a bit chastened. Then she pulled out a bag of jelly bean sours and stared out the windshield.

No way was Parker taking her word that she'd meet him at her house. He followed discreetly behind her. And if she noticed him, too bad. He wouldn't apologize. This was too important.

They drove to a neighborhood bordering Waverly Hills that had some of the most ridiculous looking homes. They were all meant to appear nautical or just Cape-Cod-like, a somewhat subdued version of the Newport cottage scene. But most of them fell short and sat on the wrong side of the street to enjoy an ocean view. He was surprised to see Ginny turn onto the gated driveway of a good-sized home that could've been attractive but crossed the line into ostentatious.

He pulled to the side of the road, wishing there was more shade or at least a spot where he could linger before the neighborhood security forces swooped down on him. But a few minutes later, she came out the other side of the circular drive, and all he had to do was wait to see which way she turned. Left if he hadn't lost his ability to find true north.

Left it was, and the closer they got to Ginny's, the closer he got to her car. It was a nice car, a Subaru, but nothing extravagant. He imagined she was more interested in the safety features than the leather seats. She pulled into her garage, and he parked in the driveway, glad to see no sign of Lee and all the windows prepared for whatever might come.

She let him in the front door quickly, then led him to the living room where she sat in an elegant wing chair while he took a seat on the couch across from her. She didn't offer him a coffee or anything else. She simply stared at him, looking as if she wanted to be anywhere else.

"First, Tilda isn't your child. Honestly. She's not."

Instantly the hackles he'd thought he had under control rose and the slow simmer in his gut turned up to medium high. She'd better start talking soon because once his thermostat ratcheted up to boiling, it wasn't going to be pretty.

"A month after I started Juilliard, Meg showed up at my off-campus apartment. I lived there by myself so I was able to practice long hours on my piano without disturbing a roommate." Ginny looked down at her hands and stopped rubbing them together. After a deep breath she met his gaze again. "Meg wasn't alone."

Parker kept his expression neutral. She'd brought a guy with her? So?

"Bundled in a blanket underneath her coat, she had a one-week-old baby. I hadn't even known she was pregnant, but I had a good idea who the father was."

Parker leaned in, his elbows on his knees, his heart rate elevating rapidly.

"She begged me to find the child a good home. And she made me promise not to tell anyone, including you and your mother, even if I could have found you."

"What the hell?"

"She said her boyfriend had ordered her to have an abortion, and if he ever found out she'd lied about not having one, it would be bad. For both her and the baby."

"Who was this guy? Was he the same one she'd gone to Florida with?"

"Yes, I'm pretty sure. Meg didn't tell me too much about him. Other than that he was going to be someone important someday. And rich. His boss had taken notice of him, and he was rising up the ranks quickly."

The ranks? Yeah, that didn't sound unsavory at all. "Doing what?"

"I'm not sure, but I got the impression it was something sleazy." Ginny wet her lower lip, and despite all he was hearing, the shocks reverberating down his spine, he couldn't help watching.

When she jolted up, he thought she would kick him out for staring at her lips, but all she said was, "I've got to have something to drink. My mouth is as dry as the Sahara. You want anything?"

He nodded but didn't move to join her. "Water's fine."

She hurried into the kitchen, leaving him alone to ponder who this mystery man was and what could be so dangerous about him that fear would have prompted Meg to abandon her baby. He sure hoped the guy wasn't involved with the mob. Or worse, a drug cartel.

Ginny returned, her steps quick, handed him a large tumbler filled with ice cubes and water and sat down with one of her own. She'd already downed a good portion of it, and suddenly he needed to do the same.

"You said his name was Danny."

"Right. I knew that from before." She took another quick sip. "Oh, I remember now. Meg had mentioned something about him being connected or wanting to be connected. I thought she may have meant he was working with the Mafia, but I don't think they exist anymore, do they?"

"I'm sure the new generation is around in some form or another."

Ginny nodded grimly. "She said he dressed well. Mostly tailored clothes, and he'd started taking her to fancy dinners and to meetings in extravagant hotels. She was wearing designer clothes herself. But for all I know I'm completely off the mark with that Mafia business. What I am sure of is that something had changed—she was more frightened than impressed with him when she found me at Juilliard." Ginny's brow furrowed. "I mean, when she first told me about him, she was excited about how he was on his way up the ladder. But by the time she had the baby, she didn't want her to be his kid. Or around him."

"She'd obviously gotten away from him to take the baby to you. Why didn't she keep going? Run?"

"Where to? She was afraid she'd already told him too much about me. You guys were in the wind. She thought her father had run off with another woman. Besides, it wasn't as though he'd been holding her captive. He'd been away on business and thought she'd gone to get the abortion."

"She could have found us somehow."

"Parker. Think when that was. How scared she must have been. How bad it would have turned out if this guy found out about her family and used that to keep her in line."

Parker stared daggers.

"Look, please understand all of this speculation is in retrospect. I was a kid too at the time. I asked her to go to the police and she just laughed. Now I understand she was probably right not to."

"Yeah, but—"

"Let me finish." Ginny stood, and paced behind the chair, back and forth, rubbing her hands again, not looking his way. "She asked me to find a home for her baby."

"You said that already."

After a quick glare she regained her stride. "She wanted to make sure he could never find a way to get to Tilda. Or to me. But I didn't exactly follow her wishes to the letter."

"What do you mean?"

"It was overwhelming, her showing up like that with a child. A baby girl. She hadn't named her yet. A week she'd had that infant, and she'd only called her sweetie. I said I'd help, but it wasn't a simple matter. I couldn't go to my father because he'd have put the child in the welfare system before letting me think it through. I couldn't let the school find out about Tilda because everyone there knew I hadn't been pregnant. They'd have questions and would probably report me to the authorities. So I took some money out of the trust fund set up by my mother's family, and got Tilda what she needed, including a reliable babysitter.

"I still had to practice long hours and keep up with my studies. But every day, I fell a little more in love with her. I wrote her a lullaby," she said, with a little smile and an air of wistfulness that Parker tried to process. "I taped it. It helped her fall asleep. Then I started skipping school to make sure she had her checkups and vaccinations. It was too easy to forget she wasn't actually mine."

"Meg's daughter."

Ginny had stopped pacing; he wasn't sure when. But when he looked into her eyes, he could see she'd been crying. Tears were still running down her cheeks.

"Did Juilliard kick you out?"

"No. I left as soon as I could. I had to make sure people would believe she was mine. I brought her to Temptation Bay and moved back home."

"Your father?"

"Was filled with rage. At me. At Tilda."

Parker shot up from the couch.

"He never hurt either of us. Not physically. But after trying to bribe me, browbeat me, threaten me, he realized I wasn't going to change my mind. So he left. I had the trust fund, which helped a lot in the beginning, but it wasn't enough to keep us going."

"Didn't your dad wonder about the pregnancy? Did you have a boyfriend at the time?"

"I made one up. It was perfect because I used the excuse that I was going with 'Caleb' to spend Christmas with his family, which meant my dad hadn't seen me for months by the time I came home with Tilda."

"So he bought the story that you'd gotten pregnant and hidden it."

Ginny nodded. "I think he must've checked and seen that I'd drawn money from my trust fund, which supported my story. Anyway, he wouldn't have imagined I'd lie about something like that."

Despite still being pissed at Ginny, Parker

would've liked to have a word or two with her worthless father. "So he just walked out…"

"We've been estranged ever since. He feels as though I didn't just betray him but my mother, as well. After a while, I began to understand that I was supposed to follow in her footsteps. He wanted me to be just like her, but for me, when it came to choosing between the piano and Tilda, there was no contest."

"I'm sorry, but I still don't understand something. How could Meg have met someone like… Danny?"

"I think it was at Grand Central, right after she'd gotten off her train. She'd looked lost and Danny had swooped right in. He was good-looking and charming, and he spent money on her."

"That's it? Looks and money?"

"Competition had a lot to do with it too. It wasn't easy for her at Roger Williams. The top tier could be brutal to everyone who wasn't one of them, and Meg felt that deeply."

"Felt what, exactly?"

"That she was one of the have-nots. I think that's why she wanted to fit in with me and my friends. I'd never been in the running to hang out with the really wealthy crowd, but then there was Cricket whose father is a popular local surfer with roots in the fishing community, and Jade, whose family are fish people, as well. Even Harlow was more like me, on the lower end of the financial spectrum. None of us liked the rich kids."

"I never even understood why she wanted to go to that school."

Ginny looked down for a second, and he knew he wouldn't like what she was about to say. "Mostly though, I think she wanted your dad's attention. I'm sorry, but she idolized your father, and she thought he didn't care about her or his family. Danny was older and made her feel special. I guess, in a way, he could've been a substitute."

Parker's chest tightened, all his muscles preparing to fight off something no fists could stop.

"She honestly had no idea what Danny was truly like. Not until it was too late. And I'm guessing eventually she knew too much and couldn't just walk away."

"She could have come to me. Or even my father before he passed. He could've protected her."

"How? You'd disappeared. All of you."

The anger grew inside him, like lava trying to erupt. How could Meg have been so stupid? And his father, the big *hero*, who'd put his family last? Parker hadn't been much better. How could he have been such a lousy brother? Of course Meg hadn't come to him. He'd been too caught up in his own bright future at Princeton, with his eye on Yale Law. No one had been there for her. No one.

He turned to Ginny. "Meg did find us on Facebook. I know it took a while, but we did make ourselves known. Did you even try to let us know what was happening to her? Or tell us about Tilda?"

Ginny's wince didn't register as anything but guilt to Parker. She hadn't tried at all.

"It was too late by then. I'd become Tilda's mother. She was my daughter in every way that counted. You do know there's more to the mother/child bond than blood, right? Besides, Meg didn't even know I'd kept her."

He turned to face the covered window. The turmoil outside was hidden from view. But he could hear the wind and knew the sea was probably roiling—an echo of what was going on inside him.

"But if you'd told her you kept the baby, that you hadn't placed her, don't you think it might've given her more reason to get away from him?"

Ginny blinked, her face paled. "Maybe," she said slowly, her voice husky with emotion. "But for what? To live an uncertain life on the run?"

Like his family?

Parker knew she'd had the same thought but possessed the good grace not to verbalize it. Ginny had given up a lot for Tilda, there was no disputing that. And Tilda was happy. Well-adjusted. With a great future ahead of her.

It was his turn to walk away. "I think I could use some coffee. You mind if I make some?"

"No, go ahead. I could use a pickup myself."

He hesitated, waiting to see if Ginny was going to follow him, but she went down the hall toward the downstairs bathroom.

It was odd to know where she kept the coffee, and exactly how to prepare it to her tastes. But mostly, the idea that he had a niece spun around in his brain. He liked Tilda. She was straightforward and for a girl her age, pretty sensible. Thanks to her upbringing, he suspected.

Ginny let him know she was headed his way by clearing her throat. Another thoughtful gesture to pin up on his mental board of how to feel about all she'd done. So many cons. But there were lots of pros too.

The coffee maker gurgled, and he turned around to face her. She was leaning against the center island. "Do you know where she is now?"

"Meg?" Her eyes were dry but rimmed with red. "No. I don't. They moved out of the country some time ago."

"And you really haven't been in touch with her?"

"It's been almost a year since we talked."

It still irked him that Meg had phoned Ginny but had communicated with their mom only through Facebook. "Was that because she stopped calling or because you were afraid she'd come back and would find out about Tilda?"

The look Ginny gave him hit him hard. He hadn't even meant for that question to come out.

"I haven't lied about anything. I swore I would tell you all, even though I know how hard it is to hear. In fact, I'm sorry, but I'm afraid that Meg might be..." Ginny's eyes closed tight, as if she was using all her strength not to say the next word.

"Dead?"

She sniffed, looked at him. Nodded. "The last time we spoke Meg was depressed and felt hopeless, like all she'd done was screw up everything. She didn't see much hope of escaping her life."

Parker cursed. "She should've been calling *me*."

Ginny's voice had gotten softer, while his had become louder. He didn't want to hear any more. It hurt to think his little sister had been in a version of hell he couldn't even comprehend. For so many years. On her own. And after a while he'd stopped looking for her. He hadn't done anything but blame her for abandoning the family. For being just like their father.

If Ginny was right, he'd never have the chance to tell Meg how sorry he was. How he'd misunderstood so much. How he should have paid more attention. Done something. Did she even know about their father's disgrace? That he'd left their mother in such terrible straits. Nearly penniless without his pension?

Did Meg believe her family had abandoned her? She must...

"What else?" The words came out sharp, directed more at himself than at Ginny.

She blinked. "Nothing important."

"There must be more to make you think she's dead."

Ginny looked away, brought down two cups and poured them each some coffee. They both took a little breather, getting prepared to dive deep once more, but finally, they were back in the living room, facing each other.

"Meg knew that Danny had been seeing other women for a while. Much younger women. Which meant she was becoming more dispensable. The upside to that was more freedom. Not that she was ever let out without some kind of bodyguard. There was very little chance of her doing anything like going to the authorities. But almost two years ago, they were in the country, in New York, and she told me she'd managed to get a safe-deposit box in a Manhattan bank. That she wanted it in both our names. In fact, she sent me a form, with a return envelope to the bank, which I signed because they wanted my signature on file."

"She wanted it in your name too?"

"Yes. Although I didn't think much of it at the time. But then, after that last phone call, I got the feeling she knew it wasn't looking good. She reminded me that I had a key."

Parker waited for her to continue, but she seemed hesitant. "No sense holding anything back at this point."

She sipped her coffee, then cleared her throat. "Before she could tell me anything more, the call was cut off. Well, she was cut off. I heard yelling in the background. It was terrifying and I just knew she'd been caught.

Then the connection was gone. I never heard from her again."

Parker put his cup down on the coffee table and spilled some. He hadn't used a coaster, but he couldn't move to wipe it up. Not while he was imagining all the possible horrors his beautiful sister had faced on her own. That monster needed to be put down.

He cursed his father. If he'd been any kind of a decent man, he would have been in the perfect position to save Meg. To have crippled that bastard and whatever organization he was working for. All the misery his father had caused by siphoning money from a raid, and for what? To end up in humiliation and failure. Betraying his honor, his name and his family. For dirty money that had been confiscated, anyway. And all he'd ever been to his kids was a hero. A hollow man, with nothing but failure inside him.

Parker glanced up at Ginny, and the pity he saw on her face gutted him. As if he wasn't broken already. He didn't want sympathy, and there'd be no redemption. "If you'd talked to Meg, you must have known she'd contacted us on Facebook. But she'd never said where she was, who she was with. Anything meaningful."

"Stop," Ginny whispered. "Please."

He had to. It wasn't Ginny who'd let the ball drop. He should have done his own homework. Traced Meg somehow. Found her. Not just dismissed her without ever trying to understand how young she'd been. How much trouble she had found herself in.

"Do you have any idea what's in the safe-deposit box?"

"Keepsakes? Personal things she wanted kept private? I honestly don't know."

"Didn't it occur to you that she might have stashed incriminating evidence in that box? Something that could have helped her?"

Her head reared back as if she'd been slapped. "I told you. The conversations were awkward and short. For a long time, everything had seemed good with them, if secretive."

"Do you remember which bank?"

"Actually, I do know. It's in Midtown Manhattan."

"What?"

"I only remember because I got a notice last week. The payment was due on the box, and the bank sent me a letter. I'd never gotten one before, which means Meg had been paying it herself."

"Did you pay it?"

"No. Not yet."

"And you still have the key?"

She nodded.

"Why haven't you gone there? It's possible that whatever's in that box should go to the FBI. I can't believe you didn't—"

"I'm sorry, it was just a week ago, and with the reunion and everything… It never occurred to me there would be anything that could help take down Danny."

He stood, stared at Ginny, disbelieving. "Don't you want justice for Meg?"

CHAPTER FOURTEEN

GINNY WISHED SHE hadn't told Parker about the safe-deposit box. Of course she wanted justice for Meg. Everything she'd done was to protect her friend and her child. Even now, thinking that she'd never see or talk to Meg again broke her heart. She also wanted Danny Whoever-He-Was to be thrown in jail for the rest of his life. He deserved much worse, in her opinion.

But she had to put Tilda's safety first. Giving her the best life possible was a close second. And if Parker wanted to get ugly about it, he could find a way to rip Tilda away from her. She'd tried to help him see that everything she'd done was out of love for both his sister and her child, but he still had a lot to process. She couldn't imagine trying to make sense of all the information he'd gotten in one tense sitting.

Besides, the Nolans weren't innocents in all this. They'd vanished for years. Ginny had picked up the slack and moved heaven and earth to protect and care for Tilda. Even the idea of sharing Tilda with Meg's family made her sick to her stomach. Selfish, perhaps, but that's how she felt.

"Ginny," he said. "The name. Of the bank?"

His voice startled her. They'd both been distracted. She'd let fear swallow her up which was a mistake she couldn't afford. Right now she had to be on her toes. When she'd glanced his way, he seemed to be lost in his own thoughts. Now, though, he was staring at her with intent.

Instead of answering him, Ginny rose and went into the family room where she could see the TV. She turned the flat-screen on to the weather channel.

Parker walked to the bookcase, arms crossed. His anxiety showed with every breath, making the muscles in his back, shoulders and neck stand out. The news about the storm was better than she'd anticipated. The tropical storm was going to come in earlier than their original predictions, but it shouldn't hit the bay too hard or before midnight. The winds were picking up, but the airports hadn't shut down, although the call had gone out for all boats that weren't already being prepared at the dock to do so immediately.

"We should try to get ahead of the storm,"

she said. "We can continue this discussion later."

He turned, his jaw muscles flexing. "Trying to get rid of me?"

"I said *we*, didn't I?"

He didn't seem to be truly listening but was preoccupied with something else. "When did you get the bank notice?"

"I told you. Last week."

"Last week when? You still have it, don't you?"

The way he was asking felt...ominous. She nodded, her mouth gone dry.

"Go get it," he said. "Now."

Ginny stepped back, a frisson of trepidation sweeping through her. "I think I should consult an attorney before I say anything more."

His expression changed to one of disbelief and distaste. If she'd been apprehensive a minute ago, it was nothing compared to what she felt now.

"There'll be plenty of time to talk about legalities, but right now we need to act. If you received the bank notice, then so did Meg." His hands fisted. "But if you're right, and she is dead..."

Okay, something had changed. A light had dimmed, not just in his eyes. She couldn't stand thinking about what had happened to

Meg, and she'd been living with the idea for almost a year.

"There's a very good chance this Danny guy has his hands on that bill. Are you following?"

She stared blankly at him, her thoughts shooting in a dozen directions.

"It wouldn't be difficult for him to track you down, Ginny. You and Meg lived in the same town. I'm sure he's heard your name before, probably in the beginning. And he'd want to know what you know, and I doubt he'd take any chances about it."

"Dear God." How had that not occurred to her? It should have been the first thing she thought of when she got that notice.

"Look, I'm not trying to scare you," Parker continued quietly. "But there's no way of knowing if and what he's found out about Tilda."

She gripped the back of the couch, afraid she'd fall without the support. "He couldn't know anything. Even Meg thought I'd found a family for her."

"Who knows what Meg might have told him in a fit of anger? But that isn't what I meant. Some scumbags wouldn't think twice about using a child to get to their mother—he could use Tilda to hurt you. We need to act quickly. I need to know exactly which bank so we can get to it before he does, in case there is any information that could put him away. With the storm on its way, we have to move. Tilda has to—"

Ginny had started shaking as Parker's voice had gotten softer and softer. She had to go get Tilda. Get her out of Temptation Bay. Out of Rhode Island. Somewhere safe. Now. Right now.

Arms came around her, and she jerked away, only to be held in place. She tried to push Parker away, but he wouldn't let go. Sounds were starting to penetrate though, and his soft hushes and soothing tone helped her realize he was only trying to comfort her.

"It's going to be all right, but we need you now. We need you to be strong, and here and with us. Can you do that?"

She nodded, knowing his actions weren't personal but tactical. Which was exactly what was called for.

"Did Meg give you any idea where she was calling from?"

After a quick breath, she was able to speak again. "No. She told me they moved around a lot. And that it was getting riskier to enter the US."

"Good. If they've been jumping around it would take the mail longer to catch up to them.

That might have bought us the window we need."

"And the storm, right? New York is being hit hard. He'd have to get there, but I think the airports have been closed..."

"That's right," Parker said as if he was speaking to a child, and that's when she realized how foolish she was being. Danny could send anyone to do his dirty work.

"Is it too late?" she asked, looking into his face. "You can tell me."

"I doubt it. That being said, we can't afford to count on anything except our own actions. We need to fly to New York today and empty that box."

Something felt wrong about that sentence, even though she knew he was right. "We have to get Tilda. She can't come with us, and I can't leave her here."

Parker eased his grip on her and seemed to calm himself from the head down. His jaw stopped clenching. Even his breathing was steady. "You're right. I have an idea about that. A way to keep her safe." He bent his knees just enough so that he looked into her eyes from the same height. "We can put her on a plane to my mom's. In Boise."

Jerking out of his reach, she shook her head, terrified to her bones that sending Tilda away would mean forever, and that was not going to happen. She'd run, pack as quickly as she could for both of them, take only what they needed for a few days. And they'd go to the airport and pick a destination. Somewhere no one would ever look for them.

"Ginny, wait. We wouldn't tell my mom that Tilda's her…that's she Meg's daughter. All I'd say is that you've had something come up and would she mind looking after your child for a few days. She'll agree. She remembers you well. And she trusts me. I know she won't ask questions."

It bothered her that he was acting as if it would be a pretense, as if Tilda wasn't hers. He knew very well that wasn't true—she was Tilda's mother in every way that mattered. He was also talking to her as if she was a fragile flower who'd wilt the moment she was touched. That wasn't true either, and if he thought—

"Look, there's more to talk about. I know that. But right now it's more important to get Tilda somewhere safe, away from Temptation Bay. And we have to do it before the storm hits and they shut down the airport."

"It's not going to be that bad this far north."

"A minute ago you wanted to leave and get ahead of the storm."

Ginny exhaled.

"Even if they don't close the airport, I still need to be able to fly us to New York. Understand? We have to get there before anyone else does, or everything you've done to protect Tilda and keep her safe might be for nothing. So I need you to put a bag together for Tilda while I call and book her a flight. Can you do that? Pack for her? And maybe for yourself too. We can't be sure things will go like clockwork."

Ginny still felt as if she was being conned, although the packing wasn't a bad idea. If, on the way to the airport, she got any hint that Parker was trying to pull a fast one— She sucked in a breath so hard she felt light-headed. What he'd subtly tried to tell her had finally sunk in. Getting to the bank first wasn't just about getting justice for Meg. It was about preserving Ginny's identity. Erasing her link to Meg. Obviously the bank had her name and address, but Meg had been careful. Ginny's name wasn't even on the invoice.

"I swear to you, I won't say a word to my mom about Tilda. If that's what's bothering you—"

A sound came from the kitchen. Like someone had kicked one of the cabinets. Not loudly. If she hadn't muted the TV, she wouldn't have heard it. Someone had come in, and panic shot through her like a lightning bolt.

A second later her father walked into the family room. The back door had been locked. Apparently he'd used his key. Which he never did, not since he'd left the house thirteen years ago. He hadn't been back more than a dozen times since, usually to get something from the attic or the garage. And he'd always, always called first and knocked on the front door. He couldn't have missed Parker's Jeep in the driveway, so he knew she had company, which made it even stranger.

"Dad," she said. "What are you doing here?"

He didn't say anything, but he did look Parker over for longer than necessary. Finally, her father glanced at her. "I couldn't reach you. It kept going to voice mail, to which you never responded. I thought I'd better come down and make sure you and Tilda were all right."

"Uh, okay. This is Parker Nolan. An old friend," she said. "I'm sorry I didn't get back to you but the storm isn't supposed to be that bad. We might lose electricity, but Lee gassed up the generator, so we'll be fine."

He inhaled deeply. Her father had always had the gift of masking his feelings. That was one of the things that made him such a successful attorney. But the way he looked at her, she could see there was something wrong. How long had he been standing in the kitchen? He could have heard everything they'd said about Tilda.

"I'm glad to see the windows shuttered, although I think it'd be a good idea to put your car in the garage. Is Tilda home?"

Could it be that her father hadn't heard a thing, but that he'd been concerned about her well-being with a strange car in the drive? That seemed ludicrous. She was thirty-two years old. For him to start caring now would be completely out of character.

"Nice to meet you, Mr. Landry, but if you'll excuse me, I've got to make a call." Parker nodded at him and headed into the kitchen.

Once she and her father were alone, he stepped closer, and with each step, his mask slipped.

"How dare you lie to me. After all I've done for you, leaving the house so you'd have a place to stay with your daughter. Were you really planning on letting me pay for some other woman's bastard's education? Isn't it bad enough you threw your own life away? Your mother's legacy? And for what? A kid that isn't even your own blood?"

"Stop right now. Tilda is my daughter."

"Right. It's a little late for backpedaling. I

heard enough to know that's a lie. And now I imagine you're planning on blowing up your second chance, as well?"

"What are you talking about?"

"The philharmonic. It may not mean anything to you, but they're going out of their way to include you as a guest soloist."

"It's only been a couple of times, and it certainly wasn't to do me a favor. I worked hard and played well. Besides, I didn't call them, they called me."

"For God's sake, I'm talking about you going on tour with them. Their first East Coast tour. What your mother would have given to see you—" He stopped. Snapped his mask back on, using his intimidation face instead.

"How do you know anything about the tour? Or me? It's not even official—"

"It doesn't matter what I know, except that I don't have a granddaughter. I've never had one."

Ginny gasped. A few things about the surprise call she'd received from the executive director of the philharmonic started to make sense. "What did you do?"

"What did I—" Her father's dismissive frown fueled her anger.

"Did you give them a huge donation? Bribe someone? No, wait. You probably got someone important out of a jam, someone who would owe you a favor."

"Oh, come on, Virginia—"

"You have no right interfering in my life. I'm not a charity case." Keeping her back as straight as a board and her chin held high, she felt like a fool. She'd honestly believed it was her talent that had earned her an invitation to appear in the lineup. "How much did it cost? What's the going rate to buy a daughter a piece of her future these days?"

"You've always been a bit dim when it comes to these matters. I greased the wheels. I used a few connections. That's how the world works. Your talent was never the issue. You should know that. If you hadn't been good enough they would never have asked you to be a guest, never mind touring with them. I committed no crime. I never lied to you."

The hurt and embarrassment was so strong she wanted nothing more than to tell him to leave and never come back. So he wouldn't take care of Tilda's education if she didn't get a full scholarship. She'd make that work somehow. The philharmonic pay wasn't all that great anyway, and she'd survived this long on teaching. And yet, there was a piece of her that felt very young and vulnerable, and he'd just managed to squash her like a bug for the second time in her life.

"I'm running late," she said. "I'll walk you to the door."

"I'm not leaving. We haven't even spoken about the legalities concerning Tilda. We have a great deal to discuss, and I'd appreciate it if you didn't do anything foolish before we've worked things out."

She walked to the front door, and opened it, not even checking to see if he'd followed. He had, albeit grudgingly. And just as he was about to step outside, she stopped him. "Whatever you heard or think you heard about Tilda, don't worry about it. You never bothered to be a grandfather before, and as far as I'm concerned, you'll never have the privilege of being one now."

PARKER HIT SPEED DIAL and waited for his mother to pick up. He'd already booked a flight for Tilda to Boise—he was lucky to get the last seat and a reasonable connecting flight. It would be a long journey for her. What was more worrying at the moment was this call. He'd spoken to his mother two days ago, letting her know he'd had no luck with finding Meg. But he knew her well enough to realize she'd be—

"Parker?"

He'd known she would be excited. Expecting great news. He heard it in her voice, in that one word. It hurt to have to break her heart again. "I'm sorry, nothing new about Meg. But I need a favor."

There was just enough of a pause that he could picture her face, imagine exactly how she'd process the news and force herself to act as if it was all fine. "Sure, honey, what do you need?"

"It's an odd request but we're in a time crunch with the storm approaching. I'm with Ginny Landry. She has a daughter, Tilda, and it would help a lot if you could look after her for a few days. She's fourteen, smart as a whip, an all-around great kid so she won't give you any trouble."

Another much briefer pause was followed by his mom's cheery voice, the one she'd always used when his father's plans had changed. Again. "Of course I will. Where is she now?"

"Here in Temptation Bay, but she can be on a flight in three hours. You'll have to pick her up at the airport. I know this is last-minute but it's complicated, and I can't explain it all now. But if you could keep her until we get things squared away it would be much appreciated."

"Well, you just tell me when to be at the airport. I'll have a home-cooked meal all ready for her."

Parker had his own moment to get through. They'd lived their whole lives with secrecy and lies, and now he was repeating a cycle he'd sworn he never would. Lying to his mother was a betrayal he could hardly bear. And when the truth came out? Would she hate him the way she'd hated her late husband?

There was nothing to be done now but to ensure Tilda's safety. And Ginny's.

"I don't know...there might be another problem. Once she has your meat loaf, she'll never want to come back."

His mother laughed. "Give me the details of her flight, sweetheart, and I'll take care of the rest."

Once they'd disconnected, he went to the kitchen door to scope things out. While he'd been on hold with the airlines, he'd heard Ginny and her father talking. They hadn't been loud, but Parker could tell the conversation was contentious. A couple of times, he'd heard more than he should have. He wasn't surprised that Robert Landry hadn't known Tilda wasn't his daughter's child, but the way Landry spoke about her friend's "bastard" made Parker want to deck him.

It made it hard not to sympathize with

Ginny. Her father was a real piece of work. He'd basically abandoned her when he thought she'd had a kid, then reclaimed her again when he thought he could get something out of it.

Then again, she'd lied to him, which Parker could understand. Ginny had also lied to Tilda, if only by omission, but that was one big omission. What confused him was that Ginny was smart enough and had sufficient resources to be independent of her father, so why hadn't she hired a private investigator to find Parker and his mother? He'd need to ask her about that later. Actually, he'd need to ask her about a lot of things. Like why she'd tried so hard to get rid of him. How she'd obviously never wanted him to know about Tilda's true heritage.

But that would have to wait until after they'd taken care of the business in New York.

A brief look into the living room told him it was clear. Even Ginny was no longer there.

"Ginny?"

When she didn't answer, he went to the back door to check the driveway. His Jeep was still blocking the garage, so she couldn't have gone far. No way would she have left with her father.

Upstairs, he heard soft rustling coming from Tilda's bedroom. He climbed the stairs and found Ginny holding on to a stuffed teddy bear, her back to him. A suitcase was open and some clothes were already in it.

Clearing his throat made her jump and she set the stuffed animal down, but she didn't turn around. He could tell from her sniffling that she was trying to hide her tears, but it was too late.

"Did you get ahold of your mother?"

Her voice was scratchy and low, which told him almost as much as her hunched shoulders and the air of defeat she wore like a cloak. It made him want to go after her father again, but he shook off the thought.

"I booked Tilda the last seat on United. It's going to be a long flight, including a two-hour layover before she lands in Boise, but I was lucky to get a ticket. My mother will be there to pick her up. She'll be well cared for, I promise."

Ginny's small cry didn't give him any satisfaction. Not that it should have, he supposed.

"She's going to hate that I packed for her." Ginny finally turned, her eyes red and distress written all over her face. "She's going to be confused and scared. I have no idea what to tell her. We're sending her across the country with no explanation. I've never put her in a situation like this before. What am I going to say?"

Parker harshly reminded himself that Ginny was at the root of this whole mess. If she'd given a moment's thought about that letter from the bank, most of this could have already been taken care of. "I have no idea," he said, probably a bit too coldly. They still had to get through this, and he would need Ginny's full cooperation.

"Maybe we could tell her it has to do with Meg." Ginny winced at her own words, but she lifted her chin and went on. "I've talked about her all Tilda's life. She knows Meg was my closest friend, and that I miss her every day. She'll understand that if it's about Meg, it must be important."

He wanted to argue. Remind Ginny that her lies had brought this on. But he didn't miss the irony in the fact that lying again was their best option.

"Don't forget to pack for yourself, and hurry it up. It's going to take a lot of luck and tricky driving to get her to the airport on time."

CHAPTER FIFTEEN

IT FELT ODD to have Parker driving her Subaru, but that was the least of Ginny's worries. Tilda was seething in the backseat while they struggled through traffic. Typically, the ride took a little over half an hour. Today, they'd already been on the road for more than an hour.

"I'm not a little kid. I'm already taking college classes," Tilda said, her voice congested with tears. "I don't understand why you can't just tell me what's going on. Keeping me in the dark is cruel and you know it."

"I would if I could," Ginny said. She sounded as weak as she felt. "But I don't have all the facts yet, and until I do—"

"You're going to send me off to someone I never met, in Boise, Idaho—a place I've never wanted to go to—and stick me there for an unknown amount of time, during which anything could happen to you and I wouldn't have a clue. For that matter, anything could happen to me and you wouldn't have a clue either."

"You can always text me, and I'll text you.

Mrs. Nolan isn't completely a stranger. She's Parker's mom. And Meg's. We've talked about Meg since you were little."

"Right, so, you're dragging me away from my best friend to go stay with your former best friend's mom while you run off with her brother. That makes me feel so much better."

Ginny turned around as far as she possibly could without undoing her seat belt. Tilda's eyes were flaming, and not just from crying. She was furious and had every right to be.

"I don't know what to say to make this easier. Not yet."

"At least you can tell me how long I'll be there. I mean, come on. I feel like I'm being sent to prison. With no parole. You can't do this. It's not fair."

"I know it's not fair, but it's far from prison." Ginny wished she knew how long Tilda would have to stay. It was the hardest thing in the world to put her on a plane by herself, knowing the state she was in. Parker was right though. They had to act quickly. "So much depends on the storm and what happens on this end. The second I know, you'll know."

"This can't be about the weather. You think I haven't heard that it's been downgraded to a tropical storm? I haven't been on Mars."

"Just because it's been downgraded now

doesn't mean there won't be a lot of damage. We could be without electricity for days or even weeks."

"The bay rarely gets hit hard. You know we're mostly protected there. And even if we weren't, we have the generator, and we'd be fine."

Sighing, and trying not to show her own fear, Ginny used the most rational tone she could muster. "It's not just about the storm. It's complicated."

The way Tilda stared at her, openmouthed and wounded, broke Ginny's heart.

"Kaley's parents use that lame excuse all the time, but I never thought I'd hear that from you."

Ginny had watched her beautiful girl go through surprise, betrayal, fear, worry, manipulation and now all of them together in one big ball of disappointment.

Unsnapping her seat belt, Tilda leaned forward and whispered, "I know you've been crying. Mom, I'm completely freaked out. If you care about me at all, you'll tell me what's going on. Is he holding you hostage or something?"

Ginny kissed her cheek and whispered, "No, sweetheart. It's nothing like that. Your grandfather and I had a disagreement. That's why

I was crying. Now, please, put your seat belt back on."

Tilda obeyed, but the look of fear and confusion never left her face. "I probably shouldn't say this, but sometimes I don't like Grandfather very much."

"Sometimes I don't either," Ginny said. "I know I'm asking a lot, but it's hugely important that you trust me right now. Trust that I'm doing the very, very best I can for you. You're right. I've never done this before, but now I have no choice. Can you please try to believe that? Know that I love you more than anything in this entire world, and I'd never, never do anything to hurt you. We're a team, you and me. We have each other's backs. Now it's your turn to do something very hard, but I believe you can weather this like the champion you are. I mean it. You're amazing, and I also know that you're a mature young woman now, and that's why we can get through this. Okay?"

Tilda inhaled as a couple of tears got past her sudden stoicism and made their way down her tanned cheek. "Fine. I'll do it. But you have to text me all the time, okay? Don't even worry about waking me up because I doubt I'll sleep."

"Deal." Ginny smiled, but she didn't get one in return. Not that she expected one.

"We're almost there," Parker said, turning off the exit to the Providence airport. "And I think you'll likely be back home very soon."

"Good, because I've got a barbecue to go to this weekend, and I'm supposed to bring the potato salad."

That was the first Ginny had heard about a barbecue or salad, but that was all right. It got Tilda thinking positively. Even if there was no way to know if Parker was correct.

It was silent in the car until they pulled up at the curbside drop-off. Ginny wanted to walk Tilda to the gate, but she knew security wouldn't allow it, nor would doing so make it any easier. Either way, she'd have to say goodbye. She slid out of the car.

So did Parker. He opened the trunk and got out Tilda's bag and her backpack. Then he walked the long way around the car, taking a moment to tell Ginny to make it quick before he closed the trunk and gave them some privacy.

When Ginny and Tilda were alone and the ticket and boarding pass were in Tilda's hand, they hugged so hard Ginny thought she might leave bruises. But then it was time, and she watched her baby enter the building.

"You think we need to worry about her pulling a fast one and ditching the plane?"

Parker's voice made her jump. She hadn't realized he'd come around again and opened the passenger door. She shook her head. "Did you mean it about Tilda making it back for the weekend?"

He didn't answer until they were both in the car and he'd inched into the flow of traffic. "I don't know. It all depends on what happens in New York."

The Subaru shuddered under a buffeting wind, and she gripped the dashboard. "We should have taken a commercial flight."

"I tried. They had no more open seats. Even to Newark."

As they made their way back to the freeway, Ginny trembled with every fear she'd had since the moment Tilda had been put in her arms. She had no idea what was going to happen, and she'd sent her daughter away without an explanation. It felt like being in hell.

THE WIND HAD picked up. Considerably. Traveling south to the airfield, there was far less traffic than driving north, but still more than Parker had expected. He heard Ginny's thumbs hitting the keys on her cell phone. Probably a text to Tilda. Ginny hadn't asked if it was still safe to fly, but it was obvious her whole world had narrowed to her child.

Which pissed him off.

Her child? Meg's child. What would life have been like if his mother had had a granddaughter to look after?

He glanced at Ginny but only for a moment. She seemed empty and fragile. Not the way he was used to seeing her.

"Are you worried about flying with me? My De Havilland isn't a commercial jet, but it's not a puddle jumper either."

Without looking at him, she shook her head, turned to stare out the window until he could barely see her profile. But when her phone signaled a text, the corners of her lips curled up.

After she finished typing back, she looked out the windshield.

"Not that you asked," he said, "but I'm keeping close tabs on the weather. Besides, I won't have clearance to fly if it gets too dangerous."

She nodded so slightly he almost missed it.

"If it does get too bad and we're grounded, we'll spend the night at a motel near the airfield and take off the minute we can."

"Okay," she said.

It felt as if she'd spoken from clear across the country. Which made sense, since most of her was with Tilda. But something had shifted.

He hadn't been looking at her, but she'd started tapping her fingers against her phone. Her right leg bounced. "What's wrong?"

"Are you sure your mom won't slip and say something to Tilda?"

"Like what? She doesn't know anything except that she's doing us a favor by watching your kid."

Her leg had stopped and so had the tapping. Probably because he'd snapped at her, but this was still new to him. He hadn't known a thing until yesterday. He hated putting his mother in this position. She'd been through too much already.

The silence that followed made things easier. The closer they got to the airfield, the more he gained control of his emotions. Then his cell vibrated and he turned on his Bluetooth ear-bud. The news wasn't completely unexpected. They wouldn't be flying today.

"The wind is too strong for us to fly. We'll find a place for the night."

"If we don't leave until tomorrow, do you think we'll still be able to make it back before the weekend?"

He sighed and tried to pull back his irritation. Did she honestly not remember asking him the same question not ten minutes ago? Did she not recognize the danger she could be in? The possible danger to Tilda? They didn't know much about Danny but if he had the resources to live abroad and stay on the move, the guy had to be pulling in some big money.

She might not have had the ideal family life she'd always wanted, but she'd been sheltered as her father's daughter. She didn't even know what a truly hard, uncertain life was like. "Do you think getting back for the weekend is more important than making sure she's safe?"

The way Ginny turned to him, as if she wanted to slap him, gave him a sick sense of satisfaction. Even he could recognize there were issues at play, and that he needed to watch his temper. And his words.

"Look, I'm sorry your father's being an ass."

Ginny shrunk against her door.

He'd just told himself he needed to watch what he said, and he'd blown it already. "Believe me, I understand how a parent can mess you up. It had to be difficult, being without a mom, and then to have your father turn away from you like that."

"Did you hear it all? Everything he said?"

"No. I was on hold a lot in the kitchen. You weren't exactly being quiet though. I gathered he didn't suspect anything about Tilda not being yours."

Ginny let out a soft whimper. "She is mine.

She's my everything. And I don't give a damn what he thinks of me or what anyone else thinks. Anyway, I didn't lie to him. She is my daughter."

Parker had overheard more than he'd admit. He couldn't imagine the humiliation Ginny was feeling over that piece of nasty business with the philharmonic. Landry was a jerk, all right, but Parker agreed with him that Ginny's talent had done more to get her the soloist spot than whatever strings he'd pulled.

Out of pure sympathy—no matter how short the supply—he swallowed back the argument he'd been nursing since yesterday. "I didn't mean to get you riled up. We're both tense. Tilda's flight will be leaving soon, and that's all you need to worry about for now. But when we get to the motel, we'll have to talk. Not about your father. About what we're going to do once we're in New York. All right?"

She closed her eyes. He let her be, watching instead for the exit he needed. There was a motel near the airstrip, and while it wasn't anything special, he'd heard it was clean and well kept. It also was next to a decent seafood restaurant that had a bar.

They both needed to relax if they were going to get through what could be a very precarious situation. And since she was having difficulty keeping her eyes on the goal, he'd have to take the reins. But once they got back to Temptation Bay, all bets would be off. She was going to have to come to grips with the fact that her secret was no longer hers alone.

GINNY HELD ON to her cell phone for the rest of the ride to the motel. They were inland, but not that much farther than her house. The wind was fierce. "We're only twenty minutes from my place. Why don't we stay there tonight?"

"I'd rather stick close. We're five minutes from the airfield, and I don't want to have to fight traffic if all the lights go out. They could give us the go-ahead by early tomorrow morning, and we need to hit it. Regardless of the contents, we need to get to that deposit box before Danny decides you're a threat and puts you in his crosshairs. I'm thinking he doesn't have your address. But until we know more, I don't want you or Tilda anywhere near your house."

The way he looked at her reminded her far too much of her father's decrees about her and her life. "I assure you I'm taking this seriously. I understand there's the potential for real danger and I'm not suggesting we don't stay alert and aware. You're right about not going to the house, but it's not necessary to scold me like a

child. This has all been alarming, and I'm not
used to being separated from Tilda, or sending her off into the unknown. I know it's my
fault, okay? I know the notice from the bank
should have raised an alarm."

"Hey, I'm—"

"I'm not finished," she said. "I also realize
you don't have to be doing any of this. You
could have easily flown to Alaska and never
looked back. I appreciate that you didn't. And
that you were kind to Tilda when she was so
frightened."

"Ginny, Tilda's my niece. I wasn't about to
leave once I understood what was at stake."

For Tilda, she knew. Who was now on her
way to his mother's house. Where they'd claim
they had every right to keep her since Ginny
wasn't much more than a legal guardian. She
couldn't say she blamed him, but... Okay, yes
she did. It was obvious he didn't understand
what it was to be a de facto parent. But she
didn't dare think about anything but the next
twenty-four hours, or she'd go mad.

By the time they got to their rooms—side-
by-side, but not adjoining, thankfully—she
was ready to collapse. As she slid her key into
the door, her phone rang.

Tilda.

"Hi, sweetie. You on board?"

"I should have made you put me in first class. It's awesome up there. They have free snacks and better everything. Even booze that they get right away. Not that I would get booze, but still."

"Is it really so bad in coach?"

"The guy next to me is already snoring, and we haven't even started to move yet. It's gross."

"Use your headphones and watch a movie. PG-13 rated, please."

"Mom, I'm not a baby."

"I trust you to make the right decision."

The sigh was as clear as if Tilda had been standing right next to her. "That's even worse than telling me I can't."

Ginny smiled. "I miss you already."

"Me too. But I have to turn off my phone now. I'll call when I land."

"You're going to have a stop to change planes. Call then too."

"I will."

"Okay, honey. I love you." She disconnected, and realized Parker was still at his door. He'd listened to their whole conversation. What on earth did he think she was going to say that he had to monitor? Keeping her annoyance out of her expression, she turned her key and pushed the door open. He stopped her on the threshold.

"What time do you want to go have dinner?"

"I'm not hungry. I'll pass."

"Nope. We need to get our ducks in a row and we both need to be well fueled and ready for anything. It won't be a long flight to New York, and I've arranged to land at La Guardia's cargo terminal. It shouldn't take us long to get to the bank, but we don't know what we'll find there. We can't afford not to be at our best."

Ginny stared down at the cement for a moment. He was right. And if she wasn't so upset with herself for all the mistakes she'd made, she wouldn't be feeling so belligerent. She wasn't in the right frame of mind to call the shots. She had to trust Parker to do it, and she was grateful to have his help.

"How about seven o'clock? Does that work for you?" he asked, his voice quiet and almost sympathetic, as if he understood her internal struggle. "I'll knock, and we can go to the restaurant next door. That'll give us both time to rest and as long as we've got electricity, we can watch the weather."

"Fine." She looked up into his concerned eyes. "I just hope we can get Tilda to that barbecue. I know it doesn't seem important to you, but…"

He put up a hand. "The next forty-eight hours will tell. There's nothing we can do to make it happen faster." He inserted his key. "Another thing. I understand you're worried about Tilda, but try to relax. Maybe you'll remember something else Meg might've told you about Danny. The name of a friend, anything that could give us a clue about what we're up against would help."

"I'll try."

She took a step inside but stalled halfway. She desperately wanted to ask him what he saw happening. Not in New York but after, when the threat was over. But that would be foolish. She needed to believe this was all going to work out for the best. It had to...

"Wait."

He'd been about to enter his room but looked over at her.

"Spider. I think that was his nickname at one time." Ginny tried to recall more of the long-ago conversation. "Meg mentioned something about getting a spider tattoo, but it was years ago. Back when she was still in the giddy stage."

"Good," Parker said, nodding, his mind clearly working double-time.

"I could be totally wrong."

"That's okay. Little things like that may

make it possible to identify him. I'm betting the NYPD has a file on him."

"The police?" Ginny's stomach clenched. "What are you talking about? We can't tell the police. We can't tell anyone."

He stared at her as if she'd gone over the deep end. "We're talking about the man who might have killed my sister. You don't think we should gather as much information as we can on him, not to mention have some muscle behind us."

"I trust that you'll have my back. You'll keep an eye out. Make sure no one's following me inside the bank."

Parker sighed and shook his head. "Listen to me—"

"No, you listen. If we find evidence against him we can send it to the police anonymously. I can't have this blowing up, everyone knowing about Tilda. What would that do to her?"

"Ginny, we don't know who this guy is or what he's capable of."

"She's all I have. She's everything to me. I won't subject her to any of this."

He took a deep breath, then another. His expression had lost its incredulity and it was clear he was trying to ease the tension between them.

She could admit that she might not be at

her best, but the police were still out of the question.

"I know you're on edge, and you're worried about Tilda, but I don't think you're being completely rational right now."

"Promise me you won't call the authorities until we talk more."

"Fine. Now you promise me you'll try to relax. We both need to be smart and make no mistakes. It's not just about Tilda finding out. It's about her being safe. I know that's what you want." He didn't understand about her daughter. How could he? But he was also right. Ginny had to calm down. Think things through. Or she'd be no use to anyone. Least of all Tilda.

CHAPTER SIXTEEN

THE ROOM WAS nothing to write home about, but it was clean and had a decent bathtub. As Ginny put her few toiletries away and hung up her one blouse, her thoughts were as jerky as a Ping-Pong match. She obsessed about Tilda finding out from the police or the news…or Parker. She wasn't going to relax until she saw her daughter again and had her safely at home.

Her thoughts bounced back to Parker. How could she both despise him and feel incredibly grateful in equal measure? Fear had to be the answer. It bled through her muddled thoughts, even when things were spinning so fast she thought she'd explode. Last week the future had seemed crystal clear. Now it was a big black hole of uncertainty.

One glance at her watch brought her thoughts back to Tilda, who was probably watching something Ginny wouldn't approve of, drinking too much soda and eating who knows what. Nowadays the airlines had menus and all kinds of things for purchase, and she'd not only given Tilda cash but one of her credit cards. It honestly didn't matter what she spent on the flight, but Ginny didn't want her to be ill in case of turbulence. Tilda had a phobia about vomiting, and she was all alone, and...

Oh, lord why was she crying again? It didn't help anything. It was important to be strong. Strong enough for herself, Tilda and Meg. Strong enough to weather this storm and have the resources to be open and flexible when necessary. The burden felt too heavy, but tough. She'd faced hard times before and gotten through them. When Tilda had gotten so sick two years ago that she'd had to go to the hospital, Ginny hadn't wavered despite being scared to death.

Talk about putting on her big-girl panties.

That made her grin. It was something Tilda said a lot—so often it made Ginny a little nuts. But right now it made her stand taller. She got out her cell and called her daughter. It went straight to voice mail, as she'd known it would, but she wanted this to be the first thing Tilda heard when she got off the plane.

"I love you, kiddo. So much it's crazy. I know how hard this is. But I also know that you've got a core of steel, because I've seen you face really hard things and sail through. Thank you so much for trusting me on this.

We'll see each other very soon, and I'll keep my phone on, so call me anytime. I'm hugging you right now in my thoughts."

After disconnecting, Ginny wanted to delete the call and try again. The assumption that Tilda trusted her was a little far-fetched, and knowing her daughter, she'd probably send her back a snide text.

No. No she wouldn't. Tilda truly was the strongest kid she knew. She might be fourteen, but sometimes she acted as if she were twenty-five.

Stepping out of the bathroom and looking out the window, she saw there was almost as much mayhem outside—with the wind whipping the trees and blowing debris everywhere—as she felt inside herself. She should have told Tilda the truth about Meg. About everything. Trusted her with the information instead of letting fear keep her secrets.

Ginny sank to the bed, her shoulders hunched and a headache throbbing at her temples. She'd planned on telling Tilda the truth many times. Initially, she'd decided twelve would be the right age. Her daughter would be old enough to understand, even though it would take time to process the information. But when her birthday came, Tilda had been going through her first serious case of unrequited puppy love, and there was no way Ginny was going to make that worse.

At thirteen, she decided to tell Tilda the truth in stages. First, that she'd been adopted. Ginny would see how she handled that, then she'd know how to approach the second phase. But then, Tilda had entered her first science fair, and as with everything else that mattered to the little brainiac, it had become her whole universe. After Tilda had gotten the blue ribbon, Ginny had figured she'd tell her. But then, like a fool, she'd gotten distracted by the initial calls from the philharmonic.

Oh, there was always a reason, and none of them justified letting things go so far. It all had to do with her own personal demons and the fear that something would damage the bond between her and Tilda.

This time, when the tears came, she didn't even think of stopping them. Instead, she curled up on the unfamiliar bed, clutching her cell phone in one hand and a wad of tissues in the other as she let it all out. It wasn't as if her eyes weren't already red and swollen, and she'd kissed any idea of makeup goodbye early this morning.

Time drifted as she went through tissues and sobs, until finally the chest-heaving, racking pain eased into a steady stream of tears wetting the pillowcase.

She thought about calling Cricket, but the truth was she didn't need a lawyer. Not yet, at least. Parker knew everything there was to know, and soon enough so would his mother. All Ginny could do now was pray the family would show her some mercy. If nothing else, they'd want Tilda to be happy. Of course, that would depend on Tilda not hating her after learning the whole story.

Another prayer went up, and she hoped the weather wouldn't interfere with God's reception. Because she needed all the help she could get.

The knock on her door startled her into a small panic. Sitting up, she dropped her phone. "Just a minute," she said, jumping up to wash her face and do some damage control.

PARKER HAD ASKED for the quietest booth in the restaurant, but he hadn't needed to. The place was almost empty. He'd figured it would be sparse because they catered to tourists. But he'd expected to see more folks who'd not been able to escape the storm.

It didn't matter. Ginny had ordered shrimp scampi while he'd settled on a halibut steak. Only he was actually eating, while she was mostly pushing food from one side of the plate to the other.

"You're going to need the protein. If the shrimp isn't doing it for you, we can try something else. You're already pale, and I don't want you passing out tomorrow."

Ginny sighed. "I tried to think of something else that would be helpful, but I just couldn't."

"That's okay." He almost told her just how much the moniker Spider had helped, but then she'd have questions he didn't want to answer.

"I called the bank, and man, they have some tight security on those safe-deposit boxes. I don't see how Danny or anyone else he'd send could get in there without setting off major alarms. But better to be prepared for any eventuality."

His phone went off but he saw it was just Ruby and let it go to voice mail. How he got so many whiney babies on his delivery schedule, he'd never know. While he had his phone out, he checked the weather. There was nothing new to report. The storm was rising, but it wouldn't hit its zenith until later on. They'd be back at the motel before the worst of it.

Ginny sipped on her drink. He'd encouraged her to get something a little stronger than iced tea, but she'd declined. Her cell was sitting right next to her plate, and between glances around the room, she kept a hawk's watch on the phone. He knew it wasn't on silent mode, but there was nothing he could say that wouldn't upset her more, so he did his best to ignore the vigilance.

He did drink some of his scotch and soda. He hoped it would relax him enough to help Ginny settle down. It was obvious she'd done more crying, and while he tried to hang on to his anger, he had to admit he sympathized with her. When he thought back on what he could have done differently—which he'd done a lot of since learning the truth about Meg— he understood how selfish he'd been. He'd written her off, never once questioned if she could have been in trouble. Used helping out his mother as his Get-Out-Of-Jail-Free card and blamed everything bad that had happened on his father.

At least Ginny had tried to help Meg.

Didn't mean she shouldn't have tried searching for him or his mom, but there was a lot to be said for her taking charge when the chips were down. Like he was doing. Finally.

His cell went off again. Denali. Nope, he wasn't going to get involved with him, not now.

"It's all right," Ginny said. "You should

probably answer those calls. It might be important."

He shook his head. "It's just customers complaining that I'm taking some time off. They'll get over it the minute I'm back."

She nodded, then took another bite of shrimp. Probably to show him that when he wasn't acting like her father, she could be cooperative.

Damn, he missed his cabin. The quiet. The fishing. He'd like nothing better than to be out on the water in his kayak right now, listening to the wild creatures as they set about catching their evening meals. Yep. Life was simple out there. No one around to depend on him. He had, on occasion, disappointed his mom by not flying to Boise for the holidays. But after everything they'd gone through with his dad, she understood better than anyone how much Parker needed the solitude. What he didn't need was emotional entanglements. Life was too short to let it get messy.

His lousy phone beeped again, which he ignored.

"Huh. I'd gotten a very different impression of your life in Alaska."

He didn't care for the way Ginny was studying him. "What do you mean?"

"I thought you were such a lone wolf. A

mountain man. All alone in the middle of the woods, chopping firewood to heat your cabin and cook your meals."

"That's true. Except when I need to make deliveries, it's just me."

"But you get calls all the time. You're clearly missed. A lot of folks depend on you."

"No one depends on me," he said, a little more sharply than he'd intended. "And that's the way I like it. The only reason I get called is because of work, and I've got to earn a living somehow. I barely even see my business partner, let alone anyone else."

The way her eyes widened, he could see she didn't believe him. It only made things worse when she carefully ate some more shrimp and rice.

Okay, so a lot of his folks...his clients... hounded him. That was because they wanted so many extras every stupid run. Like those clams. He could barely believe he'd considered filling his ice chest to take mollusks to Alaska. As if there wasn't enough seafood there.

Fine. She wasn't entirely wrong.

"Let's talk about tomorrow," he said. "We'll take a cab to the bank. We don't have time to rent a car, and there's no parking there, anyway. The first thing you should do is talk to the manager and find out if anyone's been asking about the box. The hurricane hit the city pretty hard. As of an hour ago flights were still grounded. Hopefully that slowed Danny's men down—and that's only assuming the bill was intercepted. We could be worrying for nothing. Nevertheless, warn the manager, tell him or her that your friend's ex-boyfriend will probably come looking and he's not someone to be toyed with. I'm sure it won't be the first time they've been warned about something like that."

Ginny stared at him funny. "You said Danny's men."

"Did I?" *Damn.* "Okay. So?"

"Why do you assume he wouldn't go himself?"

Parker hesitated a second too long.

"You found something out about him, didn't you?"

"A little. He might be an arms dealer, but I don't have nearly enough information to be sure." Parker didn't like the way she kept staring at him. "Let's get back to the plan. The assistant manager will be the person who'll usher you inside the vault to open the box."

"How do you know that?"

"I told you I called the bank about their security."

"Right." She put her fork down. "What if

they tell me someone has been pressuring them for access or information? Do I leave? Make sure we aren't being watched before I take anything out?" Pausing, she searched his eyes. "I guess I should call you, right? I mean, you'll be just outside. Won't you?"

"I'll be right beside you, Ginny."

"Oh. Okay. Good." She took a deep breath. "Wait. Shouldn't you hang back and watch to see if I'm followed?"

He wished he could be completely honest, but not when he thought the truth might trip her up. "Leaving the bank is when we'll be at risk. I'm going to have the cabbie keep the meter running so we can get in and slip right into traffic. Anyway, I want you to take whatever is in that box and put it in your purse."

"My leather overnight bag is bigger. Should I take that instead?"

"Good thinking." He took another sip of his scotch. "Something else we need to consider. We can't take our cell phones into the bank with us."

"What? Why not? What if Tilda calls?"

"The problem is, if Danny is sophisticated enough, he can download everything in your phone before you can blink, and you'd never know it."

"Where would we leave them?"

"In the cab."

"In New York City? Are you crazy?"

Parker had to wonder if it wouldn't be easier if he admitted they weren't in this alone. It wasn't her anger that worried him but the potential for irrational fear impairing her judgment. "We can't risk them finding out anything about you. How about we leave your phone in the plane? I'll take a chance with the cab."

"Okay, but what if—"

"Tilda doesn't expect you to be at the ready twenty-four/seven. She'll leave a voice mail."

Ginny sighed but didn't argue "What if they come after us?"

"I'm going to have a little talk with the bank's security. Ask them to keep an eye out, tell them that you're carrying a lot of cash. That won't surprise them. Nothing out of the ordinary."

"A security guard, not the police?"

"Right."

"And you're sure about that?"

"With the security measures in that bank? I'm sure."

"What about when we're done? Can we fly right back?"

"If possible, yes. There's a hotel right around the corner. I've booked us a room just in case."

"Why? Once we empty the box, why

wouldn't we be able to come home? The weather shouldn't be an issue."

"Look, if Danny is who I think he is, we have to be twice as cautious. The guy is ruthless, and so are the men who work for him." When her mouth dropped open he quickly added, "I might be wrong. I hope I am, but we can't let our guard down." He watched her nibble at her lip. "We can always change our minds and bring in the police."

"No."

"I still think our timing is good. With him living abroad and with the storm battering the coast, we have luck on our side. I think we'll be fine."

Ginny seemed surprised. She just stared at him for a long minute, making him wonder what was going on in that head of hers. "You've really thought this through."

"Well, yeah, it matters. Anyway, you know me. I love researching everything to death. That's one of the things I liked about studying law."

She didn't respond. Only looked at him funny again.

He almost put his hand on hers. Wanted to. She'd done a lot that made him angry, but regardless, he still felt that pull. More than he should. He'd even thought about the fact that if she had given Tilda up for adoption as Meg asked, he and his mother would never have the chance to know Meg's daughter. If she hadn't been a good friend to Meg they'd never know why Meg left or what had happened to her. It wouldn't be pleasant for his mother to learn the truth about Meg, but perhaps she'd have a chance to heal from that, especially if she got to spend time with her granddaughter.

"Tell me about her?" Parker asked.

Ginny's brow creased.

"Meg. Was she at least happy in the beginning?"

Ginny inhaled deeply. It made his chest tighten, but what hadn't in the last couple of days?

She flagged the waitress over and asked for a gin and tonic. He asked for another scotch. Once the waitress left, carrying their plates, he gave in and put his hand on Ginny's.

She studied it a moment, then said, "I know you got the impression that we talked a lot, but we didn't. More in the beginning, probably, but as time went on I think she found it harder to have a private conversation."

They lapsed into silence, him listening to the wind. Ginny lost in her own thoughts.

"You don't have to worry about holding back," he said finally, seeing she was gearing up to tell him some unpleasant things. Before she said anything, the waitress was back with their drinks. But he was the only one who took a sip.

"It took a long time for Meg to get over the devastation of you guys leaving like that. She came back to an empty house. Nothing was there, not even an old sock or a piece of paper. She said it was like she'd woken up in an alternate universe, where she'd never had a family at all."

Parker didn't believe Ginny was intentionally stabbing him with a broadsword, it just felt like it. But he had asked, and part of him was glad she wasn't whitewashing the whole thing. That would have been worse. This would at least help cauterize the wound.

"But she did settle down after a few months. She wouldn't stay at our house, but she called me a lot. We were all so shocked that you were gone. Even my father used some of his sources to find out what happened, but no one could tell him anything. His guess was that you had to go into witness protection for some reason, and that Meg was just acting out because she didn't want to move. He ordered me to stay away from her if she ever came back. But she didn't, and I wouldn't have listened to him, anyway."

Parker smiled. Then, as her earlier words sunk in, he closed his eyes. "It was a terrible thing they did. We did. My mom begged the agent in charge to wait, at least until someone heard from my father. But no one listened. They herded us out, didn't even let us pack. They did it all. Even my mother's most personal things were brought to us days later, in the terrible house they put us in."

"I'm sorry."

He put his hand back around his drink, wishing he'd ordered a double.

"Danny showered her with attention back then. He took her to the Virgin Islands and Jamaica. She loved the trips. He bought her nice things, and they stayed in fancy hotels. She used to call me from whatever bathtub she found herself in, tell me where they'd gone, what kind of car he'd rented and what he'd bought her." A sad smile tugged at her mouth. "Come to think of it, I think Danny probably liked hearing her brag about him and all his money, especially when the trips started becoming more lavish. And then, all of a sudden, the communication died down by a lot."

He nodded, barely able to breathe, thinking of what that bastard could have done to his little sister. He wanted to kill him with his bare hands.

"Meg didn't realize she was pregnant for a few months. She swore they'd been careful, but it happened, anyway. She didn't tell him. Not then. It turned out Tilda was small, and Meg didn't start showing until around six months. He told her she was getting fat, and she'd better take care of it. Check into a fat farm if that's what she needed, just do it pronto.

"Two months later she told Danny about the baby, although she didn't admit how far along she was, and he told her to get rid of it. He wanted it done before he got back from a business trip to Argentina. Luckily it was a long trip and she was able to have the baby while he was away. She brought Tilda to me when she was a week old. She was so tiny. But perfect. When she cried it was all wobbly, and her little fingers and toes would clench."

"It must have been hard for Meg to walk away."

"It was. But she knew she had to. If she'd disappeared, Danny would have come after her. He didn't like to lose his things. If she'd tried to keep the baby, I can't even imagine what he would have done. She saved Tilda's life."

"You didn't think she would come back?"

"I'd hoped she would. But she couldn't take

the risk that Danny would find her and get rid of the baby."

That hit Parker so hard, he almost lost it right there at the table. His sister had been so young. She'd given birth only a year after she'd graduated from that lousy prep school. To have gotten in so far over her head... It made him ache for her down to his bones, and it wasn't nearly what she deserved. "She was a sweet kid when she was little. Always asking questions. She wanted so much from life."

Ginny was the one to touch him this time. Her warm hand had nothing on the sorrow he saw in her eyes. "I'm so sorry it didn't turn out better."

He wanted to explain that he appreciated her taking the baby. Up to a point. Being given the responsibility of determining Tilda's future had also given her more reason to look for him and his mom. But he couldn't be a bastard now. Not now. "Tell me about Tilda."

That made Ginny smile and the pain eased a fraction.

"She was an amazing baby. Hardly ever cried. I found a great agency, not too far from Juilliard, where they only sent licensed and bonded nannies that had stellar references. But I still worried. The woman I used was great with her, and she taught me a lot about how to take care of an infant. Tilda and I learned together. She wasn't finicky, but early on we had to be careful about milk. She grew out of that pretty quickly. And for a couple of years she was allergic to strawberries, which she loved."

Parker watched Ginny's whole demeanor change as she talked. It was as if he'd been with someone else all through dinner. This woman was glowing, even with puffy red eyes.

"Then, we got to the *terrible twos*, and let me tell you, that's a real thing. She was always crabby and demanding and…well, by that time I'd left Juilliard and gone back home. So it was just the two of us. I nearly tore my hair out, read every book I could find on child-rearing. But they didn't help all that much. We got through it, and by the time she was three she talked a mile a minute. Could count to one hundred and play 'Mary Had a Little Lamb' on the piano all by herself."

"An overachiever, huh?"

"Oh, yeah. She was always smart. Which didn't make life easy. Insatiably curious, she wanted to know how everything worked. Why the sky was blue, why there were waves, who lived on the moon."

Parker's grin came easily. Meg had been that

way too. "From what you've said, she hasn't changed all that much."

"No. Although she's more mature than most of her classmates, and she's got the kind of discipline even my father could admire."

"How's that possible? Meg was the most impatient child I've ever known. She wanted everything right away, no waiting for her. She could throw a tantrum like nobody's business."

"Tilda was no angel either. But she was determined. She didn't give up on anything, even when I wanted her to. Headstrong and bright, she was reading so far past her peers it was kind of scary. She loves books, loves learning. Loves numbers and computers. Honestly, she could be anything she set her mind to be."

Parker wasn't enjoying this so much anymore. In fact, he wanted to tell her to stop. These were things his mother should have known, things Meg should have experienced. He liked Ginny, more than he should, but he wasn't going to let her twist things so that she was the hero of this story.

Just as she was telling him about Tilda's first crush, the whole building shook. It stopped them both.

He looked at his watch. "If we don't go now, we might get stuck here."

"I don't care," Ginny murmured, turning

to look out the window. Outside a large tree was bowing to the wind. "As long as we get to New York by tomorrow."

CHAPTER SEVENTEEN

AS THEY WAITED for their check, a second gust of wind, fiercer than the last, shook the whole restaurant. Ginny held on to her glass, afraid it would topple. Parker had his cell in his hand, checking something—probably the storm's progress. She'd been impressed by the storm mesh window coverings when they'd first come in, but now being able to see outside was too frightening.

Glass shattered in the back of the restaurant, probably in the kitchen. It sounded like something big had broken.

She could just make out the words that were leaking through the swinging doors, almost all curses. A man's voice rose above the din. Ginny was pretty sure she knew the family who owned the restaurant through their son, Justin Whittaker. He'd gone to the local public school and sold fish at the open market with his grandmother on weekends.

"I told you to board up those windows early!" a woman shouted. "Now look what's happened. Cover the pots. Hurry. And get everything in the fridge before the wind turns."

"I'm not the one who was supposed to board the windows. I'm sixty-two years old. That's why we hired that cousin of yours. Where the heck is he, anyway?"

"Sounds like trouble brewing," Parker said. "Might be more dangerous than the storm."

Ginny actually smiled. She had to hand it to him, despite how he had to feel about her, he'd remained civil. Oh, she wasn't so foolish as to believe his anger and disappointment had disappeared. He was just good at setting his emotions aside for the greater good.

Another gust felt like it might raise the roof, but the building stood—although the power failed.

It was pitch-dark at the table, but Parker put on his cell phone flashlight and made it possible for them to see the waitress carrying a small LED camping lantern to their table and placing a larger one a few tables away—although Ginny thought she and Parker were the only two customers left.

His cell light went off, and even with all the noise, the lantern made it feel a little cozy. Her thoughts slipped away from the oncoming doom as she wondered what it would have been like if the lanterns had been candles instead, and the dinner had been a romantic getaway. Her sigh was swept away in the warm wind that had sneaked through the door and picked up just enough to ruffle Parker's dark hair.

Just as he was about to say something, her cell phone buzzed. It was a text, but not from Tilda. Ah, it was Lee, which was strange. He should have finished with all his houses before now.

Remember that table we put out for Tilda's party a couple of weeks ago? There's a chance the wind could send it into the window. I'm thinking about putting it somewhere safer, but there was a gent here earlier. Think he might have come back and done that already?

Well that verified how Parker had found her at the gas station. As for Lee? Naturally, he'd risk life and limb to make sure all his folks were safe.

"Everything okay?"

She looked up at Parker, who'd gotten to his feet while she'd read the text.

"It's the man you met this morning putting up the storm shutters. There's a table on the patio he's worried could break the big window.

I wouldn't care, except it's possible the piano could be damaged. Where are you going?"

"Sounds like they need help in the kitchen," he said, his words punctuated by another loud curse from the back.

"I think you're right. In the meantime, I'm going to run home for a minute and move the table—"

He caught her upper arm as she rose and turned to the door. "The storm is getting worse by the second. You shouldn't be driving out there. If the wind did pick up the table, it could be a real mess. Besides, we have to be ready to get to the airfield at the first green light."

Freeing her arm, she took a quick breath. "Don't worry. I'm not going to run out on you. Not with Tilda at risk."

He gave her a dry look. "I'm concerned about your safety. The last thing I want is for you to get into an accident. Look at how those trees are blowing out there."

She didn't bother looking out the window, not when she could tell that he was being sincere. "I'm sorry. That remark was uncalled-for. Go help in the kitchen. I'm going to text Lee and tell him to stay put and take care of his family. Even if the table—" Her voice caught. Quietly she cleared her throat. "It doesn't matter," she said. "It's only a piano."

Parker hesitated, probably thought she would try to sneak out, which she had no intention of doing. Not even for her beautiful Fazioli grand piano. She held in a sigh.

Finally, he walked away, his shadow larger than life against the dining room wall. She watched him push through the swinging doors, her gaze moving down his back until she couldn't see him anymore.

She shot out the text, then followed Parker into the back and met not only the owners and another waitress but three other people, all of them relatives it seemed. Two were younger than Mr. and Mrs. Whittaker and one a much older woman sitting in a captain's chair and barking out orders. It was all very dark and shadowy, with pots hanging in clusters from ceiling-mounted racks. She could only see the faces of the others when they walked to the side where the camp lamps had been placed. Almost all of the crew had the distinctive chin she remembered on Justin, except for the two older women, who looked Mediterranean.

"Don't be a dope," Mrs. Whittaker said, not sparing Ginny a glance while she was shaking a finger at her husband. "Go make sure the cioppino is cool enough to put in the fridge. Cory and Stella can take care of the window."

She turned to look at Parker. "With some help from this kind young man."

The two younger Whittakers had already put on yellow rain slickers and Parker had put on his jacket. His hair was going to get wet, but she supposed he didn't care. They left as a group, with Stella making goo-goo eyes at Parker.

Finally, Mrs. Whittaker turned to Ginny. "I know you. You're the piano teacher from Waverly Hills. Lara Pearson's son goes to you on Wednesdays."

"That's right, he does. He's got some talent, that boy. I was wondering what I could do to help."

"Take over the restaurant?" she said with a wry expression in her dark eyes. She wore a dress underneath a white apron, and thick-soled sensible shoes. "This stupid tropical storm isn't even fifth on my list of things that are trying to kill me. But since you asked, you could help me make sure they got all the glass cleaned up off the floor while I get the food put away."

As Ginny swept, she listened to the pounding of nails outside and the creative curses from the two women inside the large kitchen. They both had typical Rhode Island accents, but there was extra flair when they spoke, primarily using their hands, which did make the job go a bit slower. On closer inspection, the copper pots and pans looked as if they'd been around since pirates had claimed the bay in the 1800s. But it was the pasta maker she truly coveted. She had one—it was fancy and made great noodles, but it was all electric, and there was something satisfying about making food by hand.

By the time she'd finished checking the floor, she knew the boards were in place outside as the noise level decreased by several decibels. That ended her thoughts about pasta as she wiped down counters.

Finally everyone came in from the wind, flushed and ruffled but smiling. Parker's gaze went straight to her and didn't leave for longer than was polite. Mrs. Whittaker broke the spell and put him to work schlepping big pots to the built-in refrigerator, while Stella took on the task of transferring everything they could to the large freezer. Five minutes in, she realized she'd seen Stella at the fish market, early in the mornings, usually when the bluefish were in the bay.

"Mamma, please, it's too dark in here," Cory said. "I'm going to start the generator."

"What if we don't have power for days?"

Cory sighed dramatically. "We have enough fuel for a week. Stop worrying."

"It's my job," she said. "Go. Start it. But you'd better be right."

"I am." Cory grinned. "That's my job."

She snapped a towel at him before he disappeared into what looked like a closet.

Parker, who had at least towel-dried his hair, shook his head. Ginny hid a smile. It would have been much easier to have worked all this time with the lights on.

When the generator kicked in and light flooded the kitchen, he was once again coming out of the huge fridge. He found Ginny and they traded stares, as they had every time they'd passed each other. This time he smiled, which was different from and better than the worried look he'd worn most of the day.

Thoughts of Tilda distracted her again.

Ginny had been running the gamut from remembering when Parker had kissed her breathless and left her trembling to wondering if he thought she was the biggest fool and most terrible person on the entire East Coast. She had to be to not recognize the consequences of getting that renewal from the bank. How had it not crossed her mind that she could be tracked down so easily, given that the notice gave her full name as well as Meg's?

"You know," Mrs. Whittaker said, her voice lower in the lights, "you're not like the rest of them."

"What do you mean?" Ginny was wiping her hands after washing the last ladle. "Like who?"

"Most of the Waverly crowd. You're actually willing to chip your manicured nails. Pitch in to help. Our customers are tourists for the most part, but when certain summer people come in, it's as if they want to be treated like royalty. So we indulge them, but it gets old after a while."

"Oh, yes, I understand. I know quite a few of them." Her father, for instance, but she kept that to herself. "And don't let this manicure fool you. I splurged for my fifteen-year class reunion." She glanced at her fingers, amazed she hadn't chewed off the tips.

"Ah, right, the big to-do they had at the Seaside. We thought we'd get some business from it, but nah. Only the golfers and regular tourists."

"Good thing," Mr. Whittaker called from somewhere in the back. "We were busy all weekend."

His wife rolled her eyes. "Not that busy."

Ginny smiled and left to go get a dry towel. Why had she been reminded of her father?

Until this morning she'd honestly thought he couldn't disappoint her any more than he already had. Why wasn't there a switch she could flip to turn off her thoughts? She wondered how much he'd donated to the philharmonic or what kind of favors he'd called in to finagle her solo performances. Utterly humiliated by her actions and her naïveté, she wished the storm would blow her away. Anywhere, really. Just not here.

No such luck. One glance Parker's way and all she could focus on was how pathetic he must find her and what a terrible disservice she'd done to Tilda. Once the truth got out, which it inevitably would, everyone she knew would see her incompetence and her duplicity. She'd be a social pariah, and her dream of recharging her career was a lost cause already.

Mr. Whittaker eventually declared that the cioppino could be stored, the last of the perishables had been boxed to take to the Whittaker's home and the place was all but locked up.

"You two, come back tomorrow night. Dinner's on us," Mr. Whittaker said. "Only the best for you both."

"Are you crazy?" his wife said. "We won't be ready for customers tomorrow night. Who knows what's going to happen with the storm?" She shook her head and sighed deeply.

"The offer stands, the night after, or anytime it's convenient. All you have to do is call. We'll make sure it's a dinner you'll remember."

"Thank you," Parker said. "It was no problem at all. Glad we could help."

And though Ginny smiled and said her goodbyes, she used the opportunity to pull herself together. It didn't matter what Parker thought. What anyone thought. As long as she could stay strong for Tilda.

As THEY MADE their way back to the motel, Parker kept stealing glances at Ginny, wondering where she'd gotten the fortitude to have accomplished all she had. He'd overheard the conversation she'd had with Mrs. Whittaker and realized how true it was. Ginny wasn't at all like most of the folks on the hill. He'd barely blinked when Lee had said as much. It had to have been a tremendous sacrifice to leave Juilliard when she'd been so gifted. It would have made so much more sense to have arranged an adoption than to have raised Tilda into the amazing young woman she was now, all on her own. No help from her father, no mother to lean on. Just guts and determination. If it wasn't for his mother, he might have just walked away after learning the truth. Let

Ginny keep her secret and Tilda. It wasn't as if he could have offered the girl a better life.

As he put the car in Park, the depth of his selfishness hit him like a tsunami. What he could offer Tilda was money. The way the business had taken off had given him a nice portfolio with enough to help out his mom if she should need anything. He never went anywhere, didn't spend much except on the plane, but even there he did all the work himself.

But the truth was, he wanted his life to stay just as it was. Being alone in his cabin, with his dogs as companions, suited him to a T. Yeah, he catered to the clients, but that was just good business. Nothing more.

It didn't seem to matter that Tilda was his niece, that they shared a common heritage. He wouldn't have been willing to make half the sacrifices that Ginny had. Certainly not his career. Being able to fly a plane didn't define him. It provided a good living, but above all... privacy. The safe, contained world he'd created where he expected little and gave even less.

It was a quiet walk to their doors, despite the strong gusts, and luckily, the Whittakers had insisted on them taking a flashlight.

He held the light while Ginny slid her key into the lock, and he walked her inside. She put her purse on the bed, and the only good thing about the lack of lights was that she wouldn't notice his dour mood so easily. "Here," he said, handing her the heavy flashlight.

"No. You'll need it."

"I've got my cell phone. I'll be fine. I'd feel better if you took it."

"I've been living on my own for a long time, and I've somehow managed tropical storms, actual hurricanes and a teenager. I'll be fine."

"Just take it. I'm used to long spells of dark nights, remember? Alaska winters have trained me well."

"Fine," she said, and as she took the flashlight he caught a gentle smile curving her lips.

"Good night," he said, backing up to the door. "Your cell phone charged? You wouldn't want to miss a text from Tilda."

"It should last the night," she said. "But I appreciate you asking."

"Are you still worried about your piano?"

"To be honest, I've been too busy to think about it." When she sighed he realized he shouldn't have brought it up.

"If you want we can take a quick run and move the table." He waited with his hand on the doorknob. "You'd be able to give your phone an extra charge in the car."

She paused long enough to let him know

she was thinking about it. "Thanks, but that's okay. It really is just a piano."

He nodded, not liking the defeat he heard in her voice. "I'll knock when we get the go-ahead."

"I'll be ready. Good night."

When he closed the door behind him, he didn't pull out his cell phone yet. Instead, he let the dark surround him. It suited his mood. He hadn't been kidding. He'd come to be at home in the dark, whether it was in the sky or in his cabin. The light of day had never done him any favors.

Parker had to laugh.

He should've learned his lesson by now— just because you couldn't see something, that didn't mean it wouldn't bite you in the behind.

ALTHOUGH SHE would have loved taking a long bath, there was no telling how much hot water would be available, and she'd need it more for a quick shower before they headed to New York. In the strange light, bright, yet so narrow in scope, she got into her sleep shirt and crawled into bed. It would have been more convenient to have the television on, to have less alone time with her own mind—which had never been a particularly safe neighborhood. She wrote Tilda another text, checked her email and wished she'd brought her Kindle with her.

Finally, she opened the drapes a bit and just spent some time staring out the window. She had a decent view of the back parking lot and a strip of the street, and she watched as headlights, taillights and emergency vehicles passed by. It was more of a trickle of vehicles than a deluge, but it kept her from revisiting her past mistakes.

She just wished Tilda would get in touch. Why hadn't she asked if there was cell service at his mother's house? Or thought to check if Tilda's connecting flight had left on time? As she worried, she looked at the time, and realized it hadn't been that long since Tilda had taken off. It just felt like days had gone by.

Another set of taillights caught her eye, but these were closer. In fact, she was fairly certain they were Subaru lights, leaving the motel parking lot.

It could have been another Subaru, but she doubted it. Where was Parker going now? She hadn't even thought about asking for her keys back, and he hadn't offered. He hadn't given her any real reason not to trust him, but then, he probably figured he didn't owe her anything either.

And now, the most important thing in her universe was at stake. Maybe trusting him was the last thing she should do.

CHAPTER EIGHTEEN

IT WAS TEN A.M. before they got the call and were on the road to the airfield. She'd barely buckled up before Parker shot out of the parking lot, and she almost told him she'd drive her own car, thanks, but that seemed ridiculous at this point. If she'd wanted any control over her life she would have asked him for the keys the minute they'd parked at the motel.

"You hear from Tilda?"

She wasn't surprised he'd asked, but he sounded much more relaxed than he'd been before they'd gotten in the car. Maybe because he was going to be flying soon. Or because he didn't want to spook her. "Yes. Last night after she landed."

"Good. Did everything go smoothly?"

"It's not easy to tell. She sounded as if it did, but she's also trying not to make me worry."

"I don't know a lot about teenagers, but from what I understand, that's a rare quality. Her thinking more about you than herself."

"She's a very considerate person. She knows

that it's okay to be selfish sometimes, but that it's always important to be kind."

He gave her a look she couldn't interpret but didn't respond.

After the silence had stretched for several blocks, she asked, "Have you spoken to your mother about how things have been going?"

His mouth lifted into a brief smile. "It was awkward at first, naturally, and Tilda was fairly quiet but polite. Once they got to the house and she saw Mom's husband's professional-level telescope set up on the back deck, she got all excited. She spent a long time looking at the stars. Wade, my stepfather, is an amateur astronomer, but he takes it pretty seriously. So he was out there with her, and from what Mom said, they were talking about the differences in the constellations between Idaho and Rhode Island. Tilda was a real chatterbox from then on, asking him all kinds of questions."

"What does he do professionally?"

"He's a dentist. Has a pretty big practice in downtown Boise."

"I'm glad for your mom, that she found someone nice and stable." Ginny meant what she said, but inside, she wasn't quite so pleased. Tilda hadn't said a word about the telescope when they'd spoken. But then, she hadn't been to the house yet, Ginny reminded herself. Although now that she knew Tilda hadn't gone right to sleep after that long day, it surprised her that she hadn't received a second call. Or a reply to her texts.

It was ridiculous to feel jealous. Tilda didn't suddenly love her any less. If anything, Ginny should've felt gratitude for Mrs. Nolan's and her husband's generosity and for the fact Tilda had adjusted so quickly. But Ginny just couldn't help it. Mrs. Nolan was a great cook, Ginny remembered from all those years ago. And there was a man with a scientific bent in residence.

All Ginny had to offer were piano lessons and Tilda's favorite mac and cheese recipe.

A quick glance at the dashboard clock told her what she already knew—that Boise was two hours behind, and Tilda was more than likely still sleeping. The girl could be a world-class sleeper when she'd had too much excitement.

Staring out the window, she watched as a crew of volunteers walked the grassy highway, already cleaning up after the storm. Thankfully, the wind had died down to what Parker considered a "piece of cake" speed, and the rain had stopped altogether.

It only took five minutes longer to get to the airfield, which looked as if it had weathered the storm very well. There were a number of small planes already outside the hangar, and one plane was taking off as they slowed down in front of a white-and-red plane with two propellers. It looked new, but she knew almost nothing about airplanes. "Is that yours?"

"Yep," he said, pulling into the far left of the hangar. "It's a De Havilland DHC-3 Otter. It's not too noisy, and it's big enough it shouldn't be too nerve-racking."

"I'm not scared," she said, getting out of the car. Naturally, she'd lied. At least a bit. The plane didn't look big enough to haul much cargo, but then it had only two seats in the front, so she was probably wrong about that.

"You can come inside the terminal. They've got decent coffee, and a ladies' room, if you need it. I have to talk to someone and then do a check on the plane. We should be ready in about an hour."

"That long?"

"Afraid so."

"Okay," she said, feeling out of her depth as she followed him to a glass door, which he opened for her. The terminal was larger than she'd expected, with seats for passengers, like a real airport. But here the coffee kiosk was more casual, with only one attendant and not much fancy equipment.

"You'll be all right?" Parker asked, just before he nodded at an older man heading to what looked like the business part of the building.

"Fine, thanks. Don't worry about me."

Parker left her holding her purse in one hand, her cell phone in the other. She'd worn a blue dress, one that made her look more sophisticated and professional than her normal summer wear. She could use some caffeine before she looked around. And she could use for Tilda to call.

The coffee turned out to be very good, and she found herself at the window, watching planes load both passengers and cargo. Parker's plane seemed about midsize from her vantage point, and she hadn't seen any jets so far.

Fifteen minutes ticked by like an hour until Parker returned from his meeting.

He studied her a moment, then said, "I take it Tilda hasn't called yet."

Ginny shook her head.

"She's probably still sleeping," he said.

"I know. She had an exhausting day, plus she was nervous. I just wish I had something to do while I wait. Time seems to have slowed down."

"It won't be a barrel of laughs, but you can

come out and watch me check the plane before we take off."

That sounded okay, so she grabbed a second coffee, then followed him outside. It turned out to be fascinating.

He checked *everything*, and with laser focus. She couldn't see what he was doing inside the cabin, but the engine revved and some flaps went up and down, then the engine shut off. When he got out, he walked around the whole thing, and it seemed to her that he examined every inch of the aircraft from wings to tires to fuel.

Then her phone rang.

It was too loud outside to get it, so she hurried into the terminal. Thankfully Tilda was awake, though she'd just gotten up. Everything was going fine; Mrs. Nolan was nice and Tilda had had some awesome meat loaf and spent hours looking at the stars. They were having waffles and bacon for breakfast.

After a lengthy pause, Tilda asked, "Do you know when I can come home?"

"Not yet, sweetie," Ginny said, fighting both a smile and tears. "I'll be sure and text you as often as I can. Maybe I'll know by tonight."

"Another night?"

"Can you stand it?"

Tilda sighed. "Sure, yeah. They're nice and

all, and it's kind of pretty out here. We're going out on a walking tour downtown, which is supposed to be really neat."

"Neat, huh?"

"Mrs. Nolan actually said *hip* but I didn't want to say anything."

Ginny laughed, even though she ached all over. "I know you're being wonderful and they're already impressed."

"How do you know that?"

"I know you. Now go eat your waffles."

"I miss you, Mom."

"Same back at you. We'll talk later." Ginny disconnected and gave herself a few minutes in the restroom before she met Parker outside. He'd brought their overnight bags and helped her into the copilot's seat.

"It's bigger on the inside," she said, as he took his seat. "Guess you've heard that a lot."

"A few times."

She returned his little smile, but now that she was strapped in, it started to hit her what they were about to do. Aside from possibly facing whatever kind of criminals might be waiting for her, she'd also finally learn more about Meg and the life she'd been living. She wasn't sure what was more sobering.

"You worried about flying in this small a

plane? Or is it me flying it that's making you nervous?"

"Neither," she said. "I'm fine. I trust you completely."

His smirk in response hit her wrong, but then she should have expected it. She honestly did trust him to fly, but he'd never believe her about anything again. Although, she'd bet a great deal that if he'd been in her shoes, and a friend had shown up with a week-old baby, her whole family having done a disappearing act, he'd have done the same thing.

The takeoff was smoother than she'd expected, and then they were up. Listening to him talk to the radio tower was less interesting than watching the scenery as they climbed up into the blue sky. Everything seemed very clean, as if the storm had given the whole coast a sparkling new beginning.

Not for her though. If she lived through the rest of the day, she had no idea what was in store, but her gut said it wouldn't be good.

He flew straight over the town until there was nothing but gray sea, still turbulent and beautiful after the storm. Tilda might have been crazy about looking at the stars, but Boise was a long way from the ocean. Tilda had always been a water baby. She'd grown up with the tides and learned early to respect their force, but she would miss Temptation Bay. The stories of the pirates, the fish people, running barefoot in the sand. Boise might have rivers but nothing that could compare.

Even so, Tilda might have to adjust. She was a minor, and if Parker's family decided to fight for her, they'd win.

Ginny brushed away a tear as discreetly as possible, not wanting to give Parker any reason to smirk at her again. When she finally looked his way, he seemed to be brooding. Perhaps he'd seen her after all. Or he could just be thinking of the bank and all that could go wrong.

"Parker?"

"Yes," he said, immediately attentive although his gaze shifted from her to the controls, to the sky and back very quickly.

"Will you let me be the one to tell Tilda? About…everything?"

The look he gave her was more prolonged than she'd anticipated and more confused. "What?"

She didn't repeat herself. He'd heard her.

"Don't make me the bad guy here," he said, but he didn't seem angry, just…hurt? "I'm not a complete jerk, you know. It never crossed my mind that you wouldn't tell her."

She actually felt a little guilty about her assumptions, even though he'd given her no reason to think he'd be generous.

When he looked at her again, it was after they'd banked a bit to the west. He wasn't confused any longer. In fact, it felt as if he was examining her the way he'd checked out the plane before takeoff. "We both need to keep our minds on what's in front of us. If you want to stay alive long enough to talk to Tilda, that's the only thing you should be focusing on. Do you want to go over it again?"

"Are you purposely trying to scare me? Now? Seriously? Because, guess what, there's nothing in the world more terrifying than losing Tilda. Or worse, Tilda hating me for the rest of her life."

His lips pressed together tightly. "Now isn't the time for dramatics. I wasn't trying to scare you. You should be scared all on your own. And you should also have realized I'd never cut the ties between you and Tilda. But I won't have to if Tilda decides she doesn't want anything to do with you."

Ginny couldn't stop the gasp that came out of her, or the tightening of all her muscles.

"But," he said, his voice softer even though he had to speak over the sound of the engine, "she doesn't strike me as the vindictive type. She might be confused for a while, maybe wonder why you didn't tell her sooner, but she'll also realize that you've given her the best life possible, and at great personal sacrifice."

Afraid another tear would fall, she turned her head to look out her window. How could Parker's decency make her feel both better and worse at the same time?

It took a while, but finally she felt as if she could trust her voice again. After clearing her throat, she looked at him. "You never told me how you ended up becoming a pilot."

IT WAS AN innocent topic, probably intended to make safe conversation.

Parker could shut it down with a quick answer. Raising questions or spurring her curiosity about his past wasn't something he cared to deal with. But Ginny had slid downhill emotionally—partly his fault. He couldn't let her spiral. She was so focused on Tilda that he wasn't all that sure she was adequately aware of the possible danger lying ahead of her. She could very well be walking into a trap. He figured she'd be fine while in the bank, but the moment she left with the contents of the box, all bets were off.

She'd been watching him, waiting, but then he saw her glance at her phone.

Realizing he'd clenched his jaw, he relaxed

it. Yeah, she needed something to sink her teeth into, something that wasn't about Tilda. Guess it was up to him to provide a pound of flesh.

"My dad owned a small plane, a Cessna, and he taught me how to fly when I was sixteen. I loved flying. Probably as much as I wanted to study law. But I could only go up when Dad was home…and not thousands of miles away pretending to be a hero."

Irritated with himself, Parker unnecessarily fiddled with his earphone. He needed to lose the sarcasm. It amazed him that after all these years he could still taste the bitterness of his father's betrayal. And it pissed him off that it could still get to him.

"Hey," Ginny said softly, laying a hand on his arm. "We don't have to talk at all. But if there's something you want to unload, I'm quite the authority as far as lousy fathers go. Plus, I sure as heck won't repeat anything. Not with the ax you're wielding over my head."

Even before she lowered her hand the teasing lilt in her voice had died, and Parker knew she'd slid backward, no doubt remembering the whole truth was going to come out anyway, and Tilda would know everything.

"Okay," he said, "but don't say I didn't warn you." He had her attention again but kept his eyes straight ahead. "I already mentioned my dad was convinced that his job had something to do with Meg's disappearance. His boss was right, the more time passed, the less sense it made. If they'd discovered he was a Fed, someone from the cartel would've put a bullet in his head by then. But Dad became obsessed with finding her using his undercover identity.

"His boss hadn't approved it, and he was angry, but he let things slide as long as my dad was maintaining some form of contact. It helped that my dad was responsible for a significant raid that netted the DEA a large sum of cash and millions of dollars in heroin. Yeah, his boss looked the other way real fast after that bust. He didn't even try to stop Dad from going back under a month later after he showed up at the house in Indiana again. He stayed only two days. There had been no word from Meg. He told us not to worry, he was still looking for her, then left me with a big suitcase full of hundred-dollar bills before he took off."

Ginny sat calmly, her hands folded on her lap as she listened. If she suspected what was coming next she didn't let on. Parker took a moment to decide if he really wanted to tell her everything. What was the point? The abridged version had met his objective. He'd distracted her, and it had been fourteen years since he'd

last seen his father alive. Fourteen years since
Parker's sterling image of the man had been
shattered forever.

Fourteen years.

Around the time Tilda had been born. Had
his family known about her, would it have
changed anything? He had a bad feeling Tilda
would've ended up with the short end of the
stick on that one.

"Parker? Would you like some water?"

He turned to Ginny, finding an odd comfort
in her soft green eyes and gentle smile.

"Sure," he said.

He took a deep drink and handed the bottle back to her. Their fingers brushed and the
sweet warmth of her skin did something to
him. Quieted the demons if only for the moment. Fourteen years was plenty of time to get
over all the crap that had happened. Why not
finish the whole story?

"When I said he gave me a huge bag of cash
I wasn't exaggerating. He told me he'd stashed
it away for my education. You know Princeton wasn't cheap, and Yale Law School? There
was enough for Meg's education, as well. And
he asked me to take care of my mom. Within
an hour he was gone." Yeah, fourteen years
and Parker still couldn't erase the image of his

mom standing on the small front porch, sobbing for an hour.

Ginny held the bottle out to him again, but he shook his head.

"A couple months later, still no Meg, and I hadn't gone back to school yet when my father was killed while undercover. Only, there were no awards for valor or for his long, dedicated service. No pension for my mom. The money he'd claimed he had put aside for us was confiscated by the Department of Justice. He'd stolen it from the drug bust. So, no more education. No more thinking of my father as a hero. My idol. Meg's idol.

"Once we learned the truth, we stayed under the radar, but we had to pay for everything ourselves without government support. That's why I didn't finish Princeton. Or go to law school. I had to look after my mom, so I finished putting in the hours I needed to get my pilot's license while working at a small airfield not too far from home. But I didn't move away until after my mom met Wade. As you already know, we eventually heard from Meg on Facebook, and after a while, I understood she really had just left." He let out a breath and relaxed the tightness in his shoulders. "I think that about covers everything."

"Oh, Parker, I'm so sorry." Her voice had

dropped to a whisper. "I wish—I just wish I'd—"

"We're not too far from La Guardia." He didn't dare look at her. It was bad enough to hear the tears in her voice. All he wanted was to change the subject. He'd said his piece. Now she knew everything. No other living soul had heard the story from him, and he'd be damned if he could explain why he'd told Ginny.

CHAPTER NINETEEN

LA GUARDIA WAS only eight miles from Mid-town Manhattan and the bank, but it took them a long, tense ride to get there. Parker could feel her anxiety, even though he was doing his best to be as calm as possible.

"Remember," he said, as they turned onto the packed street where the bank entrance was sandwiched between a bookstore and an Epis-copal church. "We walk straight back to the assistant manager's office."

Ginny nodded, but it was a jerky motion that had nothing to do with the stop and start of the cab. There was no parking available, only a zone for drop-offs, and it took them a while for the cab to get close enough for them to get out.

He put his phone on the floor and opened the door. "Don't forget, keep the meter run-ning," he told the cabbie. "And there'll be an extra hundred for you."

The guy smiled in the rearview mirror and said, "You got it, buddy."

"Are you sure you want to do that?" Ginny whispered, glancing down at his phone.

"It'll be fine. Did you leave yours on the plane?"

She huffed as she put her phone down next to his while he held the passenger door open for her. Their cells were probably the safest ones in the city at the moment. But he didn't dare tell her that.

She looked smart, holding her leather bag. It didn't look like a carryall, not on this street, and not with her regal bearing. She'd been clever enough to stuff it with some crumpled newspaper, making it look more natural.

He needed to remember that. She wasn't as nervous as she seemed if she could still think so rationally.

He did a quick scan of the street, trying to spot the FBI agents who, he'd been assured, were spaced inconspicuously around the entrance. And inside. Even the cabbie was FBI, and one of the best, Special Agent Archer had assured him. For whatever that was worth. Parker couldn't tell one pedestrian from another. They all might have been FBI or Danny Masters's men. Even the mom pushing her stroller could be assassin or savior.

It was time for them to go inside, and he just had to trust that their plan had all the bases covered. The FBI were supposed to be experts at this sort of thing, weren't they? He'd believed that most of his life, but his trust in the government had been shaken too badly to let it comfort him much.

He held Ginny's elbow as they walked, but he opened the heavy glass door and let her go in first—only because he saw one of the bank's guards standing next to the entry. Parker moved in quickly behind her, right in front of another woman. He hated to be rude, but he had no choice. She barely gave him a glance. Gotta love New Yorkers.

Ginny looked back as they passed the guard. "Aren't you going to mention something to him?"

"I don't think we need to."

She nodded and together they walked through the lobby, past a row of tellers to a reception desk. A young man greeted them, and after Parker stated their business, the man directed them to the assistant manager's office, first one on the left. As they entered, the woman at the desk looked up, her pen poised over some paperwork.

"I'd like to access my safe-deposit box," Ginny said with a brief smile.

The pen went down as the woman stood. She was slightly older, perhaps in her forties, and wore a severe gray suit. He doubted she knew anything about this operation at all. She simply nodded, asked Ginny for the box number and her identification.

While she pulled out her passport and driver's license, along with the renewal notice from her bag, he looked around as casually as he could. He probably wouldn't recognize anyone as friend or foe, but he couldn't help trying. Mostly he wanted to identify someone who could be FBI, but if he could spot them, so could Masters's men.

Even before Ginny handed anything over, Ms. Elward, according to her nameplate, frowned. Her gaze darted to her computer screen.

Parker gave Ginny a slight nudge, but he felt certain he already knew what was coming.

Her quick inhale indicated she did too. "I'd also like to know if anyone else has been asking about the box. Anyone in the last couple of days?"

"Actually, yes." Ms. Elward accepted Ginny's credentials and took her time examining them before glancing up. "Would you excuse me for just a moment?" The woman didn't wait for an answer but turned to look up something on her computer. "Oh, please, have a seat," she said, gesturing to the pair of visitors' chairs facing her desk, without taking her eyes from her monitor.

Ginny's movement was stilted as she lowered herself into the brown leather chair, then looked at Parker with fearful eyes.

He gave her a reassuring smile but remained standing just inside the door, keeping a furtive watch, despite knowing it was futile, his own heart picking up speed. He'd warned Ginny not to be surprised if someone had beaten them to the bank. The more he'd dug up on Danny Masters on the internet, the more Parker had realized they were out of their depth.

"Spider" had turned out to be a pretty well-known character, at least when it came to illegal arms and FBI watch lists. Interpol had also been interested in his whereabouts. The guy was not only dangerous but had become a major player in the last five years. He had no loyalty to any country, including his own, and sold to the highest bidder.

So Parker had had little choice but to call the FBI. He wasn't going to risk their lives, and besides, he wanted to see that bastard put away. Ginny would've been too irrational to understand, so he hadn't told her. But he was 100 percent positive he'd done the right thing. Besides, she had no room to complain.

It had taken him a while to get the right person interested, but when he finally did, the man had been quite informative.

Masters was very clever and hypercautious. He'd moved from city to city, country to country as he'd built his arms dealing empire.

The FBI had had a close watch at airports and docks for quite some time, but Danny always managed to slip through. It must have been getting trickier, though, because his trips to the US had become less frequent.

Special Agent Archer didn't expect him to show up at the bank himself. He'd likely send his lieutenant, a man referred to as The Shiv. That alone made Parker glad he'd picked up the phone.

Ms. Elward was taking too long. Ginny's hands were shaking and she kept darting looks at Parker. Anyone would think she was about to rob the place. He tried to reassure her with a smile, but he doubted his own tension had escaped her.

"Is there a problem?" he asked finally.

"I'm sorry for the delay. Thank you for your patience." The woman offered them a brief smile, then returned her attention to the computer. A moment later she asked Ginny to sign a form she'd printed out.

After Ginny handed the paper back, Ms. Elward had taken a phone call, which was annoying. He wished she'd hurry this up. It felt as if he had a target painted on his back standing in the open doorway.

Once she'd finished the call, the woman compared the signatures very closely. An armed security guard wandered past the office. He didn't go far and Parker figured that was what the phone call had been about. It was only after she'd buzzed them in to the private entryway leading to the vault that she explained.

"Ten minutes after we opened this morning, someone asked about the box," she said. "But he didn't have all the proper documentation."

Ginny tensed.

"Do you know his name?" Parker asked.

"I'm sorry, I can't give you that information." Her frown had faded some but hadn't left. "I have a question for you…though I'm afraid there's no delicate way to ask…"

"Go ahead," Parker said, breaking the awkward silence.

"Do you know if Megan Nolan, the other person listed on the account, is deceased?"

Ginny gasped and almost stumbled.

"I'm so sorry," Ms. Elward murmured. "I wouldn't have asked but the gentleman said he'd be back tomorrow morning with the death certificate and a court order."

Parker put his arm loosely around Ginny's shoulders, but he wasn't doing much better. "It's probably a fake," he told her, more for Ginny's benefit than hers. And for his own. Lord, how he didn't want it to be true. "I think the guy's her ex-husband."

"Ah." Ms. Elward nodded. "It happens," she said and continued on.

He kept walking because this was in Meg's honor. The very least he could do was make sure that scumbag wouldn't get away with another thing. Maybe they wouldn't catch him today, but they would get closer.

Together, he and Ginny were escorted into the vault, both keys were inserted and the box was carried by Ms. Elward to a private viewing area. It was as sterile as the vault, furnished with two plain chairs and a simple mahogany table.

Once they were alone, Ginny's demeanor slipped into a picture of misery. She covered her eyes with her palms, her body trembling.

"You're fine," he said, stroking her arm, wondering if he should go ahead and tell her about the FBI and that she was completely safe.

"Meg isn't," she said, her voice garbled. "How can this be happening? I hope Danny does follow us. I do. I'd like to get my hands on him myself."

Parker understood completely. "Stand in line."

After a moment, she lowered her hands, took a deep breath and opened the lid. Inside there was a large thick envelope that looked as if it held papers. She picked it up and held it out to him.

He didn't take it. "No, just put it in your bag. I know you want to see everything, but we need to go. The quicker we're out of here, the better."

"You think someone's watching."

"I'd bet on it."

She did as he requested, then made sure her bag was zipped up. He stopped her just as she was about to leave the viewing area. "You might want to take a minute. Maybe try to relax, and, uh…" He wiped a finger below his nose.

The ruse seemed to work. Ginny pulled a small compact out from the bottom of the bag and checked her face, which looked fine despite her fear and sadness. She took several breaths and stretched her neck, zipped the bag again, then nodded, looking a lot better before walking out to find Ms. Elward waiting nearby.

"Thanks," Ginny said, then Parker escorted her through the lobby.

The guard had returned to his post and opened the door for them. Only the cab wasn't at the curb.

Ginny whimpered, but cut it off quickly. He looked up and down the street, but there were a lot of yellow taxis and several police cars. The same had been the case when they'd arrived, so Parker didn't let it rattle him.

"Don't worry," he said. "The driver probably had to circle the block. He'll be back." Their cabbie wouldn't have been allowed to just wait. Not with all the signs prohibiting that very thing. And if he had, it would have been a neon sign to anyone watching.

"Will you recognize him? I mean, there are a lot of cabs."

"I remember which one," he said, once again with his hand on Ginny's trembling shoulder.

She jumped when two other cabs dropped off clients. Three other cars did the same— a town car, a stretch limo and then a Buick. Thankfully, the next cab was theirs.

He quickly ushered her inside, then got in himself and pulled the door closed. Only then was he able to breathe again.

She bent to pick up her phone, but he waited, looking at the mirrors he could see from the backseat as the cab inched into traffic. Naturally, they were boxed in. It was the middle of Midtown. Insanely crowded with cars, buses, every manner of transportation and pedestrians.

No wonder he missed his cabin so much. Even the traffic in Temptation Bay drove him nuts.

"Are we being followed?" Ginny asked, her voice so low and close he felt her warm breath on his neck.

"No idea." He leaned forward. "Straight to the airfield, right?"

"Yep. It'll take some time to get out of this jam-up, but soon I'll be able to get us to the highway."

Parker sat back, but kept his gaze moving from the rearview mirror to the side mirror, as if that would help them in any way. The FBI agent driving the cab was surely on top of things. It felt like hours passed before they were able to get any distance. Considering everything that had happened, Ginny had done well so far, and now the hardest part was over. He hoped.

They finally merged onto the highway, which was slightly less packed than the street. The driver was skilled, though, and wove his way through the traffic. When they were midway to the La Guardia exit, he noticed a black SUV speeding toward them in the rearview mirror.

"What's wrong?" Ginny turned around to the see the SUV almost at their bumper. "Why is that car so close?"

Parker didn't say anything, but he noticed the cabdriver's mouth moving. He must be speaking to his team, asking about the situation.

"Parker?"

He looked at Ginny, whose eyes were haunted and her face pale. Her gaze went to a dark sedan with heavily tinted windows that had pulled up and was traveling in tandem with them. Could be just any commuter. But she was scared, and he had to do something. He'd been wrong about the hard part. Ginny was heading straight to panic mode and his simmering anger at Masters wasn't helping. He mentally replayed what the assistant manager had said. *A death certificate.*

Man, he had to stop. Let it go. For now.

"Just hold it together," the cabdriver said. "The dark blue Ford is one of ours."

"What are you talking about?" Ginny asked, her voice high and tight. She turned sharply to look at Parker. "What's he mean by *ours*?"

He probably should have said something already, but it was too late now. "Look, I had to get help. I learned a lot about Danny Masters, and I knew the odds of us not being grabbed were slim at best."

She jerked away from him, her eyes blazing. "You called the police."

"No. I called the FBI."

"You promised me. You swore you wouldn't. You liar."

"And what good would that have done us? You want to get back to Tilda, don't you? You wouldn't be any good to her dead."

Her face went even paler as if all the blood had drained from her body. "Is Tilda safe?" she demanded, her voice rising as she gripped his shirt, pulling him closer. "Tell me. Is. She. Safe?"

"Yes. She is."

"Oh, God, what am I doing? Why should I trust you? You lied about everything."

Parker held his tongue. She had a hell of a nerve. But now wasn't the time to get into it.

"Ms. Landry, I'm Agent Hawkins," the cabbie told her. "Your daughter is safe. You have my word."

Just then the SUV slammed into the bumper of the cab, making them swerve.

Hawkins's gaze moved quickly between the rearview mirror and the windshield. "Brace.

They're going to go for it again. It's all right though. We planned for this..."

The bump was harder this time, and Ginny let out a cry. They both nearly hit their heads on the back of the front seats as the cab jerked then swerved into the left lane, nearly hitting another car, which smashed into the guard-rail. The SUV stayed on their tail. The Ford fell back some.

Ginny's hand gripped Parker's leg so tightly it hurt, but he just put his arm around her shoulders and held on to her.

"They're going to kill us, aren't they?" she whispered.

"No," he said, squeezing her tighter, hoping he wasn't lying again. That's when he heard the helicopter above them, lower than was legal over a freeway.

The cab put on some speed, heading toward the next exit, skimming past a car, nearly hitting the guardrail. But they made it and moved onto a less crowded road.

Hawkins pulled several impressive moves that scared Ginny half to death and didn't do Parker's heart any good. But the helicopter was still above them, and they had a lead on the SUV, while the Ford and another large car that was probably FBI were running interference.

At an almost impossible turn, Ginny squealed

louder than the brakes of the car on their right.
Parker leaned closer to her. "Hold on. We're
getting closer to the airport." That was a bluff.
He had no idea where all of this was supposed
to end.

The look she gave him should have done
him in, but she didn't let go. Her fingers dug
into his thigh. "Swear to me that Tilda's going
to be safe."

"Yes. She is. And so are you."

That's when the cabbie swore as another car,
a black, souped-up Mustang with an engine
that sounded like a jet's pulled up on the other
side of them, screaming against the metal bar-
rier. The passenger window went down and a
man leaned out, aiming a gun at their tires.

He fired, the shot muffled by the traffic
noise.

Apparently, he'd missed.

The man raised his arm and pointed the gun
directly at Ginny.

Parker shoved her down, hard, as the gun
went off. He felt a jolt to his right shoulder as
the cab jammed on the brakes, then peeled
around the Mustang. The helicopter lowered
so close it nearly landed on the Mustang's roof.

Suddenly sirens seemed to be coming from
every direction. The sound of another gunshot,
this time not at them as far as Parker could

tell, echoed inside his head like the roar of a Kodiak bear.

Underneath him, Ginny was crying, her eyes shut tight, and shaking so hard he thought she might come apart. He couldn't hear her at all, but he could read her lips as she kept repeating her daughter's name.

CHAPTER TWENTY

GINNY TRIED TO make sense of the chaos around them. FBI agents and local police had swarmed the area where the cab had finally stopped, a scrubby lot with more trash than grass. The many lights flashing from police and FBI cars made it even harder to think. Drivers honked their horns, impatient over being held up on the frontage road and on the highway above it.

This couldn't be happening. She was a piano teacher from the suburbs, with a daughter, a few close friends and a lot of acquaintances. A woman who recorded dozens of television shows and movies that she never managed to watch. Who hadn't dated in years, and honestly probably never would again.

Her gaze slid over to the ambulance just a few feet away. She could hear Parker grumbling at the paramedics, making such a fuss he reminded her of how Tilda behaved when she had to skip a summer party.

Tilda. She needed to call her, but she

couldn't yet. Not while her thoughts were still spinning and the fact that she'd almost been killed and that Parker had taken a bullet for her felt like some surreal dream.

Parker's loud curse helped bring her back to reality.

She walked over to him and the paramedics. Both Blane and Erica, according to their name tags, seemed too young to be doing such a difficult job, but they also looked as if Parker's rants didn't faze them in the least. Ginny couldn't even imagine the kinds of things they must hear.

"Sir," Blane said, "you have to go to the hospital. You've been shot."

"So what? The bullet went clean through."

"And likely did some damage on its way out. There's no other option here. We've already called it in."

"All you need to do is bandage me up. I can't stick around here—I have a business to run. As soon as I'm home, I'll get it looked at." Erica laughed. "Sure you will. Now stay still. I have to make sure you don't die from blood loss before we get you to the ER."

Parker opened his mouth, but before he could say another word, Ginny interrupted. "What's wrong with you? You have to get checked out. Can't it be enough that you didn't die, two of those jerks are in custody and they've got the whole country on the lookout for the Mustang?"

Parker stared at her blankly, and she wasn't sure if he was suffering from shock or if he just wanted her to disappear off the face of the earth.

Probably the latter. That bullet had been meant for her. He didn't have to push her down. Cover her body with his own. She wasn't even sure why he had. All of this was her fault. Seeing all that blood soaked into his white button-down shirt made her feel queasy. It wasn't just the sight of the blood though. It was still overwhelming that he'd almost been killed because of her.

"He's going to get checked out all right," Erica said. "You might need surgery. Bullets don't discriminate. They go through everything that's in the way, and you just might need that shoulder to work again."

Parker scoffed. "Then the doc in Fairbanks will make sure it does. Come on. I have dogs that need feeding. You don't want something happening to my dogs." He meant to sound threatening, but it didn't work.

Her hands clenched tightly into fists, Ginny couldn't take it another minute. "Will you be quiet and stop acting like such a baby? You're not going to be able to fly anyway, so just man up and let the EMTs do their jobs."

"If you think I haven't flown with injuries worse than this, you're delusional. I live in the woods. I have to fly to get anywhere."

"Not if I tell the doctor you're a pilot. Bet you won't be cleared to fly without getting patched up first."

His eyes blazed. "You have no right to interfere with my livelihood." Ignoring the EMTs, he focused only on Ginny. "Haven't you disrupted my life enough? My business partner's ready to throttle me, never mind my clients. What more do you want from me? I had a nice life before you. I'd finally found some peace. I was content. Then I had to run into you again, and everything went to hell."

If it hadn't been for feeling utterly paralyzed, Ginny would have walked away and never looked back. She'd have flown straight out of New York to Boise and gotten her daughter. If they wanted a fight, she'd give them one.

Did he think she didn't know all that already? Did he need to shout out all her failings to the world?

She watched as Erica finished with the bandage on his arm while Blane sneaked a seat belt around Parker's waist and went up into the front to get behind the wheel. Erica had an IV drip at hand and stuck the needle into Parker's vein a second later.

He yelped and tried to jerk his arm away, but Erica wasn't having any of that. He glared at her, then at Ginny, then at Erica again.

She got up to pull one of the ambulance doors shut. "He's in shock, honey. He doesn't know what he's saying. Just ignore him. I've seen this kind of thing before."

Ginny somehow managed to sound normal when she said, "Thanks. I figured."

But she knew she deserved every rebuke. Oh, but she was angry too. Not at Parker but at herself. She should have acted immediately when she received the bank notice. And once Parker explained why he and his mom had vanished, she should have told him everything. About Meg. About Tilda. The whole truth. He'd had every right to know that she wasn't the mother she claimed to be. That Tilda was Meg's child. Not Ginny's.

She looked down, unable to stand being stared at for the fool she was. Not that he was the only wounded party. It shouldn't have taken Parker fifteen lousy years to let her know he was alive. He'd made that choice.

Although she shouldn't be surprised or hurt. No one had ever cared enough about her to stick around. The only person besides Meg who'd ever truly loved her was Tilda. But by tomorrow, after their talk, she'd probably lose Tilda too.

"You ready?" Erica asked, holding out her hand to help Ginny into the ambulance.

"She's not coming with me." Parker sounded as if he were insulted by the idea.

Erica turned to Parker. "Why not let your wife come along? She'll just worry about you."

"My wife? I'm injured, not stupid."

Ginny didn't even blink. "Go on," she said, pasting on a smile when Erica turned back. "I have to stay. The FBI wants my statement."

Parker let out a shaky breath and closed his eyes. When he opened them seconds later he looked wretched. "No," he said in a lower, more controlled voice. "Why don't you come with me? They can catch up to us at the hospital and get both our statements together."

Ginny shook her head. "Please, go," she said to Erica. "He needs to be looked at sooner rather than later."

Parker's brows lowered and he wasn't faking the remorse on his face. She didn't doubt that he felt bad. And she wasn't trying to rub it in. She simply didn't have the energy.

Turning her back on him and anything that wasn't the next step in the excruciating journey that would give her back Tilda—for a while at least—she walked toward Agent Archer. For tonight, after she finished with the FBI, she could still dial her baby and listen to her be happy that her mom had called.

THE HOSPITAL SMELLED like antiseptic and misery, and all Parker wanted to do was bolt. Get back to his plane. Reboot his life.

The doctor had assured him that it wouldn't be a long recovery, and that the surgery itself wasn't going to be complicated even though he still had to sign all the forms.

None of that mattered at the moment.

Okay, a short recovery did, but he didn't care about the rest. He'd had no business being such a jerk to Ginny. The last thing she needed after today was him giving her a hard time.

Unfortunately, the loudmouthed paramedics had told the doctor that Parker was a pilot. He'd been grounded. Temporarily, yes, but being sidelined for even a day was a problem. They had to get back to Rhode Island. He had a choice to make—leave his plane at La Guardia and go back with Ginny to make sure she didn't make any stupid decisions about Tilda, or stay in New York and hound the doc into clearing him to fly, then go back to Temptation Bay. Or Boise. Wherever Ginny and Tilda were.

First, though, he and Ginny had to work out when she should tell Tilda and how and when he was going to give his mother the news. He dreaded having to tell his mom that Meg was most likely dead. Man, it was still hard for him to process. Since there was no conclusive proof it was tempting to delay that part. But keeping her wondering and hoping wasn't fair.

All of that was a mess, sure, but he kept circling back to that moment when he saw the gun pointed at Ginny. What it had done to him. How even knowing she'd almost been killed was a lot worse than him being shot.

If he hadn't been looking in the right direction. If he'd reacted a couple of seconds later...

He shook his head, wanting to get into surgery already. Get knocked out. Let him be numb for a while, with no worries, no depressing thoughts about his sister, no realizing how downright mean he'd been to Ginny.

Of course, then he'd wake up, and nothing would have changed, except that he'd have to find a hotel or fly on some commercial airline. Maybe he could take a train up the coast. Alone.

As if he'd be able to forget about Ginny for a minute. Ginny and Tilda and his mom. Mark was probably about to dissolve their partnership, and his clients were more than likely getting ready to send out a search party to drag him back.

The agent sent by Archer had left twenty minutes ago. The guy had had more questions than answers for Parker, but they hadn't talked long. His statement had been put off for the operation that he didn't need. The only thing he knew for sure was that Danny Masters hadn't been at the scene, and that the shooter and his driver had escaped, but they'd caught the guys in the SUV. What he needed to know was whether or not Ginny was still in danger.

"Time to check your vitals, Mr. Nolan," the nurse said as she walked into his room. She blithely pulled the curtain that gave him a modicum of privacy all the way back, so any passerby could watch her stick something in his ear, take his blood pressure and ask him a long list of idiotic questions. His arm didn't even hurt that bad.

"Here we go," she said, smiling as if her life was all peaches and cream. He knew better. Overly cheery people gave him the willies.

What annoyed him more was that she reminded him of Ginny. Her hair was almost the same dark blond and the same length. Her eyes were green, but not that vibrant green that Ginny's were. And Nurse Smiley Face wasn't even close to being as pretty.

The second the thermometer was out of his ear, she started cuffing his good arm.

"Anyone come by looking for me?"

"Hmm?" She pushed the button on the machine that wanted to strangle his biceps. "Not that I'm aware of, but I'll be happy to check for you."

"Don't worry about it."

"All righty." She picked up his chart and made some notes as the cuff deflated. "With no pain at all being a zero and more pain than you can tolerate being ten, how would you rate your pain level, Mr. Nolan?"

He wanted to scream.

He didn't.

Finally, his answers were all taken, and the nurse was ready to leave. "Would you like me to close the curtain? It won't be a minute until they come in to prep you."

Prep him? Great. "Yeah, would you please shut the curtain?"

He was tired of being stared at, even though he knew there wasn't much else to do in this purgatory.

Once he was alone, his thoughts went right back to Ginny and Danny "Spider" Masters. Logic told him that Ginny would be fine. Masters's men had failed to get any information on her, and she was no longer in possession of the envelope. Masters didn't care about her personally. He'd wanted to get a hold of whatever Meg had left in the safe-deposit box. Now that the information was in the hands of the authorities, he would be a lot more concerned with hiding from every agency that would be after him. The man was too smart and greedy to spare any time and resources going after Ginny without cause. Even if he had been the vindictive type, she was small potatoes, and he would know she'd be given protection.

Still, Parker would rather have his hypothesis confirmed by Agent Archer before he saw Ginny again. *If* he saw Ginny again.

He could just go to Boise and tell his mom the whole story and then fly back home.

But he probably wouldn't.

He closed his eyes, trying to relax before being prepped. He didn't think they'd have to shave anything. At least he hoped not.

Two minutes later, two orderlies and a nurse came in, and it was all signing this and that and getting yet another banana bag hung, just to relax him.

He fell asleep before he reached the operating room.

FOUR HOURS AFTER being helped out of the glass-splattered cab, Ginny had finally finished giving her statement to Special Agent

Archer and two other agents and was taken to the entrance of the hospital where Parker was being treated.

She didn't go inside. Instead, she walked down the busy street and thought about what to say to Tilda when she called her. And how not to cry. She wouldn't be able to tell Tilda very much over the phone. The last thing Ginny wanted was to worry Tilda even more than she already had. She knew Tilda would want to know why Ginny had been so out of touch and when she could come home. Which Ginny couldn't say and didn't know.

Maybe she should call Parker's mother and let her know... What? That Parker had been shot? That he was in surgery? That it had all been Ginny's fault?

No. That was a foolish idea. She wasn't about to interfere again. Say something she might regret.

It wasn't until she'd made it half a block that she realized she was being followed. Of course. It was Agent Morales, who'd been assigned to protect her. Just in case. She turned around, gave him a brief smile and then returned to the hospital entrance. She dialed the number printed on the door. She could have walked in, but she wasn't ready. Not yet. At this point, Agent Morales probably thought she needed to be examined herself.

Parker, she was told, was just coming out of surgery. She did lie and say she was family, and found out it had all gone well. But she wouldn't be able to see him for a while as he was still out from the anesthesia.

After she hung up, her shoulders relaxed. At least she hadn't gotten him killed. Now, if she could only go to sleep. A month might make her feel a little better, as long as she had no dreams at all. But no.

She'd be a grown-up and go see him, whether he liked it or not. After her call to Tilda.

Her shoulders tensed again.

CHAPTER TWENTY-ONE

EVERYTHING WAS BLURRY. There were things beeping and his mouth tasted funny. He didn't feel so good.

"Parker?"

He looked to his left. Didn't even have to turn his head. Ginny was right there. Sitting in a chair. She was much prettier than that nurse. He could reach out and touch her. Except her eyes were red and puffy and his mouth still tasted terrible. "What's wrong?" he asked, sounding as if he smoked five packs a day.

"With me? Nothing. How are you feeling?"

Parker shrugged. A big mistake. Whoa. "Fine, as long as I don't move my shoulder."

"You sound… Maybe I can give you some water. I have to ask. Just…rest. I'll be right back."

He closed his eyes and tried not to move. Pretty sure Ginny had lied about nothing being wrong. He'd ask her again. After she got back from wherever she'd gone.

He opened his eyes, and Ginny was sitting next to him again. "Hey," he croaked.

"Hey. I'm allowed to give you ice chips. Would you like some?"

He nodded. Tried to lift his head, but that just made his shoulder hurt. Probably because he'd asked the nurse to hold back on the pain-killers. That considered, the pain wasn't so bad.

The top part of his bed was adjustable, so he was sitting up pretty well. Ginny put a remote on his stomach, then put a spoon up to his mouth, like she was feeding a baby. He wanted to tell her he could do it himself, but when he opened his mouth she stuck the spoon in, and it was ice and water, and it felt too good to complain.

He let her do that a few more times. She'd probably leave and then he'd just do the ice himself.

His vision wasn't so fuzzy anymore, and neither was his head. At least, mostly. The day came back to him all in a rush, like a movie on Fast-forward. "Did they catch the guys in the Mustang?"

She put the glass of ice chips down on the tray at his side. "Not yet," she said. "At least not that I know of. I think Agent Morales would've told me."

"Who?"

She glanced back toward the door. "He's my babysitter."

"Protective detail?" His heart lurched. "So, they think you're in danger?"

"No. Not at all. Agent Archer said Tilda and I should be just fine. We might even be the safest people on Masters's radar. He'll know the FBI will be keeping us under watch and he won't come anywhere near us."

Right. Standard procedure. Parker still wasn't thinking all that clearly. "That's what I figured. I might be a little hazy, but I remember one of the agents saying something about having enough evidence in that envelope to lock him away for life. Something about selling arms to known enemies of the state. Meg did a great job at ratting him out."

"That's true."

He looked down at the big remote on his lap and the sling he'd just noticed, cradling his right shoulder. "I'm proud of her. She did more good than she'll ever know."

Ginny sniffed. "Yes, she did. I know she'd be thrilled to see him spend the rest of his life in a maximum-security prison."

He was sure Meg would be even happier to know that Ginny and Tilda were safe.

"You have one too."

Parker frowned. "What?"

"An agent is posted just outside your door."

"You're kidding." He could see she wasn't. And now, he vaguely recalled the agent he'd spoken with before the surgery saying something along those lines. Man, he had definitely been out of it.

She sighed. "I don't know how long it's going to last. You know, having a bunch of FBI agents lurking in the bushes. Waverly Hills will be in an uproar. Probably scare away all my piano students too."

Using the remote, Parker moved the bed up a little higher, until he was able to look Ginny in the eyes. "Don't try to be a hero. They don't need you to give them a hard time or ask them to scale back. Having them around is for your own protection. Understand? And Tilda's. At least—"

Ginny nodded. "I know. Ditto for you. Okay?"

The soft way she looked at him stopped him from making a snide remark. He hoped that was a hint about how things might be. Although he wasn't going to count on it. Not yet. He was still getting the invalid treatment.

"Although, I have to say, that's rich, coming from the man who gave those nice paramedics so much grief about taking you to the hospital. What a dope."

"What? I wasn't even really shot. It was a nick."

She rolled her puffy eyes. "The bullet went all the way through your shoulder. I doubt that qualifies as a nick."

He grinned, grabbing on to the rope she'd just tossed him. "Did you talk to Tilda?" Her eyes lost their glimmer of humor.

"I didn't tell her much, just that I miss her and love her and she can probably come home tomorrow. I'm really pushing for that to happen. She's curious and knows something is off. But I promised to explain everything as soon as she gets home."

He nodded, having no idea what the solution was going to be. He still wanted his mother to have the joy of a granddaughter, but despite all that had happened and the rotten things he'd said, Ginny truly was Tilda's mother. "We'll have to come up with a plan. I'll have to explain things to my mom too."

"Will you be doing that in person?"

Parker almost shrugged again but stopped himself. "I don't know yet. And, yeah, thanks for telling the EMTs I'm a pilot. They let the doc know, and now I'm grounded."

"Good. You're too stubborn to admit you

shouldn't fly. You're in a sling. You don't have the mobility to fly a kite, much less a plane. Now you have no choice."

He couldn't argue with that. Although he sure wanted to.

She offered him the cup of mostly melted ice. "I bet you can have something else. They probably have Jell-O or broth."

"Um, no thanks. I'm not that hungry."

She smiled. "How long are they keeping you here?"

"Gee, I'm not sure. Haven't you given the doc and nurses their instructions yet?"

Ginny actually laughed. "It's good to know you're not hurting so badly you can't be a pain in the butt."

Parker sighed, suddenly so tired he felt as if he could sleep for a week. He looked to his right and noticed a window. It was dark already. How long had this day been? Had to be more than twenty-four hours. "I can leave tomorrow morning."

Ginny didn't say anything. Neither did he. When she spoke again, it was little more than a whisper. "Shall I wait for you? We could fly back together."

"We'd have to go commercial." He hated that. Sitting in the back of a plane had never felt right. But he could overlook it knowing that Ginny was still willing to wait for him after the way he'd treated her.

"Yeah," she said. "I figured. I'll make arrangements."

"Thanks. Use my credit card. My wallet should be around here somewhere."

"I'll take care of it." She stared down at the floor. "I, uh." She lifted her head so he could see her face. "I haven't thanked you yet."

"For what?"

Her jaw dropped. "Saving my life?"

He brushed the thanks aside with a wave of his hand. "No need. I doubt a bullet could've penetrated that thick skull of yours."

Pressing her lips together, she gave her head a little shake. "Can we be serious for a minute?"

"Go ahead." He glanced at the IV bag. "I have nowhere to go."

"You were very brave, but you could've been killed, Parker. It was only a matter of luck—"

"Hey, knock that off, okay? I mean it. Enough. Look, while we're being serious… the things I said before…"

She held up her hand like a stop sign. "It's all right. I deserved it. Every word."

"No, you didn't. Now, will you just let me apologize?"

"I began my apology first and you cut in." Ginny wasn't joking, she seemed upset, and then resigned. That stop sign turned into a submissive wave.

The nurse walked in without knocking, still far too cheerful. That smile of hers had to hurt. But now that she was there with Ginny, it was clear they looked nothing alike. Ginny outshone her in every way.

The cheery smile didn't distract him from the chart and the other things she'd brought with her. It meant another blood pressure check. As if she couldn't take a readout from the one that had been marked on the chart by the surgeon's nurse. Probably wanted to ask him more useless questions too.

Before she could say a word, he pointed to the door. "No. No way. Out. I mean it. I'm not going to go through—"

The smile vanished. "Don't even try that with me, buster," she said, and he would have sworn right there she must've been a prison guard before becoming a nurse.

Ginny laughed. "I'll see you tomorrow morning. Have a good night, and don't give everyone a hard time, okay?"

"What? Wait," he said as she was scooting out the door. "Where are you staying?"

He got no answer. Just another surly look

from the former Miss Sunshine. He gave her his best glare. And then remembered he'd forgotten to ask Ginny if she had his phone.

CHAPTER TWENTY-TWO

GINNY REALIZED HALFWAY through making waffles that she didn't even know if Parker liked them. She'd been home for almost twenty-four hours, but everything still felt strange. Activity helped somewhat—hence the bacon, eggs, waffles, fresh-squeezed orange juice and coffee.

Parker had told her not to bother, but he needed to eat while he was healing. His plane was still in New York, and against his protests, she'd set him up in the guest room early yesterday afternoon. She'd picked up Tilda in Providence late last night.

Tilda had hugged the stuffing out of her, thrilled to be home in time for the barbecue. But when Ginny had evaded some of her questions, Tilda had clammed up, only willing to give one-syllable answers. Luckily, she hadn't put up much of a fight when Ginny had told her they'd talk in the morning.

The waffle iron beeped, so she added the last two to the plate in the warming tray.

She heard a rustle behind her and spun around, relieved it wasn't Tilda. Parker stood in the doorway in jeans, a brown T-shirt and a sling. His hair was a mess, his eyes blood-shot, and she imagined he must hurt a great deal since he still refused pain meds. His scowl told her his mood hadn't brightened overnight.

He went straight to the coffee maker and poured a cup, unsteadily, with his left hand. "Tilda still sleeping?"

"Yes. She was exhausted after those long layovers. I hope she sleeps for a couple more hours."

He didn't say anything, but he did look at the mess on the counter. "I'd offer to help but I have a feeling I'd be in the way."

"I'd rather you go sit."

No arguing, he just sat at the table and took his first sip. "It's going to be fine," he said.

"You don't know that." She hadn't meant to snap at him. Instead of apologizing, she turned on the stove and opened the carton of eggs. Her stomach tightened, and she was pretty certain she would end up with an ulcer or worse.

"You're right. I don't. But my instincts tell me Tilda will come through like a champ."

"I wish I had half your confidence."

His sigh cut through her. He was only try-ing to help. "Look, I get it," he said. "I've got a call to make myself today, and I'd rather tear out my own fingernails. My mother's a strong woman, but it's going to devastate her. I doubt she ever imagined that Meg might be dead. Only thing I'm sure about is that I have to tell her it's a distinct possibility. She deserves to know."

Ginny felt the verbal slap, and it sobered her. "You're going to tell her about Tilda, aren't you?" She cracked the egg too hard, and most of the shell landed in the pan. Plus she'd forgotten to add the butter. The whole mess went into the trash, and she started again, her hands beginning to shake.

"Not until after you talk to Tilda. That was the deal."

Relief swept through her…for a moment. Then the dread came back, stronger than ever. There was no escape from any of this. The life she'd built with Tilda would never be the same again.

This time she managed to concentrate on the eggs, and when they were done, she plated them with a few slices of bacon along with a waffle and put it in front of Parker.

"What's all this? I told you I wasn't hungry."

"Too bad. If you want to get back to your precious Alaska before spring, you'll eat what's in front of you and stop complaining."

"Huh." At his pause, she turned and saw a smile tugging at one side of his mouth. "I'd wondered where the drill sergeant had gone."

"What?"

He picked up the fork. "You know, the one who hijacked my phone while I was in the hospital and took it upon herself to call my business partner and tell him I'd be laid up for who knew how long."

"You were worried about your dogs. I wanted to make sure they got fed."

"Right. Just so you know, that pissed me off. Don't ever touch my phone again. Understand?"

She glanced toward the doorway and lowered her voice. "Would you have rather I'd left it with the FBI?"

"I would have rather you didn't call any of my contacts. By now, half my customers probably know I was shot, except in their versions I'm at death's door. I've already gotten three stinking voice mails."

Amusement lit her face. "What did they say?"

"I didn't listen to them."

"You truly are a big baby." She turned to pour herself more coffee. "Anyway, I'm not sorry I did it."

"Of course you aren't. You're too busy trying to force-feed me pills and food. Watching me drink my water, as if I'm twelve."

"Well, then, why don't you just leave?" She smiled. "Oh, wait. You can't drive that stick shift, can you? Or fly. Or shower without having someone help you cover your shoulder. Or change your bandage. But hey, you're so used to taking care of yourself, none of that should bother you at all."

He glared at her.

For a few minutes there, nerves and indignation had made her forget... "You're right. I'm sorry. I know you can't wait to get back to Alaska, and the last person in the world you want to be near is me. You can believe me or not, but I honestly don't want anything to happen to you."

Parker put down the fork that he'd been pointing at her like a weapon. He seemed a little chastened, although Ginny wasn't sure why. This was on her.

"That's not true. Yeah, I miss home, but the rest of it—"

"No need for apologies. I overstepped. I caused all of this. But I honestly think you'll recover here faster..." She picked up a piece of burnt bacon from the skillet, meant to eat it, but put it down when her stomach rebelled. "So, if it'll make things easier and you won't feel like I'm hovering, I can go stay at the re-sort." She chanced a glance at him. "Look, I'm not offended or feeling sorry for myself. Tilda will probably want me to leave too."

He stared at her for too long. She stopped herself from ordering him to eat before his food got cold. "How much sleep have you got-ten in the last three nights?" he asked.

Before she responded, she heard a familiar noise. Tilda was moving around upstairs.

They looked at each other, then Parker asked, "Think she'll come down right away?"

Ginny nodded.

He stood with his coffee cup. "I'll uh…"

"You don't have to go anywhere. Eat your breakfast. She might be hungry. Anyway, when it's time, we'll talk in the den."

"It's probably best I make myself scarce. We don't need to explain the sling yet."

"Oh. Right." She'd forgotten that he'd re-mained in the guest room when they'd arrived from the airport last night, precisely to avoid questions. "Thanks."

He nodded, smiled his encouragement, then picked up his plate and balanced it on his mug. "Mind if I take this to the room with me?"

Ginny felt the first sting of tears behind her eyes. She knew he was only doing it to please her. "Of course not. Let me help."

He didn't argue, so she followed behind him with his plate and utensils. After he was settled, she paused at the door. "Thank you," she said, sorry she hadn't told him first thing. "You came back and moved the table the other night."

"Oh, yeah. No problem." He almost looked embarrassed, so Ginny just smiled and closed the door.

The touching gesture had brought a few tears earlier, when she'd realized what he'd done. She lost the sentiment quickly when on her way back to the kitchen she saw Tilda on the stairs.

"You gonna tell me anything today?" Tilda asked, her hand gripping the railing.

"After breakfast."

"I'm not hungry."

Ginny took a breath. It was her turn to step up. "Fine. Pour us both some orange juice, please, and I'll meet you in the den."

Tilda nodded, her eyes widening. They never talked in the den.

Ginny turned around, rushed into the guest bathroom to grab a box of tissues. She didn't want to cry, but Tilda might break down. They probably both would.

When she got to the den, Tilda was already in the overstuffed chair, but she wasn't curled up. Both bare feet were on the carpet, the glass of juice on the side table and she was rubbing her hands as if she were chilled…an old habit when she was nervous or scared.

Ginny sat down across from her, took a sip of her juice. "Okay, so I know you have a lot of questions—"

"Mom. Please, just tell me. I'm going crazy not knowing. Whatever it is. Just tell me."

"All right. But please bear with me, I have to start at the very beginning."

CHAPTER TWENTY-THREE

DAYTIME TV WAS going to drive him to drink. He had little interest in sports, at least not on television. He didn't mind watching ice hockey, but only if he liked one of the teams... and preferably hated the other.

Giving up, he quietly moved to the living room window—even the great view of the ocean couldn't hold his attention for more than fifteen minutes. He was too restless.

He wanted more coffee. Didn't need it, but it would sure hit the spot, even as the day grew warmer by the minute.

He hoped going to the kitchen wouldn't interrupt Ginny and Tilda. There was an ebb and flow to giving people bad news, and the slightest thing could change a win into a loss.

Vividly, he remembered when he and his mother had discovered that the money from his dad had been stolen, and that she wouldn't be receiving his pension. And that his life insurance policy had been courtesy of the DEA, with a caveat, so that was out too.

Just an hour before, they had been planning a decent future. She hadn't been crying; he'd been able to set his anger aside. And then the DEA brass had come to the crappy door of the crappy house in Indiana, given them the news, and ever so *graciously*, offered to let them stay in the government-owned house for another month.

Fortunately, for the half hour Ginny and Tilda had been sequestered, he hadn't heard a peep from either of them. Not even a slammed door. So things couldn't be going too badly.

There was a scant cup of the strong Kona coffee left in the carafe, so he made another pot. Even as he was adding the grounds, he knew taking a walk would've been a lot healthier. Ginny could be a real pain, but she was right about nutrition being important to his healing.

The problem with a walk was that he'd stick out. He wasn't exactly Waverly Hills material, and with the way he was looking today, people would stare, maybe even call the cops. The neighborhood had its own private security force, with their special cars and badges. Although Agent Morales would set them straight real quick. The thought made Parker smile, but he didn't want to distract the guy from watching over Ginny and Tilda.

He waited, drumming his fingers on the counter, watching the coffee drip into the carafe and trying to figure out what he was going to say to his mom. For now, she was just glad Tilda had arrived safely, and that whatever he and Ginny were up to hadn't put them in the headlines of her local newspaper.

Finally, as the last of the coffee dribbled down, he filled his mug and checked the time on his way to the patio. Wow. Forty-five minutes now. But then it had to be a lot for Tilda to take in. Just as he closed the sliding glass door, the silence ended.

He heard Tilda, who sounded as though she was shouting at the top of her lungs. "How could you have kept that from me all this time? You had no right!"

His heart sped up as he froze in place. There was a pause, which must have been Ginny responding to Tilda. It didn't last long.

"Really?" Tilda's voice shot higher. "You thought my stupid crush on stupid Cliff Browning was a reason not to tell me? You know I'm mature for my age. You could've told me."

He might have heard a murmur from Ginny, but it could have been the wind.

"What about when I turned thirteen, huh?

What happened *then* that you decided to put off telling me?"

It got quiet again. He probably ought to just take that walk. He knew the back way in from when he'd moved the patio table.

"You're just making excuses." Tilda had lowered her voice some, but he could still hear her. That's when he realized the den's window was a few feet beyond the patio. "This is so unfair. You knew I had webbed toes just like Meg's grandmother. I mean, why won't you tell me who my father is? Why can't you at least stop lying now?" Tilda continued on, but now he could hear her sobs more clearly than her words.

It was way past time for him to be somewhere else. He shouldn't have listened to any part of this. Especially when his heart went out to both of them. Tilda wasn't wrong. But she wasn't right either.

It had taken him a while, but he finally understood Ginny had done what she thought was best. And if she'd dragged her feet telling Tilda, it was because she was scared. After all, everyone in Ginny's life had left her. Her dad. And Meg. Even he'd vanished without a word all those years ago, and she'd never have known the truth if he hadn't come back to look for his sister.

To some degree, Ginny probably felt abandoned by her mother, as well. Irrational, yes, but he knew too well how grief and betrayal could trick the mind. And now, she was terrified her worst nightmare was becoming a reality. That the only person who'd loved her unconditionally would be lost to her.

The sudden clarity hit him hard.

Tilda's voice came through again and he hadn't moved an inch.

"…instead you lied. I thought we told each other everything! My friends have always been jealous. They think you're the coolest mom ever. What a laugh. You lie just like everyone else. And now, I'll never get to know Meg." She paused. "Does Mrs. Nolan know?"

Parker couldn't listen to another word. He went into the house, headed straight toward the guest room. But Tilda stormed out of the den and skidded to a stop when she caught him in the hallway. Despite her tearstained face, she gave him a glare that should've turned him to ice. She looked as if he'd been in cahoots with her mother all along.

"So obviously you had no trouble covering for *Ginny* and lying too, *Uncle Parker*. Thanks a lot for your part in ruining my life."

He didn't say a word as she pushed past him,

purposely knocking into his good shoulder to march to the staircase.

As her bare feet slapped the wood floor, he watched her, belligerence radiating from her. But he couldn't let go of what she'd said. He didn't care what she thought of him, but calling her mother Ginny? No way he'd let that slide.

"Wait just a minute, young lady."

She stopped after two more steps, but she didn't turn around.

He said nothing. Just waited, standing quiet and still. When she finally turned, her expression was brimming with defiance, no doubt reflecting the wound to her heart.

Forcing himself to keep his tone even and low, he said, "I know you're angry and hurt, but it's no excuse to be disrespectful. I suggest you do some thinking before you pop off like that again. Whether you, or I for that matter, agree with how your mom handled things, she's sacrificed an awful lot to make sure you had a good home and a privileged life. And you know as well as I do that she's always loved you as if you were her own. I dare you to find anyone who could've loved you more."

Tilda blinked, although she didn't lower her crossed arms. He knew she was still furious, but at least she was breathing more steadily. Getting some oxygen to that big brain of hers.

"Oh, yeah," she said, as snottily as she could, which was actually a lot less snotty than her tantrum had been. "What do you think my grandmother is going to say about all this? Think she'll agree with you or me?"

That knocked the wind out of his sails for a minute but after giving it some thought, he knew the answer. "She'll be hurt and confused, just like you are right now, but when she hears everything and has some time to process what actually happened, she'll not only agree with me, she'll be grateful to your mom."

Tears streamed down Tilda's cheeks as she shook her head. "How can you be on her side? Mom lied to you too."

"It took me a while, as well," he said. "But after a few days, I got to the right place, and I know you will too. Just try to be patient. I know she'll answer any questions you have. But before you ask, think about what you would have done in her place, okay? Would you have given a child you already loved to someone you didn't know? Leave her to her fate, whatever that would be? Would you have given up the life you had all carved out for yourself to become a preschool teacher instead of a world-class biologist? Would you have done something as honorable as what your mother did? I'm not sure I would have been as strong and self-sacrificing."

Without a word, Tilda spun around and raced up the stairs. He heard her bedroom door slam.

Man, he was ready for that walk, despite the neighbors. But then he saw Ginny standing in the hallway, crying so hard he wondered if she would run out of tears.

FOUR DAYS AFTER the devastating conversation with Tilda, Ginny had finally managed to get a full night's sleep. It was nothing short of a miracle, though it probably had a lot to do with the way Tilda was coming around. Her attitude had softened in increments, and when she'd finally called Ginny *Mom* yesterday, it was as if the sun had come out after a long, hard winter.

Not all was well by any stretch, and there were still moments when Ginny had no idea what to do, especially when it came to telling Tilda about her father. But that was a bridge to cross later, after Tilda had processed what she'd already been told.

Parker was another issue. It hadn't been easy to accept that his words to Tilda had been his honest feeling. Yet, he'd been attentive and helpful. And yes, he'd also been grouchy and complained about all the calls he was fielding from Alaska, but she didn't mind. She kind of enjoyed his grumpiness and liked to give it back to him. He was quick and clever and kept her on her toes—at least when she wasn't so tired she could have slept on a bed of nails.

Best of all, the anger was gone. Not the sadness though. It was odd, how easy it was to forget that he'd only learned about Meg's fate less than a week ago. And having to tell his mother had been brutal, and she still didn't know the whole thing.

He'd gone for a long, long walk that night after telling his mom, and Ginny wasn't even sure when he'd returned. The day after had been quiet, for all of them.

Parker came into the kitchen while Ginny stirred a pitcher of her own special lemonade.

"Is that boozy lemonade, I hope?"

"It's ten in the morning. What's happened now?"

"I'm going to smash my cell phone into such tiny pieces it'll be unrecognizable."

"Ah. The calls of the wild."

"Ha. Very funny. I need coffee and whatever smells so good."

"They're almost ready. My friend is coming over in a little while. Cricket Shaw. I've spoken about her before, remember?"

"Yep. Lawyer. Dad's the surfer dude." He sat down at the table. He'd showered but hadn't shaved, and the scruff of his day-old beard made him look even more appealing.

Tilda walked into the kitchen, still in her robe, her hair all over the place, just as Ginny had opened the oven. "Do I smell cookies?" she asked, midway through a yawn.

Ginny was busy yanking on a mitt to take out the tray of double chocolate chip. By the time she set them on the stove top, Tilda was hovering. Her hand shot out, but Ginny slapped it away. "You're going to burn yourself. How about some breakfast? I can make omelets."

"Nope. Cookies."

"I have to agree with Tilda on this one," Parker said.

Ginny just shook her head, basking in the warmth that had nothing to do with the weather as she found a spatula.

Tilda poured herself a glass of lemonade and plunked herself down at the table across from Parker. "That was cool. Last night."

"Yeah," he said. "Those pictures really took me back. Meg was a wild one back in high school. Did your mom tell you that the two of them blew up the school lab?"

Tilda grinned. "Yeah. I plan on making her retelling it an annual tradition."

Ginny rolled her eyes. "We did not blow up the lab. A couple walls were damaged, that's it." She still couldn't believe she'd blabbed about it in a weak moment yesterday.

"Meg was so pretty," Tilda said. "I'd seen pictures of her before, but I never truly looked at them, you know?"

Ginny got busy making scrambled eggs. She doubted anyone would eat them, but it gave her the chance to make some peace with the heartbreak that had come with looking at those pictures of Meg. She missed her friend so much. Wished with all her heart she could have helped her. But watching Parker and Tilda go through that meeting of calm and heartache, laughter and tears hadn't been easy. It had ended up being a kind of catharsis, although the road ahead for all of them would be long and complicated. No use ignoring that.

"My mom's got a lot more pictures of Meg when she was younger," Parker said. "She'll love showing them to you. Just please, for my sake, when she tries to show you pictures of me, close your eyes."

Tilda had her glass halfway to her mouth, but she just stared at Parker as if the idea of having a *grandmother* was shocking.

It was a shock to Ginny too. Along with it came a stab of fear that went straight through to her soul. The word *custody* hadn't come up, at least as far as she knew. But there was no denying that their lives had changed forever.

Tilda took advantage of her distraction and snatched a cookie. After an enormous bite, Tilda smiled. "These are actually good. What's up with this, anyway? You never bake."

"I don't know. I just felt like it." Ginny quickly turned back to the eggs. She hated baking. But after Tilda had come home raving about Mrs. Nolan's homemade cookies and cupcakes, what was Ginny supposed to do, buy her the usual store-bought kind?

Tilda grabbed three more and headed for the stairs. Although she stopped long enough to give one of them to Parker.

He winked at her. It was unforgivably cute.

Just as Ginny was about to give up and dispose of the rubbery eggs, she saw the wrapper from the slice-and-bake cookie mix she'd bought sticking out of the trash. What she didn't notice as she did her best to hide it was Parker standing right behind her, watching the crime in progress.

He didn't say a word, but his grin was far too smug.

"Oh, shut up," she said as she straightened.

"Tilda's a smart kid," Parker said, still

alarmingly close. "She's probably figured out that you're trying to compete with my mom."

"I'm not trying to— I made cookies. Big deal."

His smile broadened. "Oh, she's going to milk you dry."

Ginny huffed a sigh.

He put a hand on her shoulder, sending a shiver right down her spine. "She loves you. Look how far she's come in such a short time. You don't have to prove anything to her."

Ginny blinked back her still-too-frequent tears. "How did you get to be so smart about teenagers?"

"They're human, aren't they?"

She laughed. "Sometimes."

He laughed too, and gave her shoulder a squeeze that meant far too much to her. Even with his injured arm, he'd been quick to offer his help. He was forgiving, great company, and had played a large part in bringing Tilda out of her initial funk. But this wasn't his life, and while she was dreading the day he left, he was probably counting the seconds.

"Hey, Mom?"

Ginny was surprised to hear Tilda's voice coming from the foyer.

She was looking out the side window by the front door. "There's a new FBI guy sitting in the car. He looks really cute. You should take him coffee or something. Find out if he's married."

Ginny coughed.

"All right," Parker said, coming up behind Ginny. "Get away from the window."

Tilda turned around, eyes wide, trying to hide a smile. "What? You aren't jealous, are you? Cause you aren't half bad, yourself."

"Funny." He jerked his thumb. "Step back. Ginny, they say anything to you about replacing Agent Morales?"

She lost the grin. "Yes." Ginny saw now why Parker was concerned. "Agent Spencer is covering for a couple days, and then we'll be free and clear. No more protective detail."

"Okay," Parker said, nodding, then taking a peek out the window himself as Tilda muttered something about calling Kaley and raced upstairs.

"Hey, what do you want for dinner tomorrow, so I can thaw the meat? We're having spaghetti and meatballs tonight." It was one of Tilda's favorites.

His mood had shifted. He had that faraway look that Ginny always thought meant he was missing Alaska. "How about I go pick up some fresh fish in the morning, and I'll grill it for dinner?"

"Perfect. I'll drive you, and then we can stop at the market for more veggies. I'll make a salad."

"I'm okay to drive on my own. My arm's much better." He glanced down at the sling. "I don't even need this anymore," he said, but he didn't take it off. "I'll be making plans to go pick up my plane at La Guardia the day after."

"Wait. You can't be healed that quickly." Panic started building in her chest. "And you have to be cleared by a doctor." She wasn't ready for him to leave. Not so soon. Not yet.

Oh, no. She wasn't falling for him all over again, was she?

"Seriously. What if you have to turn the steering wheel hard? What if there's extra turbulence, and you're all by yourself? You already busted two stitches when you tried to move the storm shutters down to the cellar."

"I'm better now. I wouldn't put anyone, or myself, at risk by jumping the gun. You need to believe me. Besides, you must be anxious to return to your normal life. Aren't you having students come back starting tomorrow? I'm sure they wouldn't be happy to see a guy like me skulking around."

"I can wait another week to pick up my schedule. I'm sure the kids will be delighted. I want you to recover. Fully. In peace."

"I'll be fine, Ginny. I think we both need to get back to normal. But first, I'm going to fly to Boise and spend a little time with my mom. Tell her the rest of what she needs to know in person. Then I'll be on my way back to Alaska."

He took a step toward the coffeepot but didn't touch it. "I'd appreciate you not calling the doctor or doing anything else to stop me. Okay?"

Ginny had no choice but to put on a happy face. "I give you my word," she said, as brightly as she was able.

CHAPTER TWENTY-FOUR

PARKER HAD GONE to the beach. Tilda was over at Kaley's, and now Ginny was down in the dumps, waiting for her friend and trying to talk herself into rising above the unavoidable.

When Cricket knocked, Ginny went to the door and did her best to be her chipper self as they hugged and moved toward the patio. The lemonade and cookies were already out there, but the thought of food didn't sit well.

"You look wonderful," Ginny said. "So much more relaxed than last week. Your dad must be doing better."

"He is." Cricket frowned, filled two glasses with lemonade, then looked at Ginny. "I wish I could say the same about you, kiddo. You look terrible. Is this about the custody issue? Because I'm staying here longer than I expected and maybe I can help in some way."

Instead of brushing her friend's worry aside, Ginny started crying. It was a curse, but there didn't seem to be a thing she could do about it. She'd never cried this much, not even when

Tilda was a baby. Now she couldn't turn off the taps.

"Oh, sweetie," Cricket said, leaning forward and putting her hand on Ginny's. "Talk to me."

She hadn't planned on it, didn't think it was smart and felt like a fool, but Ginny did just that. Talked. And talked. She told Cricket everything. About Meg. About Tilda. About Danny Masters. And about Parker. Well, not *all* about Parker.

Cricket hardly interrupted. When she did, it was because Ginny had jumped ahead, or had skipped an important bit. But mostly she simply listened.

It felt wonderful to let it all out to a friend who wouldn't judge her, or scold her or point out all the things she'd done wrong. When she was finally finished, a good hour later, Cricket got up, crouched in front of Ginny and hugged her hard. After Cricket returned to her chair, the first thing she said was, "So, you've got it bad for Parker, huh?"

After the initial shock, Ginny didn't bother with any useless pretense. "I didn't mean to, but I think I might be falling in love with him."

"Might be?"

"It doesn't matter. He's not interested in me. He's going back to Alaska. Which is where he belongs, out there in the woods. He runs a cargo delivery business, but other than that, he leads a pretty solitary life. He's definitely not the commitment type. Seriously. Aside from his mother, he doesn't have any ties."

"What about his niece?"

Ginny shrugged. "We haven't worked it all out yet. I'm sure Tilda will be spending some time in Idaho. Which, by the way, I'm still trying to wrap my brain around. She'll probably see him from time to time, but I won't."

"I don't buy it."

"You've never even met him."

"Doesn't matter. I heard you. Every word. About the night of the dance. While I was canoodling with Wyatt, who I'll tell you about later, you were doing the same with Parker, right?"

"We kissed. That doesn't come close to canoodling."

"Knowing you, same difference. And then instead of stealing Tilda away, he stood up for you. He actually sounds as if he knows you pretty well." She held her hand up when Ginny started to protest. "Yes, I know, you hadn't seen each other for years."

"We didn't know each other well back then either. Meg disappearing was stressful. Just like the last week has been. Times like that, people tend to make ill-advised emotional attachments, which is exactly what I've done. He's not as susceptible. Trust me."

Shaking her head while giving Ginny the sweetest smile, Cricket said, "He risked his life for you."

"Don't make too much out of that. He's a good man. Parker would have done that for anyone."

Cricket's brows rose. "I'm not sure about that. Having a gun pointed at you usually means panic rules. But his first instinct was to protect you, at any cost. Which, given what he's learned since he came back, is saying a lot. Despite grieving, he's also undoubtedly beating himself up. And if I know anything about human nature, it's that when people are ashamed of their behavior they lash out at the nearest target. Even when he was mean, he still listened, and put your safety first."

"That was because—"

"Tilda was part of it. Yes. But the way he handled everything, it's obvious he's trying to protect you, as well. Don't you see?"

"I'd like to believe every word of that." Ginny sighed. "I mean, you make a good argument, but then you are an attorney. But I honestly don't know what to think. His main instinct is still to get away from civilization. And quite likely me."

"Have you ever been to Alaska?"

THE DAY HAD flown by quickly. While he cooked the striped bass on the patio grill, Ginny fixed the salad. He heard her as soon as he came in after checking on the fish. "Think you could chop a little louder? I don't believe the folks in Nantucket can hear you."

Ginny didn't respond except to get louder as she diced the carrots.

They'd been busy. After getting the bass and chatting with a few of the vendors, she'd driven to the grocery store, then back home to put things in the fridge. By that time, she'd wanted something better than her own lunches, and they'd gone back to The Grind. She'd splurged on crepes and he'd had something he could handle with one hand, and they'd talked about everything that wasn't related to their situation. Like favorite books and foods.

She'd looked beautiful in her yellow dress, a belt around her trim waist and a fullish skirt that swung when she walked. Her sandals were the same color.

At least he'd shaved.

Many hours later, she still looked beautiful.

"You sure that bass doesn't need to be flipped?"

"Oh, I flipped it when I was putting it in the marinade."

"What did it do to you?"

"I don't know. It just looked fishy."

They both turned smiles on each other at the same time. The sound of her laughter made him wish he wasn't leaving tomorrow. That was why he hadn't argued when she'd insisted on doing all the driving.

She'd canceled her piano students, let Tilda spend a couple of hours on the beach with Kaley, leaving Parker and herself to spend the morning alone together.

"That was nice this morning," Ginny said, "at The Grind. I haven't felt that relaxed in ages."

"Huh. Hard to believe we were there ten days ago."

She blinked at him. "The night I brought you home, right?"

He smiled at the way that sounded. "Yep. Feels more like a year to me."

"It truly does," she said, her voice dipping into melancholy. Sadness had crept up on both of them, between the teasing and laughter. Even though he still wanted to get home, the thought had lost some of its luster. Maybe it was because he wasn't looking forward to the visit with his mother. Wade would be there for her, but she'd need to cry with Parker, who'd known and loved Meg and who understood the rocky path that had led to such a tragic outcome.

Except for Tilda, of course. He wasn't sure what his mom would want, other than to spend time with her granddaughter. Man, she was going to spoil the kid rotten.

Tilda poked her head into the kitchen. "Hey, when's dinner gonna be done?"

"Soon," Ginny said. "You finished setting the table?"

"Yes. Why are we eating in the stupid dining room, anyway? We like the kitchen table."

"Because I wanted a change. And we never eat there."

"Spoiler alert," Tilda said. "That's because it's too formal in there. And we don't do formal."

Ginny turned to her daughter, both hands on her hips. It was a great sight to behold in that dress. "And because it's Parker's last dinner with us. He's leaving tomorrow to get his plane."

Tilda came around the island to face him. "So soon? You were shot."

Parker felt an ache in his chest that shouldn't have been there. "I'm much better, and I can fly just fine. I can't neglect the business any longer. Folks need their supplies delivered." He thought about going out to check the fish so he didn't have to see the disappointment in Tilda's eyes. "Besides, I know you're anxious to get rid of me."

"That's not true," she whispered, and hurried out of the kitchen.

He wished his joke had been better.

A second later, Tilda yelled down from the stairs, "I don't have to go to the concert tonight."

Parker would miss his niece. And her mother. But soon enough, his old life would fit him once more like a handmade pair of mukluks.

"You know she's going to miss you like crazy." Ginny had her head down, focused on washing the peppers. "I'll miss you too. It's been nice having you around the house."

He couldn't think of anything to say. Nothing that wouldn't make things worse.

She turned off the water and put the vegetables on the mat to dry. "You know, I can't recall if I've ever had all the plumbing working at one time. I'm thrilled I don't have to hand water the front flower bed anymore, especially in the hot months. So, thank you."

Parker went to the sink and elbowed her aside. She was lousy at changing the subject. "Quit hogging the sink. And why didn't Lee take care of the irrigation for you? Doesn't he do all that kind of stuff?"

Her cheeks infused with pink. "I hate to admit it, but it hadn't occurred to me to ask. I've been making do with little things for so many years, I just…"

Parker heard her lousy excuse, but he was still enjoying the blush on her cheeks. She smelled so good standing next to him. Before he even knew what he was doing, he caught her hand and drew her closer.

She gasped but didn't pull away as their mouths met. Or when he deepened the kiss. He pulled her closer, wishing they were alone. That he wasn't leaving, that they had more time…

Tilda's step was hard and loud as she clomped down the stairs, but they didn't pull apart until her flip-flops hit the wood floor. Even then, it was harder than he'd imagined.

Things somehow simmered down. Smelling the fish getting overcooked helped. But his thoughts and heart rate refused to settle.

"You know I meant it about skipping the concert," Tilda said.

"No, you don't need to do that," Ginny said quickly, then bit her lip and glanced at him.

"Go to your concert. It's not as if I won't see

you again." Parker had forgotten Tilda would be gone for a few hours.

The thought of spending a little more time alone with Ginny, of kissing her again, touching her soft skin, lingered in his mind as he brought the fish to the table while Tilda brought the rest of the food.

Then Ginny walked out with the water pitcher and her eyes met his, then moved to his lips...

Everything came to an anticlimactic end when Tilda joined them and took her seat at the table. She was right about one thing. The formal dining room was way too formal.

When he looked at Ginny across the table, hunger in her gaze, it was like a slap in the face. What had he been thinking? What a jerk. They weren't going to be doing any more kissing tonight.

Ginny Landry was off-limits. Period. There was no future for them, outside their ties to Tilda. And Ginny had suffered enough pain and loss already. He didn't need to add to that.

He managed to avoid looking at her as he served them the bass; the scent of garlic, thyme and oregano splashed with fresh lemon juice was good enough to distract Tilda and Ginny. At least until they'd all served themselves squash and salad.

Before Tilda had taken a bite, she put down her fork. "I have the perfect plan."

"For tonight?" Ginny asked.

Tilda shook her head, clearly excited. "So, I've been looking at all these pictures of Alaska online. It's so amazing you won't even believe it, Mom. I figure we could all spend summers there while the tourists take over Temptation Bay, and then we can all come back here in the fall and winter, when Alaska freezes over."

Ginny's fork dropped. She tried to speak, but nothing came out except more of her blush.

Parker didn't have a clue what to say. Not a single one.

Tilda seemed to realize on her own that she might've jumped the gun.

From there dinner turned into an awkward ordeal that felt as if it would never end. Every time he tried, he made things worse. Ginny opted for ignoring everything but how good the fish was and what time she was supposed to drop Tilda off.

Finally, it was over, and he grabbed hold of that with both hands. "You guys go. I'll clean the kitchen. I know you and Kaley are worried about getting good seats, Tilda."

Ginny grabbed her purse and took out her keys as Tilda made a dash upstairs to brush her teeth. "Remember, I have to stop at the pharmacy before I come back. Do you need anything while I'm out?"

He shook his head as he picked up the remainder of the dishes, and being a coward, refused to meet her eyes. And not for lack of her trying.

Tilda hurried downstairs and they left a minute later. Making a painful decision, he whipped off his sling and got the kitchen clean in record time. The litany of his own mistakes played like a song that wouldn't leave his head. He never should have come back to Temptation Bay. He should have known better. Just telling himself that he didn't have feelings for Ginny didn't make it true.

He'd gotten far more comfortable here than he'd ever have guessed possible. Man, he'd even gotten jealous over that stupid FBI agent.

The only possible solution to all of this was for him to leave. Tonight. Not tomorrow. The second he saw Ginny again, he'd probably rationalize that this was his last night so why not spend it holding her in his arms, and that would be a terrible mistake.

Ginny needed someone she could count on. Someone who wouldn't disappoint her. Who would be a steady and equal partner. Not someone like him.

The best gift he could give her would be to walk out of her life so that she could find a man worthy of her.

He owed her that, at the very least.

CHAPTER TWENTY-FIVE

WHEN GINNY GOT HOME, she was surprised that Parker's Jeep wasn't in the garage. Before she stepped out of the Subaru, she checked her cell. No texts, no voice mail.

It seemed like such a strange thing. Had he gotten worried when she'd been gone so long? Mrs. Millner, her neighbor, had caught her at the pharmacy and talked her ear off. But if Parker had been worried, he would have called.

Inside, the kitchen was clean, the dishwasher was on the dry cycle, all the leftovers were in the fridge. Had Parker fallen asleep? That didn't explain his missing rental. Maybe he'd taken a short drive to see how he did with his arm. It made sense and she was glad he was being sensible.

The guest room door was closed so she went back into the kitchen to wait. Ten minutes later, she called his cell. Straight to voice mail.

The nice thing to do would be to go upstairs and leave him alone, but it was his last night, and she had no interest in wasting it. When he didn't show in the next ten minutes, she started to get worried. Just in case, she knocked on the guest room door. Nothing.

She knocked again, this time with her fist.

Then she opened the door. The first thing she saw was his sling on the dresser. And a note on the bed.

I found a flight to New York tonight. I'll call you later and explain.

Ginny sank down to the bed as she tried to make some kind of sense of things. But her brain was stuck and her body numb. What in the world…

They'd kissed. *He'd* kissed *her.* They'd had such a great day. Tilda's perfect plan had admittedly been a shocker, but Parker knew she was simply being a teenager, with all the usual romantic notions.

No, this was something else. If he'd needed to go so quickly, he could have called her. She'd have understood an emergency.

Leaving the empty guest room, she wandered through the house, her thoughts scattered and her stomach clenched. She couldn't help looking for him even though his note indicated he'd left. He wasn't on the patio. Nor was he upstairs. And it broke her a little when she didn't find him in her bedroom. Her fault.

She'd never been great with romantic relation-
ships.

But she'd always been good with manners.
And doing what was right. The more she paced
her bedroom, the angrier she grew. By the time
she was back downstairs, she'd already made
up her mind.

No way was he going to leave with that stupid note and no explanation. She rushed to
her car, and with her Bluetooth ready to go,
she peeled out of her garage and driveway,
breaking almost every traffic law in Temptation Bay.

When she was finally on the highway, she
instructed her car to call Kaley's mother. That
turned out to be a very quick conversation, as
she gave Sharon no choice whatsoever. Ginny
had simply lied about an emergency.

Her next call was to Tilda, knowing they
didn't allow cell phones to be turned on during the concert. "Hey, honey. Kaley's mom's
picking you guys up. I've had something silly
come up, and I might have been late, so you
get to sleep over at Kaley's house tonight. I'll
see you tomorrow. Hope you're having a wonderful time."

The smile she'd used to make herself sound
cheerful dropped the second she disconnected
the call. Next stop, Providence. Luckily, it

wasn't a very big airport, and they couldn't have that many planes heading for La Guardia tonight. And if there wasn't anything that looked right, she'd check the flights to JFK and Newark.

He wasn't going to walk out on her again without an explanation. Not in this lifetime.

WHILE PARKER WAS GRATEFUL the airport wasn't packed to the rafters, the other people waiting to board his flight to New York were already getting on his nerves and he'd sat in the least convenient spot where there were only a couple of kids with backpacks two rows back. They wouldn't shut up about some baseball game. Parker was ready to pay them each a hundred bucks to be quiet.

He looked at his watch again. It wasn't time to board yet.

He wasn't proud of leaving Ginny and Tilda like that, but in the end, it was the right thing to do. Before he spoke to them he'd come up with a good excuse that wouldn't upset them. Yep. Taking off hadn't been easy, but it had been the kind thing to do. He wasn't the man for Ginny. She needed someone she could count on, someone steady and capable of commitment. When the chips were down, he was the last guy they should look to for strength and good judgment. Instead of facing life head-on, he'd run to the farthest place he could find.

But man, he was terrible at being noble. He kept wondering if Tilda was enjoying her concert. And if the agent following her was too. Even more pressing was what Ginny would make of his note.

He dropped his head into his hands. There was no way to make this any easier. It sucked. He needed to remember that every day he could've stayed would have made it even worse when, inevitably, he'd run back to where he belonged.

The call for first-class passengers and people with small children came over the speaker. Thank God the flight wouldn't take long.

As the crowd stood up, checking their boarding passes and moving toward the attendant, someone sat down right next to him. There were a ton of empty seats, why—

"Ginny. What…?"

"I believe you owe me an explanation," she said, and he could tell she meant business. "Not this sorry excuse for running away." She tossed his note on his lap, but it fell between his feet.

She looked furious.

"How did you even get here?"

"I drove."

"No, I mean to the boarding area."

She scowled. "I bought a ticket. If it takes the entire flight to get you to tell me what's going on, fine. I've made arrangements for *your niece* to spend the night at her friend's house."

"You bought a— Are you crazy?"

"Probably."

He briefly closed his eyes. He felt trapped. Cornered. Guilty. Drowning in her eyes, even though she was staring daggers at him. He wanted to kiss her and not stop. "Ginny…"

"Oh, don't even try with those puppy dog eyes. You left me. Again. And guess what? I decided you don't get to do that."

"Look, I'm doing you a favor," he said, and she crossed her arms, waiting. "I told you, I'm a selfish man. I don't mix well in civilized company anymore. I'm unreliable. And a coward. I let my disappointment with my father run my life for years, and now it's too late."

Evidently that wasn't enough for her. She kept staring at him, waiting.

"I even failed Meg. She ended up giving up her child and probably losing her life. Believe it when I tell you, the best place for me is in the most remote piece of America I could find. You and Tilda are amazing, and you deserve to have someone in your life that—"

"Okay, that's enough." Her voice was almost louder than the attendant's call for those in the back rows to board. "I will not hear you blather on about what a loner you are, and a failure and that you can't be counted on. That's nonsense, and you know it."

Now he was getting mad. "I think I know a little bit more about myself than you do." He stood up. "I'm due to board now."

"Fine. Walk away from the kind of life you should have. Go back to the life where you get to feel sorry for yourself twenty-four/seven."

"What are you talking about? You haven't listened to anything I've said."

"But I have. I've been listening all along, you dope." She took his arm and pulled him back down to his seat. "To the way you take care of your customers. How you've always been there for your mother, through thick and thin. How, when your father ran, you stayed, and you made sure you learned what you needed to in order to give your mom a proper life. You didn't let your dad's legacy run your life—you took control. Look at how you've been with Tilda.

"In case you're searching for the right word, it's *wonderful*. You've been strong when she needed strength. Gentle when she needed kindness. When I said she'd miss you, what I should have said was that she loves you. And will keep on loving you no matter what. And I know her a lot better than anyone else on the planet, so you'd better trust I'm telling you the truth."

"I'm already a lousy uncle," he said, his head a mess of confusion. "I'll be in Alaska. Half the year, I can barely get phone calls."

She pressed her lips together. "There's something else I should've said. I love you too."

He passed a hand over his face. "Oh, Ginny, you're making this so damn hard."

"Look, I'm a strong, independent woman who's managed to raise a remarkable child on my own. I've had advantages, yes, but I have worked hard to make a good life for me and Tilda. I think I can handle you."

Parker opened his mouth and closed it again.

"Now, do you want to board the plane? Because my row is being called to get in line."

He closed his eyes. He needed time to think. To reason with her. What she'd said appealed to him and also scared the crap out of him. But he had to choose a path. Without letting fear be his guide.

"For the record, you don't know everything about me. But maybe you know more than I do…about some things."

"Such as…?"

He watched a smile slowly bloom on her lips. "I love you, all right? Happy now? I love you, and it scares me to death. You deserve everything you've ever dreamed of, and I know I can't deliver."

"I don't think anyone gets everything. But I do think we're allowed to have the things that will make our lives richer."

He wanted to kiss her. Again. But that wouldn't be an answer… "I have a business. You know that."

"Yes," she said, her voice so patient he wasn't sure what to make of it.

"I have no idea what to do about that. How to make an us out of what we are now."

"Okay. Any other concerns?"

"Yeah, at least a hundred."

"What, you imagined this would be easy?" He shook his head.

Ginny's smile widened. "The whole thing is going to be all over the map for a while. Who knows what will shake out in the end. Maybe, it'll all fall apart and we'll be sad for ages. But if we never try, we'll never know if it could be great."

He swallowed. "Well? Is there anything else you wanted to say?"

"Probably. I just can't think at the moment.

Except you're reimbursing me for this ticket. It cost me a fortune."

The last and final boarding call was going out over the loud system, and she just kept staring at him. "You're right," she finally whispered. "Love is utterly terrifying. But we're both strong enough to walk into a life we know nothing about. What do you say?"

Parker choked out a laugh. "Is that a proposal, Ms. Landry?"

She gasped, laughed too. "Sure, why not? I promise I won't tell all your customers I had to be the one to propose."

He lifted her up and into his arms as he stood, then kissed her the way he wanted to. The boarding area was empty when they finally parted.

"I love you, Ginny."

"I know." She grinned at his raised brows. "I love you too, Parker Nolan. I have for a very long time."

One Year Later...

"I'M SO GLAD to see you." Ginny met Parker's mom, Eleanor, and her husband at the door, and was promptly pulled into loving arms.

Parker had just picked his mom and Wade up at the airport. The occasion was more than just Tilda's fifteenth birthday party. It was also a celebration of Tilda's scholarship to MIT, and Ginny and Parker's new, and very complicated, life.

He'd spent time in Alaska, of course, getting things straightened out with Mark and hiring a new pilot to take over for his fall and winter deliveries. The man was someone he could trust. Someone a lot like himself—or like the man he used to be. He would also take over the cabin for the duration, and that suited both of them just fine.

It turned out, Tilda's plan had merit. In the summer, the newly formed family would go to Alaska, although they would be renting a bigger cabin. Parker would still make his runs, but he'd be home for supper most nights and have time to show off his beloved state. When they were in Temptation Bay, Ginny would still teach piano. And Parker had gotten a job as a flight instructor at the local airport. Wherever they were, Tilda would still be a teenager, getting into trouble with her friends and waiting impatiently for the wedding she insisted on planning—all Ginny knew was that it would be next spring.

Life was good. And complicated, not that Ginny would change a thing.

Well, except for the surprise they'd spring

on Tilda at the wedding. The wonderful news that she and Parker would finally become her legal parents. And perhaps, if they were lucky, that their amazing daughter might just get a brand-new brother or sister to spoil in the years to come.

* * * * *

Get 4 FREE REWARDS!

We'll send you 2 FREE Books plus 2 FREE Mystery Gifts.

Love Inspired® books feature contemporary inspirational romances with Christian characters facing the challenges of life and love.

FREE
Value Over
$20

YES! Please send me 2 FREE Love Inspired® Romance novels and my 2 FREE mystery gifts (gifts are worth about $10 retail). After receiving them, if I don't wish to receive any more books, I can return the shipping statement marked "cancel." If I don't cancel, I will receive 6 brand-new novels every month and be billed just $5.24 for the regular-print edition or $5.74 each for the larger-print edition in the U.S., or $5.74 each for the regular-print edition or $6.24 each for the larger-print edition in Canada. That's a savings of at least 13% off the cover price. It's quite a bargain! Shipping and handling is just 50¢ per book in the U.S. and 75¢ per book in Canada*. I understand that accepting the 2 free books and gifts places me under no obligation to buy anything. I can always return a shipment and cancel at any time. The free books and gifts are mine to keep no matter what I decide.

Choose one: ☐ **Love Inspired**® Romance
Regular-Print
(105/305 IDN GMY4)

☐ **Love Inspired**® Romance
Larger-Print
(122/322 IDN GMY4)

Name (please print)

Address   Apt. #

City   State/Province   Zip/Postal Code

Mail to the **Reader Service:**
IN U.S.A.: P.O. Box 1341, Buffalo, NY 14240-8531
IN CANADA: P.O. Box 603, Fort Erie, Ontario L2A 5X3

Want to try two free books from another series? Call 1-800-873-8635 or visit www.ReaderService.com.

---

*Terms and prices subject to change without notice. Prices do not include applicable taxes. Sales tax applicable in N.Y. Canadian residents will be charged applicable taxes. Offer not valid in Quebec. This offer is limited to one order per household. Books received may not be as shown. Not valid for current subscribers to Love Inspired Romance books. All orders subject to approval. Credit or debit balances in a customer's account(s) may be offset by any other outstanding balance owed by or to the customer. Please allow 4 to 6 weeks for delivery. Offer available while quantities last.

Your Privacy—The Reader Service is committed to protecting your privacy. Our Privacy Policy is available online at www.ReaderService.com or upon request from the Reader Service. We make a portion of our mailing list available to reputable third parties that offer products we believe may interest you. If you prefer that we not exchange your name with third parties, or if you wish to clarify or modify your communication preferences, please visit us at www.ReaderService.com/consumerschoice or write to us at Reader Service Preference Service, P.O. Box 9062, Buffalo, NY 14240-9062. Include your complete name and address.

LII8

Get 4 FREE REWARDS!

We'll send you 2 FREE Books plus 2 FREE Mystery Gifts.

FREE
Value Over
$20

Both the **Romance** and **Suspense** collections feature compelling novels written by many of today's best-selling authors.

Get 4 FREE REWARDS!

We'll send you 2 FREE Books plus 2 FREE Mystery Gifts.

Harlequin® Special Edition books feature heroines finding the balance between their work life and personal life on the way to finding true love.

FREE Value Over **$20**

Get 4 FREE REWARDS!

We'll send you 2 FREE Books
plus 2 FREE Mystery Gifts.

Harlequin® Romance Larger-Print books feature uplifting escapes that will warm your heart with the ultimate feel-good tales.

FREE
Value Over
$20

YES! Please send me 2 FREE Harlequin® Romance Larger-Print novels and my 2 FREE gifts (gifts are worth about $10 retail). After receiving them, if I don't wish to receive any more books, I can return the shipping statement marked "cancel." If I don't cancel, I will receive 4 brand-new novels every month and be billed just $5.34 per book in the U.S. or $5.74 per book in Canada. That's a savings of at least 15% off the cover price! It's quite a bargain! Shipping and handling is just 50¢ per book in the U.S. and 75¢ per book in Canada*. I understand that accepting the 2 free books and gifts places me under no obligation to buy anything. I can always return a shipment and cancel at any time. The free books and gifts are mine to keep no matter what I decide.

119/319 HDN GMYY

Name (please print)

Address   Apt. #

City   State/Province   Zip/Postal Code

Mail to the **Reader Service:**
IN U.S.A.: P.O. Box 1341, Buffalo, NY 14240-8531
IN CANADA: P.O. Box 603, Fort Erie, Ontario L2A 5X3

Want to try two free books from another series? Call 1-800-873-8635 or visit www.ReaderService.com.

---

*Terms and prices subject to change without notice. Prices do not include applicable taxes. Sales tax applicable in N.Y. Canadian residents will be charged applicable taxes. Offer not valid in Quebec. This offer is limited to one order per household. Books received may not be as shown. Not valid for current subscribers to Harlequin Romance Larger-Print books. All orders subject to approval. Credit or debit balances in a customer's account(s) may be offset by any other outstanding balance owed by or to the customer. Please allow 4 to 6 weeks for delivery. Offer available while quantities last.

Your Privacy—The Reader Service is committed to protecting your privacy. Our Privacy Policy is available online at www.ReaderService.com or upon request from the Reader Service. We make a portion of our mailing list available to reputable third parties that offer products we believe may interest you. If you prefer that we not exchange your name with third parties, or if you wish to clarify or modify your communication preferences, please visit us at www.ReaderService.com/consumerschoice or write to us at Reader Service Preference Service, P.O. Box 9062, Buffalo, NY 14240-9062. Include your complete name and address.

HRLP18